Erle Stanley Gardner and The Murder Room

〉〉〉 This title is part of The Murder Room, our series dedicated to making available out-of-print or hard-to-find titles by classic crime writers.

Crime fiction has always held up a mirror to society. The Victorians were fascinated by sensational murder and the emerging science of detection; now we are obsessed with the forensic detail of violent death. And no other genre has so captivated and enthralled readers.

Vast troves of classic crime writing have for a long time been unavailable to all but the most dedicated frequenters of second-hand bookshops. The advent of digital publishing means that we are now able to bring you the backlists of a huge range of titles by classic and contemporary crime writers, some of which have been out of print for decades.

From the genteel amateur private eyes of the Golden Age and the femmes fatales of pulp fiction, to the morally ambiguous hard-boiled detectives of mid twentieth-century America and their descendants who walk our twenty-first century streets, The Murder Room has it all. 〉〉〉

The Murder Room
Where Criminal Minds Meet

themurderroom.com

Erle Stanley Gardner (1889–1970)

Born in Malden, Massachusetts, Erle Stanley Gardner left school in 1909 and attended Valparaiso University School of Law in Indiana for just one month before he was suspended for focusing more on his hobby of boxing than his academic studies. Soon after, he settled in California, where he taught himself the law and passed the state bar exam in 1911. The practise of law never held much interest for him, however, apart from as it pertained to trial strategy, and in his spare time he began to write for the pulp magazines that gave Dashiell Hammett and Raymond Chandler their start. Not long after the publication of his first novel, *The Case of the Velvet Claws*, featuring Perry Mason, he gave up his legal practice to write full time. He had one daughter, Grace, with his first wife, Natalie, from whom he later separated. In 1968 Gardner married his long-term secretary, Agnes Jean Bethell, whom he professed to be the real 'Della Street', Perry Mason's sole (although unacknowledged) love interest. He was one of the most successful authors of all time and at the time of his death, in Temecula, California in 1970, is said to have had 135 million copies of his books in print in America alone.

By Erle Stanley Gardner
(titles below include only those published in the Murder Room)

Perry Mason series

The Case of the Sulky Girl (1933)
The Case of the Baited Hook (1940)
The Case of the Borrowed Brunette (1946)
The Case of the Lonely Heiress (1948)
The Case of the Negligent Nymph (1950)
The Case of the Moth-Eaten Mink (1952)
The Case of the Glamorous Ghost (1955)
The Case of the Terrified Typist (1956)
The Case of the Gilded Lily (1956)
The Case of the Lucky Loser (1957)
The Case of the Long-Legged Models (1958)
The Case of the Deadly Toy (1959)
The Case of the Singing Skirt (1959)
The Case of the Duplicate Daughter (1960)
The Case of the Blonde Bonanza (1962)

Cool and Lam series

The Bigger They Come (1939)
Turn on the Heat (1940)
Gold Comes in Bricks (1940)
Spill the Jackpot (1941)
Double or Quits (1941)
Owls Don't Blink (1942)
Bats Fly at Dusk (1942)
Cats Prowl at Night (1943)
Crows Can't Count (1946)
Fools Die on Friday (1947)
Bedrooms Have Windows (1949)
Some Women Won't Wait (1953)
Beware the Curves (1956)
You Can Die Laughing (1957)
Some Slips Don't Show (1957)
The Count of Nine (1958)
Pass the Gravy (1959)
Kept Women Can't Quit (1960)
Bachelors Get Lonely (1961)
Shills Can't Cash Chips (1961)
Try Anything Once (1962)
Fish or Cut Bait (1963)
Up For Grabs (1964)

Cut Thin to Win (1965)
Widows Wear Weeds (1966)
Traps Need Fresh Bait (1967)
All Grass Isn't Green (1970)

Doug Selby D.A. series

The D.A. Calls it Murder (1937)
The D.A. Holds a Candle (1938)
The D.A. Draws a Circle (1939)
The D.A. Goes to Trial (1940)
The D.A. Cooks a Goose (1942)
The D.A. Calls a Turn (1944)
The D.A. Takes a Chance
  (1946)
The D.A. Breaks an Egg
  (1949)

Terry Clane series

Murder Up My Sleeve (1937)
The Case of the Backward
  Mule (1946)

Gramp Wiggins series

The Case of the Turning Tide
  (1941)
The Case of the Smoking
  Chimney (1943)

Two Clues (two novellas) (1947)

The D.A. Goes to Trial

Erle Stanley Gardner

An Orion book

Copyright © The Erle Stanley Gardner Trust 1940

This edition published by
The Orion Publishing Group Ltd
Orion House
5 Upper St Martin's Lane
London WC2H 9EA

An Hachette UK company
A CIP catalogue record for this book is available from the British Library

ISBN 978 1 4719 0938 2

www.orionbooks.co.uk

CAST OF CHARACTERS

Chapter One

STREAKS of eastern color appeared behind the mountains separating the rich orchard land from the desert. The night had been cold, although not cold enough for smudging. A light layer of frost coated the lower levels where the railroad trestled its way across the dry, sandy wash.

Out on the mesa land could be heard the hoarse bark of tractors as ranchers, bundled against the cold, pulled plows across the fertile soil.

In the freshness of the coming of dawn, it seemed that a note of weariness could be detected in the exhausts of those tractors. Their steady pound became a monotonous diapason of the fatiguing process by which farmers must fight a living from the soil. There was no wind. The cold of early dawn held the countryside in the breathless grip of an icy hand. The eastern color grew to red, deepened into scarlet, and turned to gold. Objects in the dry wash became visible as gray outlines, although there was not, as yet, enough light to show color.

A brush rabbit, moving as silently as a flitting shadow, slipped from a clump of sagebrush across to a patch of cactus, pausing within the shelter of the spine-studded sanctuary to look back toward the opposite bank where a coyote was silhouetted against the dawn. The coyote squatted on his haunches, raised his head, and with swelling throat poured forth staccato barks

1

which became increasingly high-pitched and rapid until the dry wash was filled with a pandemonium of sound.

The clouds grew brilliant. Enough daylight filtered through the saddle in the eastern mountains directly beneath the glowing clouds to show objects plainly.

The body lay beneath the trestle and slightly to one side. Frost had formed on the man's clothes, on the blanket roll which lay some fifty feet beyond the body. The corpse was sprawled in the grotesque rigidity of sudden death. As the sun climbed up through the notch in the mountains and sent its cold, reddish rays sweeping over the countryside, the dry wash became silent, still clinging to its cold, its shadows and its dead.

The brush rabbit scampered out from the cactus to the higher slopes of the western bank where it could catch the first rays of sunlight. Standing up on its hind legs, it stretched delicate nostrils to the tender shoots of the lush wild greenery which bordered the cultivated strip of land. A jack rabbit, loping up the wash, came to an abrupt stop within ten feet of the body. For a moment it stood frozen into rigid immobility. Then it thrust its powerful hind legs deep into the sand and went racing away in a series of long, zigzag jumps.

The sun cleared the rim of the mountains and started its slow march up into the bluish-black vault of the Southern California sky. The sun's rays, warming the rails on the trestle, caused the steel to snap and crackle with reports which sounded like miniature firecrackers. A breeze, springing up, brought the smell of freshly plowed loam to the frozen nostrils which could not smell it.

From the east came the rumble of an approaching train. The blasts of the whistle for a grade crossing sounded sharp and clear in the frosty air. A few minutes later, the rails crackled as the long string of desert-dusted Pullmans, dragging behind a powerful locomotive, swung around a curve in the track and slowed slightly for the trestle. The outlines of steam dribbling upward from the hissing safety valve were sharply etched. The smoke, rolling out of the stack, had the hard-packed appearance indicative of a dry, cold atmosphere.

A mile away, Madison City glinted white in the morning sunlight.

The locomotive of the limited clanked and hissed its way across the trestle. Abruptly the fireman stiffened to attention, grabbed the engineer's shoulder and pointed. The two faces peered anxiously down at the huddled, inert body.

The limited did not stop in Madison City. An ordinance restricted its speed to twenty miles an hour. Promptly at seven-thirty-eight every morning, it rumbled its slow way through the city, moving faster as it reached the city limits, roaring then into flashing speed as it made its last sprint for Los Angeles.

A few persons were on the station platform to watch the limited roll through—a man to catch the mail sack which would be tossed to the platform, and a sprinkling of the curious whose brief glimpses of early breakfasters through the windows of the dining car furnished a vicarious sense of travel.

As the locomotive *"clack-hiss-clacked"* its way past the derailing switch at the far end of the yard, the engineer gave a series of quick, short blasts on the whistle. The station agent came out to stare curiously. As he saw the waving arm extended from the cab, he walked close to the track and held up his extended left arm. As the locomotive rumbled by, the fireman neatly dropped a light bamboo hoop over the extended arm. The station master unfolded the note attached to the hoop, and read:

3

Body of man lying on the north side of trestle 693A. Roll of blankets about fifty feet beyond body to the west. Notify authorities.

The station agent, walking quickly to the telephone, thumbed through the dog-eared directory, found the number of the county coroner, and swiftly spun the dial of the desk telephone.

Harry Perkins, coroner and public administrator of Madison County, was also the town's leading mortician. His living quarters were over his undertaking establishment. In the privacy of his apartment, his bony face naturally tended to relax into lines of whimsical humor. His professional expression, as befitted his occupation, was one of fixed solemnity. He was reading the comic strip in *The Clarion* when the telephone rang. He picked up the receiver, said, "Hello," and listened to the report of the station agent.

"Okay," he said, "I'll go right down. Better not tell anyone for about ten minutes, because I want to be first on the scene."

He rang his assistant who slept in back of the mortuary, and said, "Get the bus warmed up, Sam. I'll be down right away. There's a case out in the wash a mile east of town. Looks like it's on the county, a hobo, probably knocked off the trestle by a train."

He dropped the receiver back into place, and took time to finish reading the comic strip before replacing the philosophical smile of his relaxed features with his business expression of professional gravity.

Chapter Two

SYLVIA MARTIN, reporter for *The Clarion*, entered Doug Selby's private office with the assurance of an old friend. Her jacket and skirt showed the youthful contours of a distinctly feminine figure, yet managed to blend those curves into a smooth line of business efficiency.

The young district attorney of Madison County was frowning into a law book as she opened the door. He raised his eyes, smiled at her, waved her to a chair, and again regarded the law book in level-browed concentration.

Sylvia studied his profile with approving eyes. His hair, swept back from his forehead, caught the lights from the windows. The forehead ran smoothly into the lines of a high-bridged nose. The mouth was sensitive and well formed, but the jaw was that of a fighter. Responsibilities of office had dropped a mantle of maturity over the district attorney, and Sylvia, who had known him long before he took office, who had in fact been partially instrumental in getting him elected, took stock of the changes with eyes that shone, yet in which there was a trace of something wistful.

After a moment, Doug Selby made a note of the volume and page, slid the book to one side along the desk, and looked up with a grin. "Hi, Sylvia," he said.

"Hi, yourself."

"What," he asked, "is new?"

"I want to find out something, Doug."

"Afraid you've come to the wrong place, Sylvia. This office is as destitute of news as a defeated politician of optimism for the future of the country."

"No, it isn't, Doug. I want to know something."

"What?"

"A hobo was struck by a train last night, and when I looked at the body, making a routine check up, I noticed ink smudges on the tips of the fingers. Now then, what I want to know is why the coroner took his fingerprints?"

"Didn't you ask the coroner?" Selby inquired.

"Certainly not," she said.

"Why?" Selby asked, his eyes quizzical. "Aren't you and Harry Perkins getting along?"

"Of course we are, but he's one of these impartial fence-straddlers who feels that he has to be friendly with both *The Blade* and *The Clarion*. If he's trying to conceal something and knows that I'm tracing it down, he'll tell me all he knows and then, as soon as I'm out the door, reach for the telephone to call *The Blade* and give them exactly the same information."

Selby laughed. "Whereas *I* can be counted on to give you the low-down and let *The Blade* fish for its news. Is that it?"

"Exactly," she said. "You have the virtue of loving your friends and hating your enemies."

"No," he said, "my enemies hate me."

"Well, it amounts to the same thing, Mr. District Attorney, and you're avoiding the question. *Why* did Harry Perkins take the fingerprints of the hobo who was struck by a train last night?"

"Because I told him to," Selby said.

She pulled some folded sheets of print paper from her purse, whipped out a black 6-B pencil, and said, "Ah-ha, the plot thickens."

"No," Selby said, "there's no plot, and it doesn't thicken. It's simply routine, Sylvia. I've told the coroner to take fingerprints of every itinerant on whom he held an inquest."

"Why, Doug?"

6

"Because lots of times men who are wanted take to the road and start drifting around as hobos. Sometimes those men have criminal records. Sometimes they're wanted for rather serious crimes. By taking fingerprints, we enable the F.B.I. to close their files when a dead transient happens to be a fugitive from justice. So you see, there's no story in it. It's simply regular routine."

She flashed him a scornful glance. "Just regular routine, eh—no story in it, eh? Well, Mr. District Attorney, wait until you read *The Clarion* tomorrow morning. You'll find a nice little article about the businesslike methods which the new district attorney has inaugurated. You'll learn that, thanks to him, Madison County is being brought up-to-date in the administration of criminal law.

"You'd be surprised at how much good things like that do, Doug. People here have a civic pride in this community. They like to feel they're modern and up-to-date, even if it is a rural community. Now that you're elected to office, you don't want to forget that you have to keep before the people. In short, Mr. District Attorney, I'm afraid you have no nose for news."

He laughed and said, "Well, don't give me the exclusive credit for it. Remember that Rex Brandon, the sheriff, is in on it, too."

"Was it his idea?" she asked.

"No, it was mine, but he needs publicity as much as I do, and he deserves a lot of credit for putting in a fingerprint department. The county couldn't afford to hire an outside expert, so Brandon hired Terry and gave him books to study. Young Bob Terry has educated himself on fingerprints and photography and done a mighty fine job of it."

Amorette Standish, Selby's secretary, opened the

door from the outer office and said, "Harry Perkins is here, and wants to know if he can see you."

"Tell him to come in," Selby said, and when the coroner had entered the private office, said, "Hello, Harry, what is it, anything private? If it is, Sylvia can wait outside for a few moments."

Perkins said, "No. I just dropped into the sheriff's office to leave the fingerprints we'd taken from the body of the man who was struck by the train last night."

"Anything on him to show identity?" Selby asked, with a significant sidelong glance at Sylvia Martin.

"Yes, a billfold in the inside pocket. Three one-dollar bills in it, and one of those cards enclosed in celluloid—In case of accident notify, and so forth. He had a brother in Phoenix, Arizona. . . . Funny thing about that, Doug. The man was a hobo, but his brother seems to be some pumpkins. Evidently has quite a wad of dough. Wanted to be sure it was his brother, though. Rang me up when he got my wire and asked me to describe him. When I did that, he said it was his brother all right. Didn't seem particularly sorry, either. He wants a cremation and the ashes sent to him at Phoenix by air express. I told him we'd have to hold an inquest, and he said to make it as fast as we could. I dropped in to see if you wanted to telegraph Washington about those fingerprints before I held the inquest."

"No, that's not necessary," Selby said. "Any money on the body except the three dollars?"

"Fifteen cents was all. It's lucky he had that card. It saves the county the expense of a burial. Well, I'll be seeing you, Doug."

"You gave the fingerprints to Bob Terry?" Selby asked, as Perkins started for the door.

"No, Terry's away, taking a prisoner up to San Quentin. I left them with Rex Brandon."

"You're sure a train struck him?" Selby asked.

"Sure. One side of him is pretty well caved in, quite a few broken bones, and, I think, a skull fracture. Doc Trueman can tell. He's going to 'post' him this afternoon. I may hold the inquest this evening. The brother seems wealthy and there'll be a bit of cash in this for me. I didn't want to fix the time for the inquest without consulting you."

"All right," Selby said. "Let me know if anything develops at the post-mortem."

When the coroner had left, Selby grinned across at Sylvia Martin. "Well, I did the best I could for you," he said. "I thought perhaps there might have been a story."

"There is," she said. *"Penniless hobo identified as brother of wealthy man*—not much, just a stick or two. But there's a human interest angle to it anyway. Well, I'll be seeing you, Doug. Don't take those law books too seriously."

"I won't," he promised.

Chapter Three

Doug Selby had glanced through the morning's mail, was reading the paragraph in *The Clarion* about the manner in which the sheriff and district attorney of the county were bringing the facilities for crime detection up-to-date, when Rex Brandon himself opened the door of Selby's private office, saying, "Amorette said you weren't busy, Doug, so I busted right in."

Selby grinned and folded the newspaper. "Reading about the efficiency of our respective offices," he said.

Rex Brandon, some twenty-five years older than the district attorney, smiled, and as he smiled the skin of his face, tanned to a leathery brown from years in the saddle, crinkled into a network of deeply etched lines. "Some little press agent we have there, Doug," he said. "She certainly is a loyal friend."

"Sometimes I think she overdoes it," Selby said, staring thoughtfully at the paper.

"Shucks, no," Brandon protested. "You *can't* overdo anything like that. The voters put you in office. They want to know what you're doing. The big objection against you was that you were too young. Now you're elected, the thing to do is to capitalize on that youth. Let them feel that as a young man you're more progressive and up-to-date."

Selby laughed aloud. "You're becoming a politician."

The sheriff's granite-hard gray eyes softened to a twinkle as he looked at Selby with paternal affection. "Say, listen, Doug. I *want* to talk politics with you."

"Talk," Selby invited.

Sheriff Brandon settled back against the cushions of the big chair, elevating his feet to the rungs of another chair. He fished a cloth tobacco bag from his pocket and spilled grains of tobacco into a brown cigarette paper. "Mark Crandall from the other side of the river is in the office," he said. "I want to bring him in here and let you talk with him."

Selby nodded, and waited for the sheriff to go on. The "other side of the river" was always a sore spot in county politics. The San Felipe River ran diagonally through the county. Madison City was the largest and most important city. There were three smaller cities on the north side of the river. On the south side was Las Alidas standing alone, in the county but not of it. No Las Alidas man had ever been elected to county office. The north and south sides of the San Felipe River constituted a political barrier. Over on the south side, Las Alidas was queen of a rich agricultural and horticultural district. At one time the city had been slightly larger than Madison City, and an attempt had been made to shift the county seat over to the south side of the river. The north side, working together as a unit, had blocked the move. Whereupon the citizens of Madison County clinched their victory for all time by voting a huge bond issue to build a new county courthouse, hall of records, and jail.

Thereafter, Madison City had prospered. Las Alidas had barely managed to hold its own. The "south side of the river" nursed a political aloofness, a pride, and a bitterness for which there had, in the past, been ample justification. Its tax money had gone to develop the north side of the river. The county officials sought the Las Alidas vote at election time, but paid the community only lip-service after election.

"Now Mark Crandall," Sheriff Brandon went on, "is one of the big men over on the south side of the river. Whenever he comes over to the county seat, he feels as though he's going into a strange country. He never asks any political favors. He acts on the assumption that all he'll get out of the county seat is a double cross."

Selby nodded.

Brandon said, "Let's change all that."

"How?" Selby asked.

"When Sam Roper was district attorney," Brandon went on, "he made Las Alidas the goat for everything —and I guess that's been true about as far back as we can remember. Of course, around election time Sam went over and made a couple of honeyed talks—and we did, too. I think we got the Las Alidas vote, not because they expected anything from us, but because they were sore at Sam Roper—in fact, the Las Alidas vote always goes against the incumbent in office, and in favor of the one who's trying to get in."

Selby nodded.

"Now, let's change things around," Brandon said. "Let's remember those people are taxpayers and entitled to everything we can give them. Let's made them feel they're more than welcome whenever they come over to the county seat."

Selby nodded. "What does Crandall want?"

"Sort of a ticklish situation," the sheriff said. "Looks like a man he recommended for a job has embezzled a bunch of dough."

"Who's the man?" Selby asked.

"Man by the name of John Burke," the sheriff said. "Accountant for the Las Alidas Lumber Company."

"I've met him," Selby observed, "just casually."

"I've talked with him a couple of times," Sheriff Brandon said, "just passing the time of day. He seemed to be a harmless coot."

"The way I figured him," Selby went on, "was as a washed-out individual who'd never be anything but a cog in a machine. About all I can remember of him is the thick-lensed glasses that distorted his eyes, and that little trick mustache of his."

"Well," the sheriff said, "I'm going to let Crandall tell you the story himself. I tried to make him feel at home, showed him all the stuff in the office, the collection of weapons that have figured in murders, the Chinese opium pipes, our new fingerprint equipment, the stuff Terry's been working on, the riot guns, those tear-gas bombs the supervisors got for us, and in general tried to make him feel I looked on him as a taxpayer and therefore, one of my bosses. I think it made a big hit with him. I told him to wait a few minutes and I'd run down the corridor and see if you were busy—figuring that I'd slip in and tip you off before I brought him in. I think if you'll adopt the same attitude toward him I did, it's going to make a lot of difference in the way he feels toward us, and we certainly can use a few real friends over on the south side of the river."

Selby grinned. "Thanks for the tip-off, Rex. You're on the right track, and I'm for it, not only with Crandall, but with anyone who comes in from the other end of the county. We're county officials, and it's up to us to see the taxpayers feel that we're representing them."

Sheriff Brandon said, "Thanks, Doug. I was hoping you'd look at it that way. I'll be right back."

He strode out through the exit door of the private office and returned a few moments later with a tall, fleshy man in the early fifties.

Mark Crandall had a certain impressive dignity about him despite the fact that he seemed entirely un-affected in his manner and speech. He was gray at the temples, and there was the suggestion of a droop to his lips. Past fifty, his step nevertheless was quick and springy. His shoulders were held well back, and his handclasp was firm and muscular. "Hello, Selby," he said, as he shook hands with the district attorney.

"Glad you ran over to see us," Selby said cordially. "You don't get over this way very often, do you?"

"No more than I can help," Crandall replied, and then as though wishing to soften the barb of the re-mark, added quickly, "My business is all in Las Alidas. Of course, I get into Los Angeles frequently. But I make even those trips as short as possible."

"Sit down," Selby invited. "How about a cigarette?"

"No, thanks, I'll have one of my cigars. How about you boys?"

Sheriff Brandon said, "I'll take one, but Selby is pretty well wedded to his pipe."

"Oh, I smoke an occasional cigar when I'm being polite," the district attorney said, taking a crusted brier pipe from his side pocket. He opened a humidor, pushed the pipe down inside, and filled the bowl with moist, fragrant tobacco.

The men lit up and smoked in silence for a few seconds. After a while, Selby asked, "How are things over in Las Alidas?"

"Pretty good," Crandall replied. "We don't have the business you folks do over here because we don't have the through highway, and we don't have any other towns to draw from. But I don't know but what that makes us stick a little closer—gives us a little more civic spirit. I came over today to speak to the sheriff about an embarrassing position in which I find myself. He thought we'd better go over it with you."

"Anything I can do," Selby assured him, "I'll be glad to."

Crandall said, "Ten years ago, I had a brokerage business in Chicago. John Burke was my chief accountant. I found him sober, industrious, efficient, and honest. I've never been one to stay in a business unless that business paid me for staying in it. So when the bottom dropped out of the market, I dropped out of the brokerage business and liquidated my holdings. While I hoped for a return of prosperity, I didn't allow my desire to color my judgment. As a result, I gradually drifted away from the larger industrial centers, and finally decided to invest in horticultural land. I located in Las Alidas and have never been sorry I did. The people are friendly and loyal. I can assure you, Mr.

Selby, it's an entirely different attitude than that which I've encountered in the larger cities."

Selby nodded.

"Some six months ago I met John Burke on the street in Los Angeles. He was out of work and down on his luck. I brought him back to Las Alidas with me and spoke about him to George Lawler who runs the Las Alidas Lumber Company. I knew they were dissatisfied with the bookkeeper and accountant they had and were intending to make a change. They gave Burke a try-out and were very much pleased. The man has exceptional ability. I was only too glad to vouch for his integrity.

"After he'd landed the job, Burke told me he was married and had a baby. It was the first intimation I'd had he wasn't still a bachelor. He explained he hadn't wanted to tell me about his wife before he got a job because she and the baby were on relief, and he was ashamed of not being able to support them. Remember that the man was very despondent when I met him in Los Angeles. Apparently, he just escaped a nervous breakdown."

"Thanks to you," Sheriff Brandon said.

Crandall's nod showed that he appreciated the sheriff's comment. "Tuesday," he went on, "I went to Los Angeles to consult my brokers upon a matter too important and delicate to be discussed over the telephone.

"I was in the private office of the junior partner, Alfred Miltern, when it became necessary for him to get some data of a highly confidential nature. As he opened the door to step out to the corridor, I had a glimpse of John Burke leaving one of the other offices. I heard Mr. Miltern say, 'Good morning, Mr. Brown. Are they taking care of you all right?' And Burke said, 'Everything's coming fine, thank you,' or something to that effect, I can't remember his exact words. I was utterly stunned, because I could tell from the manner in which Mr. Miltern had addressed him that he was considered an important customer.

"Fortunately, I had several minutes to think things over while Miltern was in the other department. When he returned, I said casually, 'Does Brown give you all his business?'

" 'You mean Allison Brown?' he asked.

" 'Yes,' I said, 'the one you were talking with in the corridor just now.'

" 'Do you know him?' he asked.

" 'I've known him for more than five years,' I said.

" 'Perhaps you could tell us something about him,' Miltern said, and I laughed and said, 'Not until you answer my question. I want to know how he considers you before I divulge any information.' Thereupon Miltern said, 'He's a very peculiar chap. I believe he lives out your way, but he never uses the telephone or the mails. I'd like to know more about him. I am wondering if he lives in Las Alidas.' "

"What," asked Rex Brandon, "did you say to that?"

"Fortunately," Crandall said, with a smile, "I was in the position of a customer so far as Miltern was concerned. It enabled me to say with some dignity, 'Under the circumstances I would want to have Mr. Brown's permission before I said anything. I think it would be better for you to ask your questions of Mr. Brown.' "

"What did Miltern say to that?" Selby asked.

"There was nothing much he *could* say. However, I gathered Mr. Brown was a valued customer. I gathered that his transactions ran into rather large figures. Knowing, of course, that Burke was entirely dependent upon his salary and that I had recommended him to a position of responsibility, I became uneasy.

"I returned to Las Alidas Tuesday night and rang

Burke's house. Mrs. Burke answered the telephone and told me her husband was laid up in bed with the flu and had been in bed all afternoon. She thought he was over the worst of it, but he was still running a temperature and she was keeping him absolutely quiet. I intimated that I'd like to see him, and she told me, tactfully but firmly, that she thought it would be better if he had no visitors, that he was inclined to be nervous, and that she wanted him to rest quietly. There was, of course, nothing I could do except express my sympathy, extend my wishes for a speedy recovery, and hang up."

Crandall's face showed anxiety as he surveyed the two men. "What," he asked, "do *you* think of it?"

Brandon ganced at Selby, then back at Crandall. "Sure of your identification?" he asked.

Crandall said positively, "There's no chance of a mistake. I saw the man and I heard his voice. The man who was in that brokerage office was John Burke. Frankly, gentlemen, I don't know what to do. There is, of course, a possibility that Burke's wife may have received some money by inheritance and Burke doesn't care about letting me know about it. He's a secretive chap. The way he acted about his wife and child proves that. I've tried to dismiss the matter from my mind and can't.

"Now it occurs to me that you gentlemen might pretend you were investigating some crime and . . . well, sort of check up. Incidentally, there's one other matter . . . I hate to mention it . . . However, it's one of the things which made me come to you, so I should give you the information."

"What is it?" Brandon asked.

"It happens that Arthur White, who is employed at the First National Bank in Las Alidas—a bank in which I happen to be a director—lives next door to John Burke. I'm not very proud of what I did. But nevertheless, it seemed the logical way in which I could get the information I wanted at the time. Yesterday afternoon I made it a point to call Arthur White into my office in connection with some other matter, and then casually ask him about his neighbors, the Burkes. I told him I understood Burke was sick, and asked him if he knew anything about it.

"White opened up and told me that there'd been a lot of strange goings on over at the Burke residence. Most of what he said impressed me as being a lot of petty neighborhood gossip about seeing a mysterious hobo carrying a roll of blankets come down the alley back of his house around seven o'clock Tuesday night. He doesn't think Mr. Burke was home at the time. White saw the hobo turn into the alley, thought he might be coming to his house, so kept a watch on him. He saw him go to the Burke place, saw Mrs. Burke come to the backdoor, fling her arms around him and embrace him passionately. There's a lot of other stuff that I won't dignify by repeating. I was sorry I placed myself in a position where I had to listen to it. But one thing it does establish definitely, and that is that Burke didn't have influenza.

"After I talked with White, I called the Burke residence again and got no answer. Then I telephoned the lumber company. Lawler told me Burke was in Phoenix, Arizona, on a matter of business. That made me feel better about the whole thing, and I tried to put it out of my mind, but it just wouldn't stay out. If there's any shortage at the lumber company, I'll be morally obligated to make it up, of course. . . . And yet, Burke handled thousands of dollars for me and was never short so much as a penny. . . . Well, frankly, I'm worried. Burke got his job because of me. . . . I suppose I'm an old woman listening to a lot of neighborhood gossip . . . but . . ." His voice trailed away into silence, then he suddenly blurted, "I wish you men would investigate."

Selby glanced dubiously over to Rex Brandon. "Well," he said, "we . . ."

The telephone on Selby's desk rang. Selby picked up the receiver and Amorette Standish said, "Harry Perkins is calling and seems very much excited. He says it's very important." "Put him on," Selby said.

The switch clicked, and he heard the coroner's voice, high pitched with excitement. "Doug, this is Harry. Listen, you remember that hobo that was hit by that train night before last?"

"Yes."

"Well, you know, we got in touch with his brother in Phoenix, and the brother telephoned, instructed me to rush through the inquest, take the body to Los Angeles, have it cremated, and ship the ashes by air express to Phoenix. He wired me five hundred dollars, which was very generous considering the service he wanted. . . . You're listening, Doug?"

"Yes," Selby assured him. "Go ahead."

"Well, we had an inquest. Doc Trueman made a post-mortem. We rushed the body to Los Angeles, had it cremated, sent the ashes by air express to the address in Phoenix—and the express company has just notified me that they can't make delivery, because there's no one of that name at the address given."

"You got the five hundred dollars all right?" Selby asked.

"Yes, it was transferred by wire."

"And your telegram was delivered all right?"

"Yes."

"You took the man's fingerprints?"

"Yes. Rex Brandon has them."

"Any other means of identification—did you take any photographs of the body?"

"*We* didn't, but the Southern Pacific men did. Their detectives showed up on the scene around noon yesterday and got busy. They took photographs of everything, the place where the body was found, the body, and all that."

"What was the name of the brother in Phoenix?" Selby asked.

"Horatio Perne, care Inter-Mountain Brokerage Company, 690 East First."

"Street or Avenue?" Selby asked. "As I remember, it makes quite a difference in Phoenix. I think they have both streets and avenues, streets running in one direction, and avenues in the other."

"I don't know. Six-ninety East First was all the address I had. But I sent a wire to that address and it was delivered."

"I'll find out about it," Selby said, "and let you know." He hung up the telephone and said to Rex Brandon, "I think we'd better investigate. I have a couple of matters I want to clear up. It'll take me about ten minutes. Suppose I meet you out in front at that time. We'll go over to Las Alidas in the county car, and see what we can find out."

"Okay," the sheriff said.

"I have my car here," Crandall volunteered.

"No, that would put you to the trouble of making another trip back. You'd better go on over and we'll look into it and get in touch with you later."

Crandall pushed forth an impulsive hand. "I voted for both of you. It wasn't so much a vote for you as it was a vote against Sam Roper and his crowd. I didn't expect any particular co-operation from you. You could very well have referred me to the chief of police in Las Alidas, and I rather expected that's exactly what you'd do. However, I have a hunch this calls for a little more action than Billy Ransome can offer. I just want to say that you two haven't lost anything by the way you've acted. If you ever need a friend in Las Alidas, count on me. Good morning."

When he had gone, Brandon grinned across at Selby. "I guess that's going to help, son," he said. "Crandall draws quite a bit of water on the south side of the river. . . . What do you make of it, anyway?"

Selby told him of Harry Perkins' telephone conversation. "What I'm figuring," he said, "is that there might be a hookup between this mysterious hobo who was seen at the Burke residence and this man who was knocked off the trestle."

Brandon shook his head. "Not one chance in a hundred," he said. "Hobos are as thick as fleas on a dog's back. You can find men walking up and down the road, men panhandling on the sidewalks, men riding the flat cars, men hitchhiking through the county going to 'look for work' in San Francisco, Fresno, Los Angeles, or any place which happens to be a few miles distant. Farmers right around here can't get men enough to get the ground plowed and the crops in. When it comes harvest time, they'll not only be short-handed, but the men they do have will strike about the time the farmers are the hardest pressed."

"Well," Selby said, "I think you'd better send a telegram to the chief of police in Phoenix and have him investigate. That's why I stalled around. I figured it might be just as well not to let Crandall know about this development."

"Okay," Brandon said, "let's send that telegram and then go over to Las Alidas. I want to talk with Mrs. Burke."

Chapter Four

THE RESIDENCE of John Burke was a little bungalow at 209 East Center Street. It lacked a few minutes of noon when Rex Brandon swung the county car in close to the curb. "That's it," he said; "the house on the corner. That must be White's place next to it. What's the number on that . . . 213 . . . okay, Doug, you plan the campaign."

Selby said, "I don't want to beat about the bush. I'm going to say we're checking up on a hobo, that someone saw a hobo in the alley near here night before last, and ask Mrs. Burke if she can tell us anything about him. That will put it squarely up to her."

"Good idea," Brandon said, "but don't lose sight of the main issue, Doug. We want to find out whether Burke is short at the lumber company."

"I want to find out about that hobo," Selby said, "because I have an idea that's more important than we think right now."

They left the car and walked up a driveway flanked by a lawn, and approached the bungalow which was shaded by a cluster of orange trees. The two men climbed the stairs to the porch, pressed the bell button, and received no answer. Selby pressed the button a second and a third time, then said to the sheriff, "Looks as though we've drawn a blank."

The sheriff said, "The woman in the house next door is looking out of the window. Let's go talk with her."

"Okay," Selby said.

There was a low hedge separating the two houses. The men cut directly across to the hedge. Selby jumped over it lightly. Rex Brandon cleared it, but landed a little more heavily. Before they had reached the porch, the door opened and a thin, nervous woman in the early thirties with high cheekbones and black burnished eyes inquired, "Were you looking for John Burke? Is this the law?"

"We wanted to talk with Mrs. Burke," Selby said.

"Well, she's out. She went away last night. I don't think she's going to be back right away."

"Why?" Selby asked.

"She took the baby and a suitcase and drove away. There have been some queer goings-on over there. Things ain't right—if you ask me."

"Perhaps she's gone to the city, and intends to come back today," Brandon suggested tentatively, giving the district attorney a surreptitious dig with his elbow.

"No, it isn't anything like that," the woman said positively. "She was sitting over there last evening in the living room, reading *The Blade*, and all of a sudden she dropped the paper, put her hand to her mouth as though she was trying to keep from screaming. Ten minutes after that she drove away."

Sheriff Brandon frowned. "You're Mrs. White?" he asked.

"Yes. Mrs. Arthur White."

"Now how do you know she was reading *The Blade*, Mrs. White?"

"I could see her. Come in here and you can see for yourself. Her house sits back a little farther than mine. My kitchen window looks directly into her dining room. The light was on and the shade was up. I could see her plain as day."

Mrs. White led the way into her kitchen, indicated the window of the house opposite.

"Right there," she said, "is where she was sitting, reading that paper. Now I don't want you to think I'm snoopy because I'm not. I never was one to gossip. But when things start going on under your very eyes, you can't ignore them. Tuesday night she had a visitor. My husband saw . . ."

Selby said, "Can you show me just how she was sitting, Mrs. White, when she became so excited?"

"Yes," Mrs. White said. "She was sitting in that chair by the window, holding the paper out in front of her."

"Was the paper folded or open?"

"Open. She held her hands far out and about on a level with her eyes. The paper hung down below them."

"Then she wasn't reading from the front page of the paper?"

"No, she wasn't," Mrs. White said thoughtfully.

"Coud you tell what part of the paper it was?" .

"I would say somewhere on the first inside page. . . . And I guess . . . I guess about the lower left-hand corner."

"Did you gather it was something she had read that excited her?"

"I don't know as it was. It may have been that she thought of something all of a sudden—or it might have been something she read. Come to think of it, I guess there wouldn't be much on the inside page of the paper, would there?"

"You don't take The Blade?"

"No. That's a county-seat paper. We subscribe to the Las Alidas Record."

Selby nodded toward the house across the hedge. "How do they get along?"

"You mean, are they happy?"

"Yes, are there many fights?"

"No. Sometimes he'll have sort of a tantrum, but she don't argue with him much. They have a few fights, not many."

"Well," Selby said, "we're trying to find out something about a hobo. We understand that Mr. White had seen one so we thought we'd check up on it."

"I'm glad you are. . . . I've been all upset. Has he—has he killed anyone or attacked someone?"

"No," Rex Brandon said, "not so far as we know."

"Well," she said, "I ain't one to gossip and Lord knows we aren't the snooping kind, but Tuesday night my husband saw a hobo in the alley. Naturally, he watched him because we can't afford to put out feed for hobos, not that we're unsympathetic, but we just can't run a hobo hotel.

"Well, this hobo went over to Mrs. Burke's place, and the way she received him was something scandalous. And then Mrs. Burke and some man, I guess it must have been the hobo, went out in the car, and while they were gone, her husband came home. And then Arthur thought he heard Burke go out and then, to top it all off, Mrs. Burke came back with some man who wasn't the hobo—and we never did hear *him* leave —not that we were listening, you understand—after all, what she does is her own business, but those are pretty goings on for a married woman—and her with such a sweet little baby."

Selby glanced at Brandon. "Let's go and see Lawler up at the lumber company," he said.

It was while they were driving to the Las Alidas Lumber Company that Selby said casually, "That story about the hobo being found dead was on the lower left-hand corner of the inside page on *The Blade* yesterday night—just a few lines."

Rex Brandon said, "Looks as though we're getting on to the trail of something, but I don't know just what."

George Lawler at the Las Alidas Lumber Company was standing at a bookkeeping desk which was littered with books. Beside him, evidently working on the books, were two men with green eyeshades and the expression of complete abstraction which is common to competent accountants.

"Hello, Sheriff," Lawler said, coming forward with a smile which seemed rather sheepish. "Glad you dropped in. I wanted to talk with you. Hello, Selby. Come in and sit down. Tell me what I can do for you."

"Taking an inventory?" Selby asked, nodding toward the counter where the two accountants had resumed their interrupted labors, apparently completely oblivious of the county officials.

"Well," Lawler said, rubbing his hand across the dome of a very bald head, "I was just sort of checking up."

"Those two people employed by you regularly?" Brandon asked.

"No, they're from the bank. The bank agreed to loan them to me. I'm making a check of my books."

Brandon glanced at Selby. Selby fixed Lawler with his eyes. "Why?" he asked.

Lawler glanced from one to the other, then lowered his eyes and fidgeted uneasily. "I don't know just what the situation is," he said, "but day before yesterday my bookkeeper didn't come to work. I telephoned his house, and his wife told me that he had a bad case of influenza and would probably be in bed for a day or two. She wanted to know if I could carry on without him. I told her I thought I could. Later on I telephoned again. No one answered. I went out there last night. No one seemed to be home. Yesterday I got a wire from my bookkeeper, 'Called away on matter of life and death will explain later.' "

"Where was that wire sent from?" Selby asked.

"Phoenix, Arizona."

"May we see it, please?"

Lawler showed it to them. It bore the signature, "John Burke."

"Today I became worried about the whole situation. I dug into the books and found two or three things that didn't look right to me. So I went down to the bank and explained the situation. The bank loaned me a couple of their best men. The first thing they did was to check the cash on hand. The books showed there'd be about a hundred and thirty-two dollars and some odd cents in the safe. Well, we found the safe had been cleaned. Every cent had been taken out of the cash drawer—even the pennies out of the stamp drawer, *but* we found a package wrapped up in a newspaper fastened with elastic bands. That package contained ten thousand dollars in one-hundred-dollar bills.

"The preliminary audit of my books indicates a series of shortages which were covered up with false entries. There's been a steady, consistent dipping into assets. The boys figure the shortage is going to run somewhere around eight thousand dollars. I was going to get in touch with you sometime today. I was glad to see you come in."

"The ten thousand was wrapped in a newspaper?" Brandon asked.

"Yes."

"What paper?" Selby asked.

"A last week's newspaper from Phoenix, Arizona."

"You have it here?" Selby inquired.

"Yes."

Selby said to the sheriff, "Rex, if it isn't too late, I think you should have your fingerprint expert go over that paper and see what he can find."

"Good idea," Brandon said. "Bob Terry was to get back sometime this morning. He should be back to the office by this time. Let's put through a call."

He put through a call from Lawler's telephone, got

Bob Terry on the line, and told him to make time to the lumber company, bringing along his outfit for developing latent fingerprints.

Rex Brandon hung up the telephone, and said to Lawler, "Let's put some pins in the corner of this newspaper. Now we'll pin it to the wall. I don't want anyone to touch it, see?"

Lawler nodded.

"You got any theories?" Brandon asked.

"No," Lawler said briefly.

Selby glanced at Brandon.

"If it isn't asking too much," Lawler said, "how did you two find out?"

"We didn't find out," Selby said. "We were just looking things over."

The cordiality faded from Lawler's eyes.

"Well, boys," he said calmly, "that's *my* ten thousand dollars. Do you understand?"

Selby said, "We're not arguing with you—not now."

Lawler said doggedly, "This is my ten thousand bucks.—I only told you about it in confidence. The story isn't to be repeated."

Selby said, "When Bob Terry comes over, tell him we want the fingerprints on that paper and on the safe."

Lawler said, "You won't be here?"

"No, we have another witness we want to question."

Lawler shifted his eyes.

"Okay," he said.

Chapter Five

SYLVIA MARTIN was waiting for Doug Selby when the district attorney reached his office around two in the afternoon.

"Anything that breaks now," she told him, "is my meat. *The Blade* has gone to press. From now until midnight it's all mine. So please, Mr. Man, dig me up a nice mystery over that hobo."

Selby knitted his brows. "I'm afraid there's more mystery than I know what to do with."

"Why, Doug?"

"There's the possibility of a large embezzlement over at Las Alidas, and I'm not certain but what this hobo figures in it some way."

"How?" she asked.

"I don't know, and that's what bothers me. I'm not even certain there is an embezzlement. It's a whole series of suspicious circumstances pointing toward some crime which seems to have been covered up so completely we can't find out much about it. A chap named John Burke seems to be at the bottom of it, and he's most certainly juggled things around so they're in a sweet mess!"

"Can you give me the facts, Doug?" she asked.

Selby pulled out his pipe, tamped tobacco into the bowl, swiveled around in his office chair, and told her the whole story, not failing to mention that Mrs. Burke's abrupt departure had quite probably been due to reading the account of the hobo's death in *The Blade*.

When he had finished, Sylvia Martin said, "I think I can dot an 'i' and cross rather an important 't,' Doug. I happened to pick this up in my dragnet on routine police reports and stolen-car information. Bill Ransome, the chief of police, over at Las Alidas, recovered a stolen automobile yesterday afternoon. The automobile had an Arizona license, and apparently had been driven by a hobo with a roll of blankets. The car was a big Cadillac owned by a James C. Lacey of Tucson. A woman noticed the car swing in to the curb and park about seven o'clock Tuesday evening. She was surprised to see that the big automobile was driven by a man who was apparently nothing but a hobo. He parked the car, opened the rear door, pulled a roll of blankets out from the back, and walked off down the street."

Selby's eyes narrowed. "And she notified the police?" he asked.

"No, not then. She told her husband about it. Her husband said not to get excited, that it was none of their business, and not to mix into things. But the next morning when he went to work the car was still parked right where his wife had told him, and he stopped to look it over.

"It was a big Cadillac, shiny and well-groomed; but the grille work on the front of the radiator was bent and the lock on the trunk had been forced open—although the spare tire hadn't been taken. At noon it was still there. So the man notified the police. Ransome went out to look it over. The tank was about half full of gasoline and neither the car doors nor the ignition was locked. Ransome turned on the ignition switch, and the motor ran perfectly. He found the car was registered to James C. Lacey in Tucson, and a late bulletin showed the car had been stolen. Ransome didn't report the car here because he figured there might be a reward. If there was, he wanted it. That's why he handled it direct."

Selby puffed in thoughtful silence at his pipe. At

length, he asked, "Just where was the car found in Las Alidas?"

"I don't know," she said, "but I can find out. Let me telephone the paper."

She put through a call to *The Clarion* office, and after a moment reported, as she hung up the phone, "Apparently some place on East Center Street. The people who found it were Mr. and Mrs. Leonard Bell who live at 410 East Center Street."

"And John Burke lives at 209 East Center Street," Selby said. "My gosh, Sylvia, I never saw such an active hobo. He steals a car, and drives from Arizona to Las Alidas. He parks the car, walks two blocks, goes into the house of John Burke, makes love to John Burke's wife, and then manages to walk far enough along the railroad track to be hit by the eleven-ten train."

"What makes you think it was the eleven-ten, Doug?"

"Everything points to that conclusion. According to the autopsy, time of death was fixed at ten to fifteen hours before the post-mortem. The post-mortem was performed around noon. That would fix the time at anywhere from nine o'clock in the evening, but there wasn't any nine o'clock train. There's one at seven, but that's probably too early. Then there's the eleven-ten train—we only have to consider the westbound trains. He was hit by a westbound train. The position of the body and the manner in which the blanket roll was thrown show that. There's a freight at three-forty in the morning. Then the next westbound is the seven thirty-eight limited. The engineer on the limited discovered the body."

"And you think this is the same hobo, Doug?"

"When you stop to think of it, it hardly seems possible," Selby said, "and yet I have a hunch it all ties in together."

Sylvia doubled her left leg so that she was sitting on her foot. She tapped the end of her lead pencil gently against the arm of her chair. "Doug," she said, "I don't like the way this looks."

"Neither do I," Selby admitted. "I'm interested in finding out what Brandon has learned about that brother in Phoenix and why he won't accept the ashes."

Sylvia Martin smiled. "Wait until you read the paper tomorrow, Doug," she said. "Do you realize that this rule you've made of taking fingerprints has given you not only the best evidence but about the only evidence on which you can identify that body?"

Selby knitted his forehead. "I'd like to locate Mrs. Burke. She can tell us about that hobo—of course, there may be no connection, but where there are two mysterious hobos and . . . wait a minute. This sounds like Brandon's step in the corridor."

A moment later, Brandon walked in from the outer office. "Hello, Sylvia," he said. "Not interrupting, Doug?"

"No," Selby said. "Sylvia and I have no secrets from the sheriff, and the sheriff has no secrets from *The Clarion*."

"Or shouldn't have," Sylvia interposed.

"The Phoenix police called me just a few moments ago," Brandon said. "They're all up in the air."

"What did you find out?" Selby asked.

"A man telephoned Western Union and said he was expecting some important telegrams addressed to Horatio Perne at the Inter-Mountain Brokerage Company at 690 East First. He said he'd had a deal on for office space at that address and then the deal had fallen through, so to deliver any wires to him at the Pioneer Rooms, and promised that within a few days he'd have an office address.

"Well, when they got Perkins' wire, the police in

Phoenix went down to the Pioneer Rooms and found that a man named Horatio Perne had been registered there. He was a middle-aged man with peculiar eyes and a gray mustache. He wore a big Stetson, leather vest, and cowboy boots. That isn't the sort of man who would have been Horatio Perne of the Inter-Mountain Brokerage Company—at least, the Phoenix police didn't think so. And they've never heard of the Inter-Mountain Brokerage Company. Now what does that add up to, Doug?"

Selby stared at the sheriff and then said one word, "Murder."

Sheriff Brandon nodded.

Sylvia gasped, a quick, nervous intake of breath, then started scribbling furiously on the folded proof sheets which rested on her knee.

"I'm wondering," Sheriff Brandon said, "if you figure this the same way I do, Doug."

"I think I do," Selby said. "The man knew a telegram addressed to Horatio Perne of the Inter-Mountain Brokerage Company was going to be received. Therefore, he must have known of the identification card in the pocket of the dead hobo. He must also have known that the hobo was dead. How does the time element check, Sheriff?"

"It checks," Brandon said. "He put in his call to the Western Union supervisor at seven o'clock Wednesday morning."

"Now then," Selby said, "why all this elaborate preparation simply to get a man's body cremated?"

"You think that was all it was done for?" Brandon asked.

Selby nodded. "The man registers an address with the telegraph company just before the body is discovered. He urges extreme haste in his telephone conversations with the coroner. Perkins is only human. He sees an opportunity to get a generous fee for the funeral of a man who would otherwise have been a county charge. Naturally, Perkins fell for it."

"But," Sheriff Brandon said, "why should a hobo suddenly become this important? He . . ."

"I don't think he was a hobo," Selby interrupted. "Don't you see, Rex, it's a pretty safe bet that someone was masquerading as a hobo—someone rather important."

"And you don't think he was struck by a train?" Brandon asked.

"No," Selby said. "That would have made the death accidental. The man who went to such elaborate preparations to get the body cremated must have known of the death sometime before the body was discovered. I think I want to examine the front of that Arizona automobile."

"What's that?" Brandon asked.

Selby told him about Sylvia's communication.

Brandon grinned at her, and said, "Guess we're going to have to make you a deputy, Sylvia."

She didn't answer Sheriff Brandon, but said to Doug Selby, breathlessly, "Doug, what a *whale* of a story!"

Selby stared past her, his eyes fixed on distance. "Rex," he asked, "did *you* see the body of that hobo?"

"No."

"You say photographs were taken?"

"Yes."

Selby knocked ashes out of his pipe. "I think, Rex," he said, "that the next thing for us to do is to locate the Southern Pacific investigators and view those photographs. I think we'll find there's a connection between James C. Lacey at Tucson and Mrs. John Burke. There's a good chance Lacey drove his car from Tucson, disguised as a hobo. He called on Mrs. Burke and then—no, that won't do. Lacey must be alive. He reported the car as stolen. Tell you what you do, Rex. Get in touch with Bill Ransome at Las Alidas. Get him to find out everything he can about Mrs. Burke. Crandall should be able to give him some information. In the meantime, let's see if we can get the photographs of the hobo that were taken by the railroad investigators. I'll get in touch with their Los Angeles office. Get the police at Tucson to give us everything they can on James C. Lacey and find out where his car was stolen, when it was stolen, and, if possible, let's find why it was stolen. We . . ."

He broke off as Amorette Standish slipped quietly into the office, closing the door behind her. Her spectacled eyes were expressionless, her face a mask of secretarial efficiency. "Oliver Benell is waiting to see you," she said. "He's quite impatient, and says it's very important."

"You mean the president of the First National Bank at Las Alidas?"

She nodded. "He says it's about a Mr. Burke."

Brandon said, "Come on, Sylvia, let's go do some detective work, and let Selby talk with the banker."

She nodded, pushing her folded print paper into her purse. "Look here, Doug," she asked, "are there any strings tied to this?"

"I don't think so," Selby said. "It would seem to me that the more publicity we had, the better—and, Rex, get Bob Terry to rush classification of those fingerprints and wire into the Federal Bureau of Investigation. Let's see if these fingerprints are on file."

Brandon said, "I'll start Terry at work on it right away—just as soon as he gets back from Las Alidas."

Sylvia came to stand close to Selby. "Doug," she said, "perhaps it's just intuition, perhaps it's the way things are developing, but this case gives me a creepy feeling all up and down my spine. Benell is smooth. He wouldn't be coming over here to see you personally unless he wanted something very badly. Watch your step, Doug. Don't make any mistakes—people are watching you, and—oh, Doug, I feel this is going to be . . ."

He dropped his hand to her shoulder. "Don't worry, Sylvia. We're just starting. We'll have more to work on soon."

She tilted her chin and smiled up at him.

"Luck," she said.

Selby ushered Sylvia and the sheriff through the hall door and nodded to Amorette. "Send Benell in," he said.

Oliver Benell surrounded himself with synthetic dignity, as a bitter pill is encased in sugar-coating. In the early fifties, his figure reflected affluence. "Selby, how are you?" he said, pushing his stomach across the office, his face wreathed in an expansive smile. "It's been some time since I've seen you. I believe congratulations are in order on the way you're handling your office. You're making quite a record for yourself, Selby, my boy."

"Thank you," Selby said, shaking hands. "Won't you sit down, Mr. Benell?"

"Thank you, yes."

"My secretary said you wanted to see me on a matter of some importance."

Benell nodded. "About John Burke," he said.

"What about him?" Selby asked, his manner becoming guardedly aloof.

Benell avoided answering for a moment as he adjusted his huge form to a comfortable position in the chair on the other side of Selby's desk. He cleared his throat, shifted a half-smoked cigar from his left hand to his mouth, and said, "I'm quite a booster of yours, Selby. I'm very anxious to see you make a success."

"Thank you," Selby said.

"A district attorney is faced with numerous responsibilities. He has a great deal of power. He can do a great deal of good using that power. Also he can do a great deal of harm."

"Go ahead," Selby invited, as Benell paused to puff on his cigar.

"You'll understand," Benell went on, "that as a banker I am interested in the financial background of many businesses in Las Alidas."

Selby nodded.

"Take, for instance, the Las Alidas Lumber Company," Benell went on. "We've let them have money from time to time. When Lawler thought that there might possibly be a shortage in John Burke's accounts, he came to me at once. I detailed two of my best men to go over the books."

Selby again nodded.

"If there *had* been a shortage," Benell said, "I would have been the first to come to you and ask that a warrant be issued. Since there is no shortage and knowing in a roundabout way that you are investigating Burke's absence, I felt that it was only right I should report at once to you that while there have been certain trivial bookkeeping irregularities, there is no shortage. The cash on hand is amply sufficient to cover any carelessness in bookkeeping."

"You are referring to the ten thousand dollars in the safe?" Selby asked.

Benell raised his eyebrows as though surprised that the question should have been asked. "Why, certainly! One naturally includes the cash on hand in making up an account. Cash in the safe is a part of the cash on hand."

"Do the books show that there was any ten thousand dollars in the safe?" Selby asked.

Benell waved his pudgy hand in a deprecatory gesture. "I haven't gone into details," he said. "My primary concern was to ascertain whether there had been a shortage in actual assets."

"There was none?"

Back on familiar ground, the banker's manner became expansive.

"None whatever," he said.

"The accounts are in exact balance?"

Benell thought for a moment and said, "There have been numerous bookkeeping irregularities. I am afraid Burke's competency is open to question. But there can be no question of his honesty."

Selby said dryly, "If there is no shortage, and if the books don't balance, then there must be an overage."

Benell said, "There you go, Selby, putting words into my mouth. That's the lawyer in you."

"But that's the fact?" Selby asked.

"I believe so, yes."

"How much of an overage?"

"I'm sure I couldn't say. I don't bother myself with detailed figures."

"As much as a thousand dollars?" Selby asked.

"Well, in round figures you might call it that."

"Exactly what did you want?" Selby inquired.

Benell said, "You have been investigating John Burke's absence. Feeling that he might have embezzled funds from the lumber company, that's only natural. It's also very commendable. But, now that you understand there is nothing criminal in his activities, there is no reason for you to continue that investigation. Naturally, an investigation costs money—taxpayers' money. And as a taxpayer and a well-wisher I am interested in seeing that your conduct in office is above criticism. Naturally, we both of us wish to conserve the taxpayers' money."

"Then you want me to quit investigating John Burke?"

Benell's face was bland. "Why," he countered, "what is there to investigate?"

"He left Las Alidas rather abruptly under peculiar circumstances," Selby said, "and so did his wife. I . . ."

"A very nice little woman, his wife," Benell interrupted to assure him. "A *very* nice woman indeed."

"You know her?" Selby asked.

"I've met her several times. She's a depositor in our bank, you know."

"A large account?" Selby inquired.

"No, no. Certainly not. Just what one would expect of the wife of a bookkeeper. But we take a personal interest in our depositors, you know. I have had occasion to notice her financial competency."

Selby was silent until Benell's eyes rose to meet his. Then he inquired abruptly, "How about your withdrawals, Mr. Benell? Has there been any large cash withdrawal which would give you any inkling as to where that ten thousand dollars came from?"

"I couldn't say as to that," Benell said hastily. "It probably was received in the ordinary course of business, and Burke very foolishly allowed it to accumulate in the safe. The money has now been deposited to the account of the Las Alidas Lumber Company, and since that deposit made a larger checking balance than the lumber company required, eight thousand of it has been used to wipe out an indebtedness which the company had to the bank."

Benell abruptly scraped back his chair, got to his feet, and with a cordial smile said, "Well, I must be getting on, Selby, my boy. I just wanted you to know that everything was all right—and in regard to Burke, I think it would be well to drop the entire matter. The telegram received by the lumber company shows that his absence is voluntary. His wife is a very estimable woman—by the way, Selby, I understand you've been making inquiries concerning visitors in the house—a hobo, who, I understand, was given something to eat by her—that's an illustration of her charitable nature —but you know how neighbors are and how easy it is to make some ordinary occurrence seem peculiarly sig· nificant by attaching undue importance to it—so now that you understand the situation we can let this . . . er . . . hobo . . . go on his way, well fed and happy, eh, Selby?"

Benell reached over to shake Selby's hand and went on: "Thank you very much for seeing me so promptly, Mr. Selby. You're making a wonderful record in office. I've had occasion to tell my friends I thought you were a very good district attorney—and an economical dis- trict attorney. You don't squander the taxpayers' money on foolish or fruitless investigations—well, good afternoon, Mr. Selby."

It was as his hand was on the knob of the exit door that Selby said, "I don't suppose there's any chance you'd care to be frank with me, is there, Mr. Benell?"

The banker stood motionless, his face frozen in an expression of surprise. "Why, what do you mean, Selby?"

"Simply that I'm a curious individual. When a prominent citizen goes to a lot of trouble to show me how I can save the taxpayers' money, I always wonder what ax he's grinding."

Benell's face darkened. He controlled his feelings by a perceptible effort. "Selby," he said, "I'm not divulg- ing any secret when I tell you that you have severe critics in the county. You have need of every influ- ential friend you can make—or retain."

"Thanks," Selby said. "It's my opinion that what

this county needs is more officials who can concentrate on the job they took an oath to perform, rather than on how to be re-elected."

"Selby, do you mean to say you are ignoring my suggestion, spurning my friendship?"

Selby said, "I'm ignoring nothing. I particularly want you folks over in Las Alidas to feel that this is a friendly office, but I don't want the friendship of any man who tries to keep me from doing my duty. If you want to be frank with me, I'll be glad to listen to what you have to say and meet you halfway. I don't like to have you take the stand that you're big enough and powerful enough politically to make me drop an investigation of something that should be investigated."

"Do you mean that you're going ahead with the investigation?" Benell asked, his voice ominous.

Selby met his eyes. "I am."

Benell hesitated a moment as though debating whether to make some further statement, then abruptly turned, opened the door, and banged it shut behind him.

Chapter Six

SYLVIA MARTIN came running down the corridor and rapped excitedly on the exit door of Selby's private office. Selby unlatched the spring lock and opened the door.

"Oh, Doug, forgive me," she said. "But I just *couldn't* wait to go through the other office. Listen, Doug, I'm in a hurry, but promise me—promise me you won't say no."

He looked down into the dancing excitement of her reddish brown eyes, and said, "I won't say no—but I may say that what you want is impossible."

She made a little grimace. "Listen, Doug, the sheriff put through a call to Crandall direct and told him he wanted to find out something about Mrs. Burke. Crandall said he didn't know a great deal about her except that her first name was Thelma and she'd been married before—oh, Doug, I'm so excited I can hardly talk. He said he'd heard the name of her first husband, but couldn't remember it. The man had a ranch in Arizona somewhere, and then the sheriff asked him if the name was Lacey and Crandall said he thought it was."

Selby pursed his lips. "That's pretty slim, Sylvia. It's easy for Crandall to be mistaken, you know. Remember, he couldn't even recall the name."

"I know, Doug, I know, but I just feel in my bones that he *isn't* mistaken. Look, Doug, you're going down there. You'll have to now. Give me a break. Let me go with you."

"When?" he asked.

"Right now. As soon as we can. We could charter a plane and make it in three and a half or four hours."

Selby said, "I don't know. I don't think the taxpayers would care particularly about chartering airplanes for me. In fact, one of the influential taxpayers has just finished suggesting I drop the whole thing."

"Who, Doug? Benell?"

"Yes."

"That stuffed shirt! What business is it of his?"

"He's a taxpayer."

"Bunk. He has some ax to grind."

Selby smiled. "Well, his bank seems to have received eight thousand dollars on a note that may not have been worth exactly one hundred cents on the dollar— so I guess he'd like to let sleeping dogs lie."

"It isn't that, Doug. It's something bigger. You know it and so do I. The lumber company could have paid off that note. Benell's two-faced, suave, slippery and wouldn't lift a finger to help you."

"The Arizona authorities would get busy," Selby said. "They'd be glad to question Lacey for us."

"Doug, you simply *can't* turn this over to the Arizona police. They wouldn't know what it's all about, and if Lacey knows anything, he could pull the wool over their eyes. You've simply *got* to go yourself. And you've got to act fast. There's something going on here with people covering up clues and hampering your efforts to find out what it's all about. I know my paper will stand part of the expenses if it comes to that."

Selby said, "Well, we'll see."

She handed him a photograph still slightly damp. "Here are copies of the dead man's fingerprints," she said. "Terry had made the photograph and classification before you called him over to Las Alidas. He's back now and has wired in to the federal men to see if they have the prints on file.

"Thanks," he said.

"Promise, Doug, that you'll go to Tucson—and take me."

"Well," he said, "I'll think it over."

"All right," she told him. "That's as good as a promise, because when you think it over, there's only one answer. Listen, Doug. I'm on the trail of a set of those photos of the dead man. I'll have them in an hour. You can arrange for a plane and we could leave here about five o'clock. We can take along some soup in a thermos bottle, and some sandwiches, and have dinner on the plane."

"Call me back in half an hour," he said. "I'll let you know."

"Be seeing you," she told him, and turned to the door. He heard her steps as she ran lightly down the corridor.

Selby closed the door and stared down at the photographic record of the fingerprints. What secrets did they hold? A man had died. His body had been cremated, but these fingerprints remained, an irrefutable witness to the man's identity, lines etched by nature in the skin of a murdered man. Would these lines trap the murderer?

He reached for his pipe, filled it, and studied the fingerprints, letting his mind use these prints as a starting point from which to build up a theory as to what might have happened.

He was trying to account for the activities of this mysterious hobo on Tuesday night when Amorette slipped through the door and said, "Inez Stapleton wants to know if you can see her for a minute."

"Inez Stapleton!" he exclaimed. "I haven't seen her for ages. She's in the outer office?"

"Yes."

"Tell her to come in . . . wait a minute, Amorette. I'll need a plane tonight, flying to Tucson. I don't want anyone to know where I'm going. Slip down to Sheriff Brandon's office and ask him if he wants to go along. Tell him we're taking Sylvia Martin, then ring the airport at Los Angeles, and get a good, fast plane. We've had some planes from them before, and they know just about what's required."

She nodded.

"And tell Inez to come in—wait a minute. I'll tell her myself."

Selby pushed back his chair and strode to the door. "Hello, stranger," he called.

Inez Stapleton, slim, brunette, came to give him her hand, moving with that smooth-flowing grace which was so characteristic of her.

She met his eyes with a calm, steady gaze, but a tell-tale pulse was pounding rapidly in her throat.

"Where," Selby asked, "have *you* been?"

"Where I told you I was going eighteen months ago," she said.

"You mean . . ."

"Yes," she said, "studying law.—And I mean *studying*, not just playing at study."

"What progress?" he asked.

She smiled. "It was a three-year course," she said. "By studying right through the summers, I cut it down to seventeen months, one week and three days. Behold, Mr. District Attorney, Counselor Inez Stapleton, an attorney at law, duly admitted to the courts of the State of California."

"Inez!" he exclaimed, enthusiastically gripping her arm. "That's wonderful, simply wonderful!"

"Do you," she inquired, "ask me to come in and sit down or do I walk in?"

He laughed, and held the door open for her. After she was seated in the big chair across from Doug's desk, he was conscious of a change in her. There was a new maturity. She seemed more certain of herself. There was, moreover, just a hint of strain about the eyes. When her face relaxed, she looked tired, evidence of the grind which she had been through. But when she talked or smiled, the animated expression of her face and the sparkle of her eyes dissolved the lines of fatigue.

"Was it a grind?" Doug asked.

"Let's not talk about it," she said, with a light laugh. "It's over. My college work was prelegal, you know—or did you know, Doug?"

"Yes," he said, but his tone failed to carry conviction.

"You know, Doug, when I left you over a year ago, I had a mad up."

"I know you did," he told her. "I was sorry. It was something that couldn't be helped. I simply had to do my duty . . ."

She snapped her fingers. "Forget it," she said. "I don't care anything about *that*. George had it coming to him. He'd been mixed up in a hit-and-run case, and had tried to duck out and avoid responsibility. He was cutting a wide swath. Dad was simply ruining him. It was an awful blow to all of us, particularly Dad. It humbled our family pride, but things have worked out for the best.

"That judge in San Diego was very human. He said that he was going to grant George probation, but was doing it on the condition that he went back to school, that he didn't drive an automobile for two years, and didn't take a drink for five, that he be in bed by ten o'clock five nights a week, and report to the probation officer both personally and in writing at regular intervals. It's been a wonderful thing for George."

"Your father," Selby said, "couldn't understand. He . . ."

"Nonsense," she said. "Father understood perfectly. His pride had a hard blow, that's all. He sold out his interest in the sugar company and moved away. I think it was a fine thing for him as well as George—but what have you been doing, Doug?"

"Mostly routine," he said. "What are you doing back here? Are you going to practice?"

She met his eyes and nodded.

"Well," he said, with a quick laugh, "I may find you on the opposite side of a case some day."

Her voice was grave. "You may."

"Gunning for me, eh?" he asked, laughing.

"Not exactly," she said soberly, "but you outgrew me, Doug. And I let you outgrow me. When you were practicing law as a free lance, we used to have wonderful times together, tennis, hikes, swims, quick impromptu trips to the city, and all sorts of larks. Then you got elected to office and started taking things seriously. I suppose the background of Dad's money was what kept me from seeing things in their proper perspective. I did not realize, however, that—oh, well, skip it."

Selby reached across the desk to put his hand over hers. "It hurt when you left, Inez," he said, "hurt a lot. I thought, perhaps, you were bitter and vindictive and—well, I've thought of you a lot, wondered about hunting you up, and then, knowing you as I did, knew that *if* you felt that way, nothing I could say or do would change you."

"I didn't feel that way," she told him. "I simply determined to make you respect me in the field which has become so fascinating to you that you've given it every waking moment."

He changed the subject somewhat awkwardly, embarrassed by her calm frankness, feeling, as he always had, the power back of her steady, dark eyes. "How do you find the old town?" he asked.

"Very much the same," she said. "Are the two newspapers still fighting each other?"

"Yes."

"And *The Blade* fights you, and *The Clarion's* for you?"

He nodded.

"Sam Roper, the former district attorney, still out to get you?"

"Not as much as formerly," Selby said with a quick laugh. "He's lost some of his influence, and, I think, some of his grudge. He's settled down to private practice."

"And that Martin girl?" she asked. "What was her name, Sylvia? You still see quite a bit of her?"

He said, "Whenever I get on a case, she seems to be right on the job. She has a nose for mystery like a hound for a hiding rabbit."

"Well," Inez said, "you're going to see something of me now, Mr. District Attorney—quite a bit of me, in fact."

"Tennis?" he asked.

She shook her head. "No more tennis. You've outgrown that. So have I. We're going to have our battles in the courtroom, and I'm going to give you just as much to think about as I did on the tennis court."

"You had a mean serve," he said, studying her, "and a tricky return."

"Wait until we get in court," she threatened, with a laugh which seemed somehow only to lend emphasis to her words. "How about dinner tonight, Doug? We could climb in my car and slip down to Los Angeles. I know a place where . . ."

She stopped at the look in his eyes.

"An engagement?" she asked.

"Busy," he told her "I'm going to Arizona on a case."

"By train?"

"No, by plane."

She started to say something, then checked herself. "I see," she said simply. "I presume the press will be represented?"

Selby met her eyes then, and said shortly, "Yes."

It was her turn to change the subject. She looked down at the photograph of the fingerprints on his desk. "Who's the crook?" she asked.

"We don't know," Selby said, and then after a moment, added, "—yet."

"Mind if I look?"

"No, certainly not." He slid the photograph across the desk to her.

"Who made the classification?" she asked.

"Bob Terry."

"Oh, he's in the sheriff's office now?"

"Yes, he took up fingerprint work."

Inez Stapleton said coolly, "I'm not certain that I agree with his classification."

"What do you mean?" Selby asked.

"I think that what he's classified as a whorl in his denominator is in reality a tented arch."

Selby said, "Good Lord, Inez, don't tell me you're a fingerprint expert as well as a lawyer."

"Not an expert," she smiled, "but I've studied criminology and therefore know a little something about fingerprints."

"Why the criminology?" he asked.

"It's related to the law, silly. I wanted to fit myself for the work I'm doing, and I couldn't do that unless I knew something about criminology."

Selby said, "My own knowledge of fingerprint classification is rather sketchy, so go ahead and explain."

She said, "In a classification, the fingers are divided into pairs, and each finger has a numerical classification. The first is sixteen, the second eight, the next four, the next two, and the next one. The first finger of the pair goes into the denominator, the second into the numerator, then one is added. A number is only assigned to a finger when there is a whorl on that finger. For instance, in this classification of five over thirty-two, it means that there is one whorl in the numerator of the third pair, and that all of the denominators are classified as whorls."

Selby asked, "What is the difference between a whorl and a tented arch?"

"With a tented arch the ridges rise higher in the center and don't recurve, whereas in a whorl the ridges form a series of circles, or spirals, around the core or axis. Get a magnifying glass, Doug, look at this print, and I'll show you what I mean."

"I thought you counted ridges in order to get a classification," Selby said, taking a magnifying glass from his desk drawer.

"You do, but your primary classification is determined by whorls. . . . Look, see what I mean?"

Selby held the magnifying glass over the fingerprint as she traced out the course of the lines.

"I see," he observed, and for a few second concentrated on studying the ridges of the printed finger.

The telephone rang. Selby said, "Pardon me," picked up the receiver, and heard Sheriff Brandon say, "Doug, Bob Terry just told me he was changing the classification on that fingerprint."

"Thanks," Selby said, and then added, "I thought myself that he'd classified a tented arch as a whorl."

The sheriff's voice showed his surprise. "Do you know fingerprints, Doug?" he asked.

"No," Selby said, laughing. "I was just practicing by ear. How about our trip to Arizona, Rex?"

"We leave at five-thirty on the dot," Brandon said. "The plane can pick us up at the local airport. Sylvia tells me she's dug up some thermos bottles and sandwiches and is going to serve a sky-high buffet supper."

Selby said, "I'll meet you there and have my appetite with me."

He hung up the telephone to face Inez Stapleton's eyes in which there was something both quizzical and wistful.

"Just as much wrapped up in your work as ever, aren't you, Doug?" she asked.

"It's fascinating, Inez."

"One of these days," she said, pushing back her chair, "I'll be all wrapped up in my work—and when that happens, just *try* to get a dinner date with *me!*"

"Speaking of dinner dates," Selby said, "how about it? When I get this case cleared up, do we make a little whoopee?"

"When will you have it cleared up, Doug?"

"I don't know. Pretty soon, I hope. . . . Don't rush away, Inez."

"Thanks. I have places to go and things to do. I just dropped in to say hello. . . . If you don't know when you're going to be free, Doug, you'd better wait until you *are* free before extending any rash invitations. Be seeing you, and here's luck."

Her lips gave him a quick smile as she slipped through the exit door into the corridor. But her eyes were brooding.

Chapter Seven

THE PLANE seemed mysteriously detached from the world below, as it roared south and east through the gathering twilight. Sylvia had gathered up the remnants of their picnic supper, scraping the refuse into a pasteboard receptacle, crumpling the pasteboard dishes and the waxed cups into a compact bundle. Sheriff Brandon, fearing that the absence of both sheriff and district attorney from the county seat might make for criticism in *The Blade*, had decided at the last minute not to go. Selby and Sylvia were alone in the passengers' compartment.

"Let's switch out the lights while we have our cigarettes, Doug."

He nodded. She found the light switch and clicked the plane into the half darkness of twilight. Up in the pilot's compartment, the light-proof curtain which divided the fuselage into two compartments shut out all view of the illuminated instruments. A match flickered into flame, bathing their faces in red radiance. Then the fire was transformed into two glowing coals at the end of their cigarettes as Selby shook out the match and dropped it into an ash tray.

Down below, the desert streamed past—a desert which was not the flat, barren, waste of popular conception, but a desert of scarred buttes, of ancient lava flows, a desert where giant saguaro cacti thrust up arms at the skies as though reaching up at the speeding plane. Over in the west, the afterglow illuminated the horizon, leaving a trace of color over the sharply silhouetted contours of the California mountains.

"I see Inez Stapleton's back in town," Sylvia Martin said.

"Yes."

"She's a lawyer. Did you know that, Doug?"

"Yes."

"She told you?"

"Uh-huh."

"Almost two years ago she announced she was going to study law," Sylvia Martin went on. "Well, it must be nice to have the money to indulge one's little whims."

Selby said slowly, "It seems to me that's the most laudable use one can make of money—getting an education, developing character and being of the greatest possible service to the community."

For a moment, Sylvia Martin's voice was bitter. "Don't think she's actuated by any lofty ideals, Mr. District Attorney. She decided you had no respect for a wealthy playgirl. So she decided to change her spots. Whenever a good-looking young woman sticks doggedly to some course of self-improvement, you can gamble there's a man in the case."

Selby laughed nervously. "You flatter me. Inez and I are old friends. She's a level-headed girl. She realized she wasn't getting anywhere drifting through life."

"*Old friend!*" Sylvia Martin exclaimed. "Don't let her rope you in on that, Doug—oh, Doug, it's none of *my* business, but I'm so proud of you and I see so much ahead for you—things that would evaporate into thin air if you married a wealthy heiress and settled down to the smug respectability of being a very big toad in a very small puddle."

Selby patted her hand. "Don't worry," he said. "I don't intend to commit matrimony—not while I'm district attorney at any rate. When a man marries, he assumes definite responsibilities and should have a home life. The district attorneyship calls for a man who can be on the job twenty-four hours a day."

There was a long period of silence after that. Selby's hand unconsciously slid across the arm of the cushioned seat. His strong, taping fingers clasped about the throbbing warmth of her pliable hand.

"You mean you'd give up the office if you got married, Doug?" she asked at length.

"Yes, if you want to put it that way."

"Don't give it up, Doug. Don't do it until—until you've done the job the way it should be done."

"What job in particular?" he asked.

"The job of making the county seat respect you, the job of rising superior to politics, of showing a fearless, impartial law enforcement. Oh, Doug, I can't say it the way I want to say it. This job is doing things for you. . . ."

"Meaning I'm getting too serious?" he asked. "Seems to me I *have* heard that somewhere."

"No, not that, Doug. It's something good, something wonderful. It's a mental maturity—and something more. You're becoming . . . Doug, I guess I'm getting sentimental or something, but I can remember when you were running for office how much talk there was up and down the street that you were just a kid. And occasionally someone would recall your pranks— those practical jokes you used to play at lodge—and use them against you. It used to make me so mad—and I worked so hard—somehow, Doug, it seems as though this is something we're doing together, a work to which I'm dedicated with you. I can't bear to think of you ever turning your back on it." She sniffed a little and he saw that she was crying.

His arm slid around her, drawing her close to him. His lips brushed tenderly against her forehead. "Why the tears, Sylvia?" he asked sympathetically.

"Oh, I don't know, Doug. I'm just sort of g-g-goofy I guess."

She slipped a handkerchief from her purse, dabbed at her eyes, and lifted her head from his shoulder to stare at him in the gathering darkness. "You have enemies in Madison City, Doug, enemies who hate you, not because of you but because you're clean and square and capable, and they're the people who want corruption in politics so they can build up power and influence—oh, shucks, Doug, you know what I mean. Give me back that shoulder. I'm going to snuggle and be silent. Now don't talk."

They sat in silence, watching the stars grow in brilliance while the desert became concealed beneath the dark mantle of deepening night. Occasionally a rotating air beacon threw a long pencil of light, circling like some ghostly finger glowing with weird phosphorescence. Little bluish flames flickered about the exhaust ports of the roaring motors. The plane passed over a highway. Diminutive automobiles rolled below, invisible black specks that push fan-shaped fields of yellowish light before them, dragged a blood-red pinpoint of ruby light behind. Then a city appeared, laid out in checkerboard squares, outlined with the blazing brilliance of a star cluster seen through a powerful telescope. The plane swept on. Selby moved his head so that his cheek was pressed against the cold slab of the window. Looking ahead, he could see a twinkling cluster of light that spread out to the side of the plane.

"That's Tucson ahead," he said. "We've made a quick trip."

The pilot swept back the curtain over the window in the partition. They could see the glowing circles of illuminated dials against which his head and shoulders showed in a competent silhouette.

"Doug," Sylvia Martin said, "don't turn on those lights till I've had a chance to get the traces of sentiment off my face—a mawkish sentiment which ill befits a hard-boiled reporter getting an exclusive scoop in a murder case. Go up front and see what he wants."

Selby patted her cheek, slid out of the cushioned chair, walked to the door in the partition and opened it. The pilot, raising his voice, said, "Tucson ahead. We'll be down in five minutes."

"Nice going," Selby complimented.

"You want me to wait for you and take you back?"

"Yes."

"How long will it be?"

"Darned if I know," Selby said. "You'll just have to stick around and charge for your time accordingly."

With a click of the light switch, the cabin of the

plane was flooded with brilliance. Sylvia, smoking a jaunty cigarette, smiled up at him and said, "Just what's the program, Mr. District Attorney?"

"We locate Lacey," Selby replied. "Rex Brandon has telephoned ahead and a deputy sheriff will be waiting with a car. We shouldn't have very much difficulty."

"Look," she said suddenly, "did Oliver Benell bring a *lot* of pressure on you to drop this whole business?"

"Yes," he admitted. "Why?"

She frowned and said, "I don't know, and keep wondering about him."

The motors of the plane slowed in tempo. The craft tilted forward, seemed for the moment to lose buoyancy.

Selby reached across Sylvia to fasten her seat belt, then fastened his own. Her hands, helping with the snaps, brushed against his with a touch that was a caress. The plane banked sharply, and the window was filled with the illumination of city lights. A confusing sense of circular motion made Sylva and Selby feel strangely light-headed. Then, as a dark oblong stretch loomed below, the plane straightened and dipped. Floodlights illuminated a long runway. Searchlights in the wings of the plane cast long beams downward. Almost before they could accustom themselves to the thought of being heavy groundlings again, the plane had landed and taxied up to a stop in front of an illuminated hangar.

As the pilot switched off the motors and came back to open the door, an automobile slid up almost alongside the plane. Selby stepped out and surveyed the driver, a broad-shouldered, rangy individual with outdoor skin and a five-gallon hat tilted slightly toward the back of his head.

"Selby?" he asked.

"Yes."

"The sheriff over at Madison City telephoned and asked me to meet you. I'm Jed Reilly, the under-sheriff —call me Buck if you want to. Most people do."

"Glad to meet you, Buck," Selby said, laughing and shaking hands. "And this is Sylvia Martin, a newspaper reporter from Madison City."

"Swell," Reilly said, looking approvingly at the slender form of the girl. "I like reporters—particularly when they're as good-looking as this one—and you don't see many of them as are—about one in ten million."

Sylvia flashed him her prettiest smile.

"We can sit three in front," Reilly said.

"You know the man we're looking for?" Selby asked.

"Uh-huh."

"How far do we have to drive?"

"Not very far. Fifteen miles."

"Sheriff Brandon told you what we wanted?"

"Nope. Said he wanted me to find out if Jim Lacey was home. I found out he was. He owns the 3-bar-L ranch."

"Married?" Sylvia Martin asked crisply.

"Nope. He's a bachelor—was married once, but it didn't take."

"What kind of a citizen is he?" Selby asked.

"Good," Reilly announced emphatically. "A square-shooter—what do you want to see him for, if it's any of my business?"

"Just to question him about the theft of his automobile," Selby said.

"Somebody lifted it a couple of nights ago, but it's been recovered all right," the under-sheriff said. ". . . Must think it's important if you come gallivanting over here in aeroplanes just to ask him questions."

Selby turned the inquiry with a laugh. Sylvia, with

lithe grace, squirmed in under the steering wheel of the big car and took her place in the center. "Okay, boys," she said. "Let's go."

"And I wait here?" the aviator asked.

"Yes. Get your plane filled with gas, and you'd better get something to eat. If it's fifteen miles out, it'll take us at least an hour to make the round trip and get what we want. You can count on that much time. After that, be ready to take off at a moment's notice."

"Okay," the pilot said.

Buck Reilly eased in the clutch and slid the big car into motion.

For the first ten miles the road was paved, and the ribbon of cement flowed smoothly beneath the wheels of the car. Then the deputy sheriff swung the car abruptly to the right at an obscure crossroad, and his passengers braced themselves as the car jolted over a dirt road which apparently had gone for a long time without attention.

"Evidently there isn't much travel over here," Selby said.

"Oh, he uses it quite a bit, but he's an old hand and accustomed to the desert. . . . You'll realize when you see him. . . . And don't do any monkeying with Jim Lacey. He's all right when you shoot square, but he's dynamite if a man ever tries to doublecross him."

Selby's eyes narrowed. "Rather dangerous?" he asked.

"He could be."

"Ever been in any trouble down here?"

"Took a shot at a man once."

"Hit him?"

"Naw. The guy ducked behind a boulder—and ducked just in time, what I mean. He was on one of Lacey's claims; didn't think Lacey meant business when Jim told him to beat it."

"What happened after that first shot?" Selby inquired.

"The guy beat it."

Selby flashed Sylvia a significant glance. "Suppose that rock hadn't been there?" he asked.

"There'd have been one claim-jumper less?"

"What would have happened to Lacey?"

"Nothing much—probably. It was his claim."

"I see," Selby said.

The road twisted and turned, following the contour lines of a dry canyon until it finally debouched upon a mesa where clusters of ocotillo thrust spine-covered stalks high above the ground, looking in the reflected illumination of the automobile's headlights like some weird grouping of breadsticks in an Italian restaurant. Down closer to the ground where the chunky shapes of cholla cactus, and in the background the grotesque saguaros.

"What does he grow on this ranch?" Selby asked.

"Cattle, mostly. You can't judge the land from what you see up here. Over on the other side of the ridge, there's a valley—no flowing water, but good wells. He has some alfalfa fields and raises quite a bit of hay."

The road crossed the mesa, dipped down a ridge on the other side, and the dry cold of the desert air became tempered with moist scents of bottom land covered with growing green things. A gate barred the road. Selby jumped out and opened it as the undersheriff brought the car to a stop. A few moments later, the tires were crunching gravel as the car swung in a circle before the white tile of a modern adobe house.

"Well, here we are," Reilly said, "and there's a light in the living room. Do you want me to sort of break the ice, or do you want to bust right in?"

Selby hitched down his vest, squared his shoulders, and said, "I'll bust right in."

He led the little procession up the steps. The knocker was made from the iron part of a stirrup hinged in a metal sleeve and drooping against an iron plate. As Selby raised and dropped it several times, it filled the night with dull, ringing sound.

A moment later a man in the early fifties with motions almost birdlike in their explosive quickness opened the door, regarded Selby with puzzled gray eyes which flashed an approving glance at Sylvia, and then softened as they rested on the under-sheriff.

"Good evening, Mr. Lacey," Selby said. "I want to talk with you."

"Who are you?"

"Douglas Selby, of Madison City, California. Does that mean anything to you?" Selby said.

"Not a thing," Lacey said, "except that you're my guest. Come in and sit down. Why didn't you give me a ring, Buck, and I'd have had some of my hot toddies all mixed up. It must have been cold riding."

They entered the house, and Lacey gave them seats in the big living room—seats that were made from hand-hewn native wood, covered with rawhide stretched in such a manner that the occupant of the chair naturally reclined, with his feet elevated at just the right angle to insure maximum comfort.

After the incessant drone of airplane motors which had beaten on Selby's ears for the past few hours and the rushing of air flowing past the speeding automobile, the tranquil silence of the desert night seemed to beguile his eardrums into producing fantastic echoes. It was as though his ears were chasing a mirage of sound. When he tried to relax, he could hear the noise of motors until, concentrating upon these sounds, he would find that there was, after all, nothing but a silence so majestically impressive that it seemed as tangible as the thick walls on which coiled rawhide riatas were hung from wooden pegs.

Lacey said to Selby, "So you're from Madison City?"

"Yes. I'm the district attorney of Madison County."

Lacey's face didn't show any expression. He said, "I owe you boys up there something. You recovered my stolen automobile. How about a little drink?"

Reilly grinned. "If it ain't too late, and you *could* make one of those hot toddies," he said wistfully.

"I'll have one for you right away," Lacey promised.

Reilly turned to Sylvia with sudden confusion. "Guess I spoke out of turn," he said with a grin, "but Lacey's hot toddies are famous. I hope you'll pardon me getting my feet right up to the trough and speaking first."

Sylvia laughed away his apology. "I don't think I care for a thing," she said to Lacey.

"Oh, surely," he protested, "you'll try one of my toddies. It will warm you after the chill of your ride."

"Only a teeny little one," she said. "Don't load it."

Lacey looked at Selby.

Selby shook his head.

"A little tequila? A little Scotch and soda? A . . ."

"No, thanks," Selby said, adding with a smile, "I can't afford to drink when I'm on business."

"On business?" Lacey asked tonelessly.

"On business," Selby said firmly and without explanation.

"Excuse me a moment. I'll get those toddies started. I think I can find one of the servants—although they go to bed pretty early."

He stepped through the arched doorway into the corridor. His high-heeled cowboy boots could be heard clump-clump-clumping along the square red tiles.

"I don't like that particularly," Selby said, frowning.

"I wanted to talk with him before he had an opportunity to do too much thinking." After a moment he went on, " I think I'll just step out to the kitchen if you don't mind."

Reilly said uneasily, "I wouldn't if I was you, buddy. You've got to take things just so in this country. We've come to call on Lacey, and his code is to extend his hospitality before we get down to business."

Selby fished his crusted pipe from his pocket, tamped fragrant tobacco down into the bowl and thoughtfully regarded the arched doorway through which Lacey had vanished.

"Swell place he's got here," Reilly went on. "Notice all those braided ropes, those silver-mounted spurs, and these Indian rugs. Those Navajos are worth a fortune. The modern ones are Two-Gray-Hills. The older ones are . . . Here he comes now."

Lacey clumped back down the corridor. "They're as good as made," he said. "One of the Mexican servants is still up. I measured everything out. Soon as they're hot, she'll serve 'em." He stretched himself out in one of the big chairs, and inquired courteously of Doug Selby, "Did you drive over from Madison City?"

"No," Selby said, "we came by plane."

"Nice way to travel," Lacey observed, "—if you like it. I don't think I'd care much for it. I've been thrown pretty high by a bronc, and that's as high as I want to go."

"I was wondering," Selby said abruptly, "if you could give me any details about the theft of your automobile?"

"No, I couldn't," Lacey answered easily, "except that I can identity the automobile all right. But I gathered from the wire I received there's no question but that it's my car."

"Where was your car when it was stolen?"

"Right out here in my garage."

"How long had it been missing before you discovered the theft?"

"Now that I can't tell you," Lacey said. "You know, an automobile is something you use when you have to, but horseflesh is the way nature intended a man to travel. Whenever I'm doing anything around the ranch, I throw a saddle on one of the broncs and go where I want to go without bothering about highways and tourists and speed cops. When I *have* to go to town, I take the Cadillac. Sometimes once a week, sometimes twice a week, and sometimes—when I can't help it—once a day."

"Do I understand the car was stolen from your garage?" Selby asked.

"That's right."

"At night?"

"I wouldn't know. I'd been in to town Monday morning. Wednesday morning I had to go to town again. I went out to the garage, and there it was, empty."

"That the only car you have?" Selby asked.

"No, I have a station wagon and a truck. I use the station wagon for light supplies and things of that sort, and the truck for the heavy stuff."

"So what did you do?"

Lacey grinned and nodded toward the under-sheriff. "Well," he said, "I went to the telephone and called the sheriff's office and happened to get Buck on the line. I told him what had happened, and he said he'd teletype a description of the car, and I'd probably get it back. I'm willing to admit I didn't think much of my chances at the time, but sure enough I got a wire from this place up in your country—what's the name of it?"

"Las Alidas," Selby said.

"That's right. And then Reilly called me on the phone just a few minutes afterwards."

Slipshod steps sounded in the corridor. A dark-haired, dark-skinned woman with bent shoulders came shuffling into the room carrying a tray on which reposed three steaming cups. The tempting odor of hot liquor and nutmeg filled the room.

Lacey spoke quickly to the woman in Spanish as she hesitated a moment, apparently undecided. At the sound of his command, she shuffled over to Sylvia.

"Oh, but I wanted just a small cup," Sylvia protested. Then, with a quick look at Lacey, said, "And don't tell me to drink only what I want and let the rest go, because I haven't that much will power—or is it *won't* power?"

He gave her an impish, good-natured grin as she took the cup and saucer. His manner with her was in contrast to the calm courtesy he showed Selby. The servant shuffled over to the under-sheriff, then to Lacey.

"I hate to see you sitting there and not drinking anything," Lacey said to Selby. "Won't you have a little tequila? I have some very nice . . ."

"No, thanks."

The servant turned to leave the room. Reilly said, "Here's regards, and . . ." Sylvia Martin's cup and saucer dropped from her fingers to crash into slivers on the flagged floor.

The old Mexican servant hardly looked up. With the stoic patience of her race she gave no sign of resentment.

"Oh, I'm *so* sorry!" Sylvia Martin said. "I touched the side of the cup, and it was hotter than I expected and . . ."

"It's quite all right," Lacey said. "Panchita will get you another drink. A hot toddy isn't any good unless

64

it's really *hot,* and I'd had the cups warmed. I guess Panchita got them too hot."

He spoke once more in Spanish to the servant who went to a closet, took out a towel, dropped to her knees, and sopped up the steaming liquid. After she had gathered the pieces of broken crockery and left the room, Lacey said, "You'll pardon us if we go right ahead with this drink, Miss Martin. Yours will be along directly. A toddy just isn't good for anything unless it's *hot.*"

She smiled graciously. "Please do."

Selby said abruptly, "Look here, Lacey, you don't seem very familiar with Madison County."

Lacey regarded him with coolness amounting almost to hostility. "So what?" he asked.

"You've never been there?"

Lacey looked up from his cup, studied Selby intently for a moment, and then said shortly, "No."

"Do you know anyone who lives there?"

"Not that I know of. Why, what's the matter?"

"Did you know a John Burke—a bookkeeper and accountant employed by a lumber company there?"

"Burke . . . Burke . . . No, the name is familiar, but I don't seem to place any *John* Burke. Why do you ask, Mr. Selby?"

Selby ignored the question. "How about Mrs. Burke?" he asked. "Her first name was Thelma."

There ensued another period of silence during which could be heard the slippety-slop—slippety-slop —slippety-slop of the servant's feet coming back down the corridor.

Something in Lacey's attitude struck Selby forcefully. The man seemed to be tense, listening. The sound of those shuffling steps along the flagged corridor seemed to be associated in his mind with something which made him definitely ill at ease.

Selby flashed a quick glance to Sylvia. He saw her eyes narrow until they were almost closed, then flicker quickly about the room as she made a swift survey to see if the eyes of the others were on her. Finding they were not, she lowered her right eyelid in a quick warning wink.

The steps approached the door. The Mexican servant, her form concealed in the folds of a voluminous black dress, the hem of which swept the floor as she walked, entered the room and gave Sylvia a fresh cup of steaming liquor.

One more Selby became conscious that Sylvia was staring significantly at him. "Oh," she said to the servant, "there's another piece of the saucer!" The servant dropped to her knees. Sylvia leaned forward to assist the woman in picking up the fragment of porcelain. As she did so, her right hand rested for a moment on the back of the woman's dress.

"Wait a minute," Sylvia exclaimed with a little half laugh that was first cousin to a giggle. "I'm off balance . . . I've overreached myself!"

She was pivoting on her left hip which was resting on the extreme edge of the chair. Her right leg extended itself as she strove to maintain her balance, her skirt sliding up along the smooth silken contour. But Selby's eyes were on Sylvia's right hand because he realized that was what she wanted him to watch. He saw the hand make a quick motion as though clutching involuntarily, saw her fingers hook over the neck of the Mexican's dress, pulling it back some two or three inches.

Selby's eyes saw plainly the line of color demarcation. From the base of the neck up to the hair, the woman was Mexican, her skin smooth and dark. Below that point she was white-skinned.

With a quick exclamation, the Mexican woman

twisted free. Sylvia regained her balance. Lacey started to say something and caught himself. The Mexican woman got to her feet, flashed a glance at Sylvia, then, at what she saw in the young woman's face, straightened.

Selby, thinking fast, said, "Don't you think it would be better to be frank with us, Mrs. Burke?"

Lacey came to his feet with such vehemence that the hot liquor slopped unheeded over the sides of his cup. "What the devil are you talking about?" he demanded.

Selby sensed the menace in the man's attitude, saw the blazing anger in his eyes, and calmly said, "Don't make it any worse than it already is, Lacey."

The under-sheriff was on his feet, puzzled, watching Jim Lacey's right hand.

The "Mexican" woman said wearily, "Oh, what's the use, Jim? I knew it wouldn't work. The girl spotted me from the first. She dropped that saucer so she'd have a chance to look at the back of my neck. Then she pulled back my dress so *he* could see."

Reilly said, with a drawl which somehow held an ominous note, "Jim, I don't know what this is all about, but don't make any foolish moves with that right hand—there's a lot of things you can explain if you have the chance. But a foolish move with that hand . . . "

"Please, Jim," the woman pleaded, and crossed to him. But not until she had interposed her body between Lacey and Selby did the man relax.

Sylvia's eyes were large and eager, taking in every detail. The under-sheriff, puzzled but, of a sudden, wary and watchful, held his right hand near the left lapel of his coat.

Selby seemed the coolest person in the room. Sitting back in his chair with his knees crossed, he puffed at his pipe. "Don't you think," he said, "it would be a lot better if we all sat down and talked the thing out?"

Slowly, reluctantly, Lacey dropped back into his chair, the woman's hands on his shoulder gently pushing him down. Then she turned to Selby, the incongruity of her appearance emphasized now by her erect carriage and flashing eyes. The body, which had been stooped from work, shapeless in the voluminous folds of a black dress, had completely vanished. In its place was a tall, slender young matron standing supple and erect, the ill-fitting, baggy clothes disguising but failing to conceal the contours of a beautiful figure.

Selby inquired of Lacey, "Why did you go to Las Alidas?"

Mrs. Burke said quickly, "He didn't."

"How did it happen his car was there?" Selby asked.

"It's a coincidence. It's just as he said. Someone stole it. Everything else was planned perfectly, and then this had to come along and upset our plans. I knew as soon as I heard of it that the thing would never work."

"What wouldn't?"

"My leaving John."

Selby said, "Suppose you sit down, Mrs. Burke, and tell us the whole thing from the beginning—but first I want to ask a couple of questions of Mr. Lacey." He turned to Lacey and said, "Your car was parked within a block of Burke's house. A man got out of that car who was dressed in ragged clothes and carried a roll of blankets. A few moments later, a man who answered that same description was being embraced by Mrs. Burke. The consequences of lying to me may be very serious. Therefore, I'm not going to take an unfair advantage of you. I'm going to tell you those things, and then I'm going to ask you the question once more. *Why* did you go to Las Alidas?"

"I tell you he didn't go," Mrs. Burke said. "I can explain . . ."

"I want Lacey to answer this question," Selby interrupted. "It's the second time I've asked it, and the second time you've rushed in with an explanation. Now, Lacey, I want your answer to that question."

Lacey said, ominously, "I don't like your attitude."

"My attitude, as it happens, has nothing to do with it," Selby said. "I am here in an official capacity. I am doing my duty as the district attorney of Madison County, and I am investigating a murder."

"A murder!" Mrs. Burke half screamed. "Who was murdered?"

"I don't know," Selby said. "I *had* thought it was Lacey who was murdered. I came here prepared to investigate the situation, and rather anticipated I'd find some impostor who had assumed the name of Lacey—that is, if I found anyone. But Reilly's identification seems absolute."

"He's Lacey all right," Reilly said. "He's hotheaded and dangerous if you crowd him. Take it easy and he'll co-operate. Just go a little slow, Selby. I don't want to have things get out of control here. This is *my* bailiwick, you know, and Lacey's a friend."

"Of *course* he's Jimmy Lacey," Mrs. Burke said. "It's absurd to think otherwise."

"And I'm still waiting for an answer to my question," Selby went on.

"But *who* was murdered?" Mrs. Burke demanded.

"That," Selby said, "is a question I'm not prepared to answer right now."

Mrs. Burke whirled to Lacey, moved swiftly to the side of his chair, dropped a hand to his shoulder. "Please, Jim," she said, "don't answer *any* questions. No matter what happens, simply don't answer anything. Simply refuse to answer a single question. I think the law gives you that right. Please do that for me."

Selby waited until she had finished, and then said, calmly, "That isn't going to help matters any, Lacey."

Lacey's manner was truculent. "I don't give a damn whether it helps matters or not," he said. "Thelma's hunch goes with me. She's asked me not to talk, and I don't talk."

"That," Selby said, "is going to make it exceedingly difficult—for you."

Lacey shrugged his shoulders, then added, after a moment, "You're being pretty high-handed, Selby. You may find *you're* in difficulties."

The under-sheriff fidgeted nervously. "Look here, Jim," he said. "If there's really a murder and you've been doing anything that ain't connected with the murder but looks as though it mighta been, you'd better kick through and talk. This is going to get in the newspapers all over the country, and what people think first is going to have a lot to do with what they think last. If you refuse to answer questions, it ain't going to look so good."

"Please, Jimmy," Thelma Burke said, almost tearfully, "don't let them talk you into . . ."

"I won't," Lacey interrupted. "You don't need to worry about that, Thelma. I'm sitting tight as a clam, Buck."

Selby said quietly, "We've done a lot of talking, and there have been a lot of interruptions, Lacey, but so far you haven't answered my question."

"That's right, I haven't," Lacey said.

"Are you going to?"

"No."

"Do you refuse to answer?"

"Yes."

"On what grounds?"

"On the ground that it's none of your damn business."

Selby said patiently, "I haven't enough facts before me as yet to form an intelligent opinion about what happened, but I have every reason to believe a deliberate, diabolically clever murder was committed. I have every reason to believe that circumstantial evidence is going to connect you in some way with that murder or with some of the events which immediately preceded it. I'm warning you that any refusal to answer questions puts a sinister interpretation on your own movements of last Tuesday night."

"All right," Lacey said, "that's *your* speech, now I'm making *mine*. I have a right to see a lawyer before I say anything. I haven't seen a lawyer. I'm not saying anything."

Selby turned to Mrs. Burke. "How about you?" he asked.

She squared her shoulders. Still standing by Lacey's chair, she said, "*I'll* talk. I'll answer questions. This is my affair entirely. I don't want Jim involved in it."

"The best way he can keep from being involved in it," Selby said, "is to clear up his connection with what happened. Once he's done that, we can leave him out of it—if his explanation is satisfactory. If he fails to make that explanation, he's just as deep in the mud as you are in the mire, and I don't mind telling you both that's rather deep."

"Look here, Jim," the under-sheriff said, apprehensively, "this thing ain't going so good. Suppose you and I take a little walk out here in the patio and talk for three for four minutes, just as one friend to another."

"Don't go," Thelma Burke said.

Lacey sat perfectly still. "I've said all I'm going to,"

he observed calmly. "I'm not answering any questions."

"Will you please let *me* tell what happened?" Thelma Burke asked.

Selby nodded. "Go ahead and talk," he said, "but remember that we're investigating a murder, that anything you say may be used against you."

"You don't know who was murdered?"

"No."

She said, "Honestly, Mr. Selby, this has nothing to do with a murder. It's purely a private affair. Jim and I were married. I was foolish, headstrong, and impetuous. I expected too much of a man, and didn't know enough about men to excuse superficial faults. Jim was a wonderful husband, but I was a little fool and didn't have sense enough to know it. We were both hotheaded. I left him. We were divorced, and John Burke married me. As soon as the gilt wore off John Burke, I saw that he was plain brass underneath. He had polish and glitter, but it was only a superficial goldplating. I realized then that Jim Lacey was solid gold. . . . He was genuine where John Burke was counterfeit. He was true where John was false. The only thing he lacked was the spurious polish which attracted me to John."

"Why didn't you leave?" Selby asked.

"I was going to," she said, "and then I found . . ." She took a deep breath, met his eyes, and said quietly, "I found I was going to have a baby."

"And then?" Selby asked.

"So I made up my mind that I'd stick it out. About that time I read a magazine article written by a woman who said that marriage was a career, that it was up to the woman to make it successful, that by tact and intelligence *any* marriage could be saved from the rocks of divorce, that it was the duty of a woman to save a marriage where there were children. The article went on to describe what a horrible thing it was for a child not to have a father—and I fell for it."

"You don't believe that now?"

"Of course not. It's a thousand times better for a child not to have a father than to have its character shaped by living with a two-faced, selfish, deceitful, ill-tempered brute who occupies the position of head of the house."

"And I understand that your husband, John Burke, answers that description?"

"Every bit of it," she said.

"Where is John now?"

"I don't know. He . . . he went away."

"Where?"

"I don't know. He went away and left me with the baby."

Selby's eyes narrowed. "And he left his job?"

"Yes."

"And was short in his accounts?"

"Certainly not," she said emphatically. "Whatever other faults John Burke has, he isn't an embezzler. He's utterly selfish and inconsiderate. He's narrow and egotistical. He's very much of a brute in many ways. He has no consideration, and no idea of how to treat a woman. He's a failure as a husband and a menace as a father. But he isn't an embezzler. He's honest."

"You seem rather certain of his honesty."

She answered defiantly, "I am."

"What makes you so certain?" Selby asked.

For a moment there was silence, then she said, in a voice which somehow lacked assurance, "Because I know him so well."

Lacey said, "Look here, Selby. I think you're carry-ing this thing too far. I think this woman is entitled to a lawyer."

"Why?" Selby asked.

"Because you're accusing her of murder."

"Accusing *her?*" Selby inquired, raising his eyebrows. "I don't know what gave you that idea, Mr. Lacey."

"You virtually said so."

"I said that I was *investigating* a murder. Circumstantial evidence seems to indicate that . . ."

"Oh, Jim," Thelma Burke interrupted, "please don't. Please leave me alone. I know what I'm doing. Can't you see this man is clever? He's deliberately trapping you into a discussion so you'll make admissions. Let me do the talking. This is my responsibility."

"I don't like the way he's bullying you," Lacey said.

"There's nothing you can do about it, Jim. He represents the law."

"What if he does?" Lacey countered. "You go see a lawyer who knows the law. Then we'll find out just what this man's representing, what he can do, and what he can't do. It's my idea he's taking in too damn much territory, trying to throw too wide a loop."

"But, Jim," she pleaded, "it's all so absurd! I have nothing to conceal."

She turned to Selby, and said, "I may as well make a clean breast of it, Mr. Selby. I tried to stick it out with John Burke. I found I couldn't. It came to a head when John threatened to kill me and the baby—and he's just the pinheaded, emotional, egotistical type to do that very thing.

"It got on my nerves. He started carrying a gun, showed it to me a few days ago, and then I read in the paper about how some man had killed his wife and child in a fit of jealousy . . . and . . . well, I just made up my mind I was going to leave."

"Why was he going to shoot you?" Selby asked.

"Jealousy."

"Of whom?"

She pointed toward Lacey.

"Lacey had been visiting you?" Selby asked.

"No," she said quickly. "I don't think Jim even knew where I was, but John sensed that I was still in love with Jim and it made him furious. He may love me in his cracked, warped way—but I don't think any man can love a woman and treat her the way he's treated me."

Lacey stirred uneasily in his chair, his eyes dark with anger.

"So he threatened to kill you?" Selby prompted.

She nodded.

"What did you do?"

"I took Airdre—that's my little girl—and left."

"*When* did you leave?"

"Wednesday night."

"What time?"

"I don't know what time it was. I was frightened. I just made up mind we'd clear out. We drove all night; we only arrived this morning."

"You had some definite plan?" Selby asked.

"Yes."

"To come here?"

"Yes."

"Did Lacey know of it?"

"No, he didn't know a thing. I don't think he even knew where I was. I'd deliberately refrained from letting him know—well, that's all there was to it."

"How did you get here?"

"In my automobile. It isn't much, but it gets you there."

"Your husband's car?" Selby asked.

"*Our* car," she said, "if you want to put it that way."

"And why the disguise?" Selby asked.

"Because I was afraid John might suspect where I was and try to follow me."

"You told Lacey about that?"

"Yes."

"And that's the reason Lacey is carrying that gun in his hip pocket?"

"I guess so, yes."

"Where's Airdre?"

"In my room, asleep."

"The other servants?" Selby asked.

"We let them all go."

"And how about this automobile?"

"That," she said, "is just one of those coincidences that happen in real life. Some hobo walking along the road came to the door looking for something to eat. He found there was no one home, happened to look in the garage, saw the automobile, and decided to take it. He figured, of course, he could drive to California and abandon the car before the alarm had been broadcast. It just had to be fate that he left that automobile in Las Alidas."

"And within two blocks of your house," Selby pointed out.

She was silent.

Selby shook his head slowly. "That simply isn't credible."

"I know it, but it's a fact just the same. Someone stole that automobile . . . unless someone deliberately planted the car . . ." Her eyes suddenly lighted. Her manner became eagerly animated. "John himself could have done it," she said, "and it's just like him. If he'd found out where Jim was and had intended to kill Airdre and me, it would have been just like him to have gone and stolen Jim's automobile and driven it to Las Alidas so it would look as though Jim had done the killing."

"In that event," Selby said, "John Burke must have stolen the car sometime on Tuesday and driven it to Las Alidas."

"Yes."

"Do you think he did that?"

"He might have done it," she said. But even as she spoke, some of the assurance faded from her voice.

"What's the matter?" Selby asked. "Have you thought of something which means he couldn't have done it?"

"No."

"Thought of something which means a story you'd hoped to put across wouldn't stand up?"

"No," she said defiantly.

Lacey said ominously, "That'll be enough of that, Selby. I don't give a damn who you are or what you represent. You'll not insult that woman—not in this house."

Selby paid no attention to the comment. "Now let's see, Mrs. Burke," he said, "you had no one to fear except your husband. Is that right?"

She hesitated for a long moment, and said, "Yes, that's right."

"And these elaborate precautions to hide your identity by disguising yourself as a servant were solely for the purpose of keeping your husband from finding you?"

"Yes."

Selby tapped the ashes of his pipe into the ash tray, and said, "Mrs. Burke, I want to take a look through your baggage. Do you have any objections?"

"Why . . . I . . ."

"You can't search this place without a warrant," Lacey interposed.

"I'm asking Mrs. Burke if *she* has any *objection* to a search of her baggage," Selby said doggedly.

"Why, what on earth are you looking for?" she inquired.

"That's not the question," Selby observed. "Do you have any objection?"

"Why, I . . . I don't know . . . I see no reason why you should."

"Well, *I* object," Lacey said. "If you ask me, you've gone plenty far enough—too damned far."

Selby got to his feet, and motioned to Sylvia. "Very well," he said; "that, I believe, covers it. As I told you, I am investigating a mysterious murder which seems to have been cleverly planned. It was a cold-blooded, premeditated murder. I don't know all the details as yet. I felt that the disappearance of Mrs. Burke was rather significant. I wanted to check on that. . . . By the way, Sylvia, you have those photographs there?"

"Yes."

Selby extended his hand. Sylvia Martin opened her brief case, and handed Selby three eight-by-ten enlargements printed on glossy paper.

Selby crossed to where Lacey stood with his arm circling Mrs. Burke's waist. He said, "I don't want to subject you to any undue strain, Mrs. Burke. I warn you that these are pictures of a dead man taken as the body was discovered. It's not a particularly pleasant subject. However, I can't complete my questioning without asking you if you know this man or have ever seen him before."

And Selby handed her the picture.

For a moment, the two stood staring at the photograph while Selby studied their faces. Lacey held his face expressionless as a good poker player might deliberately keep expression from his face at a moment when he knew others were watching him for some betraying flicker of emotion.

Mrs. Burke stood very straight and very erect, her eyes staring steadily at the photograph. But her lips twitched involuntarily with some emotion she was unable to control. When she spoke, her voice was high-pitched. "I . . . I don't . . . My God! . . . It's John!" she screamed, and flung the photographs from her, turning to pillow her face against the lapel of Lacey's coat.

"What do you mean, Thelma?" Lacey asked. "You don't mean . . . it can't be . . ."

"It is," she said. "It's John Burke, my husband. He's dressed as a hobo, but it's John. . . . He's shaved his mustache. He hasn't his glasses . . . but it's John!"

Selby said very quietly, "I didn't want to shock you, Mrs. Burke. I'm sorry. I'm investigating a murder. I want you both to come to Madison City and answer questions before the grand jury. Will you come?"

Mrs. Burke stared at him with wide, startled eyes. "It's John," she said, "and he was murdered! Murdered! It's John! It's John! I tell you, it's John!" Her voice rose to hysterical screams.

"You poor kid," Lacey said, picking her up in his arms as though she had been a baby.

"That'll be all, Selby," he said, striding from the room, carrying the wildly sobbing woman in his arms. A moment later her shrill, hysterical laughter rang from the corridor.

Reilly said nervously, "I guess I don't have to tell you your business, Mr. Selby, but there's going to be trouble here. I know Jim Lacey pretty well. He's gone just about as far as you can crowd him. . . . If you want a suggestion, take that phone there, put through a call to Madison City, and have a warrant issued for the arrest of Mrs. Burke on the charge of murdering her husband. Then you can get a fugitive warrant here and take her into custody."

For several thoughtful seconds Selby regarded the telephone.

"No," he said, at length, "I think I have a better plan than that." He walked to the corridor and was struggling into his overcoat when Lacey's steps came pounding down the corridor. He stood, shoulders squared, facing Selby in silent, ominous hostility.

In the silence of the corridor, the hysterical sobbing of the woman could be heard coming from one of the bedrooms.

Selby said quietly, "I'm sorry, Lacey. I didn't know the dead man was her husband. I had begun to think it might be, but I didn't know."

Lacey said nothing. He continued to stand in the hallway, ominously silent.

Selby helped Sylvia into her coat. The under-sheriff seemed frankly nervous. He looked once or twice at Lacey as though he wanted to say something, but Lacey stared straight through him with stony hostility.

"All right," Selby said, "let's go."

He led the way to the front door and strode out into the cold, crisp, desert night.

Lacey continued to stand in the corridor. Reilly was the last to leave. He turned and fumbled with the knob of the door, held it so that he was facing the lighted corridor.

"Close the door, Reilly," Selby said quietly.

Reilly held the door open for a long moment, his face concealed from Selby, his eyes fastened on Lacey. Then he slowly pulled the door shut.

In silence the trio walked across the crunching gravel to the under-sheriff's big automobile. A moon, but slightly past the full, had sprung up over the eastern mountains, etching the surroundings into silver and black. The intense dry cold of the desert had taken possession of the valley, freezing out the odor of growing green stuff, cutting through their overcoats, puckering the skin of their faces.

Reilly said, "He's a square-shooter, Jim Lacey. If I could talk to him alone for a minute, I think he'd loosen up and tell *me* what he knows."

"He's had his chance to talk," Selby said.

Reilly fidgeted with the door of the car. "The woman's lying," he said, "She ain't kidding me, and Lacey ain't kidding me. Jim Lacey drove that car to Las Alidas, and you know it as well as I do."

Selby ignored the opening to say quietly, "The next thing we want to find out is whether Jim Lacey withdrew ten thousand dollars in cash from his bank sometime Monday. Do you suppose you could find that out for me?"

"I reckon I *could*," Reilly said without enthusiasm. "Suppose he did? What does that have to do with it?"

"In that event," Doug Selby said quietly, "I think we'll telephone Madison County, get a warrant issued and return to arrest him for first-degree murder."

The cold silence of the desert night seemed to magnify the sound of Jed Reilly's startled intake of breath.

Chapter Eight

JED REILLY used the telephone in the sheriff's office at Tucson, and located the bank cashier at his club. In a voice that was singularly without enthusiasm, he explained what he wanted to know and that it was important. While they were waiting for the banker to report, Reilly talked with nervous volubility about subjects not connected with the case. Sylvia kept herself as much as possible in the background. Only her eyes showed her excitement.

Reilly was in the midst of a story about three Mexicans bandits when the telephone rang. He interrupted his anecdote to pick up the telephone to say hello, then frowned darkly at the somewhat battered top of his desk as he listened to the words which came through the receiver. After a moment he said, "Thanks a lot for the information, Pete. I guess that's all they wanted to find out."

He hung up the receiver, avoided Selby's eyes for a moment, and then said, "You win. Jim Lacey drew ten thousand dollars in cash about two o'clock Monday afternoon."

In the moment of silence which followed, Sylvia's scurrying pencil point was distinctly audible.

"Well," Reilly asked, in a weary tone, as Selby remained silent, "what are you going to do?"

Selby said, "I'm going to leave that to you. I want Lacey and Mrs. Burke to come to Madison County and be available for interrogation by the grand jury. I won't place any formal charges just yet. If they're innocent, they owe it to themselves to clear their names. If they're guilty, flight won't help them very much. We'll catch them sooner or later."

"Shucks," Reilly said. "Jimmy Lacey is no more guilty of murder than I am. I'm not so certain about that woman."

"Well," Selby said, "suppose the woman *did* kill her husband, then what?"

Reilly puffed at his cigarette for several uneasy moments, then said, "Well, of course you can't blame Jim particularly. He'd naturally try to protect the woman he loved—the woman who had once been his wife."

"And technically," Selby went on, "what does that make him?"

"What do you mean?" Reilly asked.

"I'm talking from the viewpoint of a prosecuting attorney," Selby said. "If James Lacey juggles facts or commits overt acts to protect a woman who has committed a murder, he becomes an accessory after the fact. You know where that puts him."

Reilly hitched slightly forward in his chair. "Now look here, Selby," he said, "a man has to use his head on these things. Of course, laws are laws, but people ain't all alike. Now Jim Lacey's a good substantial citizen, but he's human just the same. Sometimes it ain't good business to bear right down with the letter of the law."

Selby got to his feet, stood looking down at the under-sheriff, his legs spread slightly apart, shoulders squared, eyes ominously steady. "Now then," he said, "I'll tell you something. You haven't said so in so many words, but it sticks out all over you that Jim Lacey is important politically to your office. While we were out at Lacey's place, you tried one excuse after another to talk with him where I couldn't hear what you said. Now I don't *know* what you were going to tell Jim Lacey. I know what I *hope* you'd have told him. After I leave, you're going to have an opportunity to talk with him. Now remember just one thing— I try to give a man who plays ball with me the breaks. When a man tries to give me the doublecross, I throw the book at him. I don't want to come into this county and upset your political applecart. You've co-operated with me. You were in a position where you had to. Nevertheless, I don't want to put you in a position where you're going to lose any political skin.

"I want Jim Lacey and that woman to appear before the grand jury at Madison City. If they want to co-operate, they'll start for Madison City right now. If they *don't* want to co-operate, they can't say I didn't give them the opportunity, that *you* didn't give them the opportunity, or that I didn't give *you* your chance."

Reilly got up and pushed his hand out to Selby. "Buddy," he said, "that's damn square. That's all I wanted. Lacey supported the boss in the last election. I want a chance to go to him and talk with him. I want to give him a chance to get in the clear."

"Tell him," Selby said, "that there's just one chance —that's all he'll have."

"I'll tell him," Reilly promised.

Selby turned to Sylvia and nodded. "Let's go," he said.

Chapter Nine

IT WAS almost midnight when the plane Doug Selby had chartered banked into a turn and groped its way into the Madison City airport. There was no flood-lighting on the ground, and the pilot used the moon-light and lights on his wings to come in to a somewhat bumpy landing.

The plane taxied over to the far end of the field, and Doug assisted Sylvia out of the plane, the back-wash from the propellers of the idling motors whipping her skirts about her legs.

"How about it?" the pilot shouted. "Want me any more?"

"No more," Selby said. "Can you take off from here?"

"Sure."

"Okay. Send your bill to the county."

Selby escorted Sylvia over to where he had left his machine. They stood and watched the plane taxi around for a start, heard the motors roar into power as the plane swept down the field. Like some huge night bird, the plane blotted out a section of the sky as it moved upward. A few moments later it had become merely a pin-point of light streaking down the moon-lit heavens, throwing behind it the roaring strum of motors.

"Tired, Doug?" Sylvia Martin asked.

He shook his head. "It's exhilarating," he said, "even if it is sordid. Riding in a plane through the clear moonlight makes you feel completely divorced from murders and politics and lies."

"I know, Doug. I felt that way, too. I hated to come down."

"Well," he said, "you go home and get some sleep."

She laughed. "We don't put the paper to bed until three o'clock in the morning. This night life is almost routine for me. I have a story to write."

"You want to be dropped off at the newspaper office?"

"Please," she said.

Doug drove her to the *Clarion* office. As the car drew to a stop, Sylvia placed her hand over his. "Thanks, Doug, for everything," she said. "It was wonderful. Are you going to call Sheriff Brandon now?"

"No, I won't disturb him. This can all keep until morning," Selby said, and she noticed that there was a note of weariness in his voice.

"Bye-bye," she told him, "and don't forget to read

The Clarion tomorrow morning."

Selby watched her in through the doors where the office of the newspaper hummed with a buzz of activity. Then he drove to the house where he maintained his furnished apartment, put his car in the garage, and went to bed. For almost an hour he lay trying to quiet his mind, which skipped nimbly from bodies lying in the frost-covered bed of a dry wash to belligerent Arizona cattle ranchers and then finally to the clear moonlight which had made the world below seem as a distant planet.

It was with the thought of the plane in his mind that he fell asleep.

He fought back to consciousness from a deep sleep. He had been battling his way through a wild dream in which James Lacey, riding on the cowcatcher of a rushing locomotive, had thrown a lasso around the body of a tramp lying in the wash and, with a whisk of the rope, jerked the body up in the air and caused it to disappear, much as a Hindu magician performs his rope trick. And above the mocking sound of Lacey's laughter the hysterical screams of Mrs. Burke finally resolved themselves into the continued steady ringing of a persistent telephone bell.

With his thoughts still numbed by slumber and groping his way to reality through the distorted realm of the world of nightmares, Selby said hello in a thick, muffled voice.

Brandon said, "Hello, Doug," and rattled into unusually swift speech which simply failed to register on Selby's brain. It wasn't until the sheriff had been talking for some ten or fifteen seconds that Selby's head cleared as though it had been under a cold shower. He heard the sheriff say, ". . . watchman reported to Billy Ransome. Ransome found a key and opened the door. Benell was lying there in front of the vault. The door was open. Benell had been shot in the left side of the head. Looks as though he'd been shot from behind."

"Oliver Benell?" Selby interrupted.

"Yes."

"Where?"

Brandon said patiently, "Guess you didn't hear very well, son. I told you that it was in the First National Bank. Looks as though bandits had pulled him out of bed, taken him down to the bank, forced him to open the vault, and then shot him from behind. The vault's been looted clean, all except some reserve cash that was in a cannonball safe. I'm giving you the facts the way Ransome gave them to me over the telephone. Sure glad I got you, Doug. I was afraid you hadn't got back from Arizona."

Selby said, "Let me get into some clothes, Rex. What time is it?"

"Around four o'clock," the sheriff said.

"You'll drive by for me?"

"In ten minutes," Brandon said.

"I can be ready in five," Doug told him.

"Okay," Brandon said, "I have a couple of calls to put through. I'll make 'em soon as I can."

Selby was waiting out in front by the time Brandon drove up. Bundled in his overcoat, the district attorney was shivering slightly in the cold darkness.

The sheriff opened the car door and said, "Never rains but it pours, Doug. Looks as though you aren't going to get much sleep."

Doug settled back against the cushions, and was glad of the big auto robe which the sheriff had thoughtfully provided.

Madison City was ghostly and silent as Sheriff Brandon piloted the car through the deserted streets. The tang of frost was in the air. The moon, well over in the west, bathed the streets and houses in a cold, pale radiance. In the chill of the early morning, the silhouetted fronds of palm trees against the skies seemed strangely incongruous.

"What did you find out in Arizona, Doug?" the sheriff asked. "Get anywhere?"

Selby gave him a quick résumé of what had happened.

Brandon said musingly, "Seems strange that Benell would have taken such an interest in the case—particularly in view of what you found out down there. Billy Ransome says there's no question but what it's a bankbandit job, but personally I ain't so sure. Looks as though Benell must have known something more than he told you. Maybe he was mixed up with the Burkes some way."

Selby said wearily, "I suppose so. The way I figure right now, it'll take about two cups of coffee to bring my mind to a point where it can digest another crime."

Brandon said, "We'll probably find some place open in Las Alidas. Ransome told me the whole town was awake. I've got a few deputies over there, and they've organized a posse. I telephoned Bob Terry right after I called you—got him out of bed and told him to get posses together and start them patrolling all the hobo camps along the railroad. He'll get them started and then follow us to Las Alidas.

"Ransome says he telephoned the neighboring counties and told them to watch the roads. That stuff doesn't do much good unless you have a definite description of the persons you want, but it has a moral effect and sometimes scares the criminals into holing up."

Selby sighed and said nothing.

The tractors were still plowing. Occasionally, off the highway could be seen the glare of headlights and the cough of a tractor would become audible above the smooth purring hum of the county car's motor.

Selby shivered and said, "Gosh, how I'd hate to be out there on one of those things."

Sheriff Brandon nodded. "When we get too much civilization," he said, "we forget that life is a fight to get a living out of the soil. Other things give us the conveniences, but when it comes right down to a show-down, there's where the battle of civilization is being fought, Doug." And the sheriff took one hand from the wheel to make an inclusive gesture toward a rolling sweep of land across which the headlights of a tractor were laboriously marching. "Some people get pretty far away from it, living in the conveniences of cities. But there's the front-line trench right there, son, and that chap sitting in the tractor seat with the frost seeping into the marrow of his bones is one of the shock troops. You gotta fight for a living if you want to live. Nature's made that way."

They found an all-night café on the highway near Las Alidas. Selby gulped two hasty cups of coffee, and felt new life warm his body. As they re-entered the car, the sheriff, grinning somewhat sheepishly, said, "Let's let them know the county officers are coming in," and switched on the red spotlights and cut loose with the siren.

The machine leapt into speed as the sheriff's foot pressed the throttle. Roaring through the streets of Las Alidas, the siren screaming its alarm, the sheriff slid the car to a stop in front of the First National Bank Building, cut off the motor, switched off the head-lights, grinned across at Selby, and said, "If they only knew we'd stopped for a couple of cups of coffee on the road—come on, son, remember to take it on the run as we cross the sidewalk."

Recognizing the practical political value of the sheriff's advice, Selby pushed the car door open. A group of spectators were crowded around the bank entrance. They respectfully opened a way for the district attorney and the sheriff; and the county officials went through on the run. Billy Ransome, warned of their arrival by the sound of the siren, flung the door open for them.

Big, tall, apparently good-natured, the chief of police now held his forehead puckered into a ferocious scowl of official concentration. He was overweight, but his fat was hard, and he held himself well erect.

"Hello, boys," he said. "Come in. Looks like a bad business."

They followed the chief through the swinging plate-glass doors into the marble and mahogany interior of the bank.

Ransome led the way through the door marked Executive Offices and then through another door opening into the room where the vault was situated.

The vault door was swung wide open. Sprawled in front of it, lying half in and half out of the vault, lay the body of Oliver Benell, face down, the extended right hand pointing toward the interior of the vault, the left doubled under the body.

In the vault, lights were on and two grim, white-faced men with tired eyes were making notes.

"The cashier and his assistant," Ransome explained. "You know them. We're trying to make a quick estimate of what's gone."

The cashier, whose name Selby for the life of him couldn't remember, came over toward the door of the vault and looked at the sheriff and district attorney across the body of Benell. "Can't we move that body?" he asked. "It seems brutal to leave it there. . . ."

Ransome said importantly, "That body's gotta stay there until we've gone over everything for clues. He's dead. There's nothing we can do for him—except track the guys that did this down to earth and pin a first-degree-murder rap on 'em."

"A doctor's seen the body?" Sheriff Brandon asked.

"Yeah. I got Dr. Endicott just as soon as they notified me. He's dead all right. Been dead for something around two hours, maybe a little less, maybe a little more."

"Find the gun?" the sheriff asked.

"Yes, I did," Ransome said, opening the drawer in a desk and disclosing a gun lying on a sheet of paper. "The gun was on the floor by the body. I've made a little chalk mark to show where. I didn't want to leave it where it was with people moving around in here for fear we might lose some fingerprints. So I slid this piece of paper under it and put it in the drawer."

Sheriff Brandon frowned toward the vault, and said, "We aren't going to get many fingerprints out of the vault," hesitated a moment, then added significantly, "now."

Ransome flushed and said, "Well, the night watchman let these boys in here. You see, I was in bed. The watchman telephoned me and telephoned the cashier. The cashier got here a little before I did and . . ."

The cashier interrupted to say, "We don't want to interfere with your investigations, but we have a duty to our depositors, as well as a duty to the community. We have to learn how much was taken and wire the bank examiner for instructions. We may . . . well . . . I don't think I'll make any statement right now, but we certainly aren't going to have people in the bank moving around in this vault until we've taken steps to make some sort of an inventory. That's final."

"Seems to be," Brandon remarked cheerfully. "If you've got a piece of chalk there, Billy, let's make an outline of the body. Bob Terry will be following me over with a camera. I told him to get in touch with some of the boys, and start posses around the hobo camps. Here he comes now."

The sound of another siren grew from a faint wail in the distance into a harsh shriek. A few moments later, Bob Terry came in, carrying his fingerprint apparatus and a camera.

"Let's get some pictures, Bob," Sheriff Brandon said. "Fingerprint the outside of the vault door. It's probably too late to do much with the inside now. There's a gun to be fingerprinted. As soon as you get done, they can move the body."

Brandon turned to the chief of police as Terry started setting up a big tripod. "Did anyone see them enter the bank, Billy?"

"Apparently not."

"Where's his car?"

"That's the thing that makes me sure it's a gang job. His car's at his house in the garage. He'd evidently put the car in the garage and gone to bed."

"Was the house broken into?"

"No, he must have opened the door. Looks as though someone rang the bell, got him to answer the door, stuck a gun on him, forced him to dress, drove him up to the bank, made him open the vault, and then shot him from behind."

"You've been out at the house, Billy?" the sheriff asked.

"Yes, I took a quick run out there and put an officer in charge to see that no one goes in and touches anything."

"Let's go take a look out there," Brandon said.

"Okay. Go in your car or mine?"

"Ours is better."

Terry asked, "Where's that gun?"

Ransome opened the drawer and showed it to him. "I'm turning it over to you now," he said.

"Okay," Terry said.

"Shoot some pictures," Brandon instructed, "do what you can here, then beat it out to Benell's house. I have an idea we'll find more there than we will here. . . . How about the neighbors, Billy? Do they know anything?"

"No. Nothing that'll help. The house on the north is vacant. The people on the south heard a car drive up, heard voices over at Benell's, and saw the lights switch on. They say it was some time after they'd gone to bed, which was around eleven-thirty. They don't know how much after. A man and his wife—neither of them woke up enough to pay much attention. The man heard the car drive up. The wife heard voices over there afterwards. She thought one of them was a woman's voice. Then the car drove away."

"Were the lights on or off in the house when you got there?" Selby asked.

"Off."

Brandon frowned. "A man being stuck up wouldn't switch the lights off when he left the house," he said, "and it doesn't hardly look as though bandits would have done it."

"They might have, at that," Ransome said. "They might have figured a house lit up at that hour of the morning would attract attention."

"There's something to that," Selby admitted. "Well, let's go."

On the way out, Ransome seemed quite proud of his activities. "Of course," he said, "I'm not organized to do much with a crime like this. They keep me short-handed and my men overworked. I rounded up every man I had on the force, telephoned the police in adjoining counties, put a guard out at the house, and

93

told him to interrogate the neighbors, and then keep the place closed. We may find something out there."

"We'll see," the sheriff said.

Ransome gave them directions on the streets to take. The sheriff pulled to a stop in front of an attractive modern house of Spanish architecture, with white stucco walls and a small front porch roofed with red tile. In the rear was a garage with a driveway leading past a white-walled patio. Lights were on in the house and the figure of an officer was illuminated by the porch light.

"How'd you get in?" Selby asked.

"The cashier at the bank knew where Benell kept an extra key in his desk," Ransome said. He spoke to the officer on guard. "Anything new?"

The man shook his head.

"Nobody been trying to get in?"

"No one."

"We'll go on in," Brandon said. "When Bob Terry comes, let him in. Don't let anyone else in. Be careful not to touch anything, boys. Where's his wife, Billy?"

"Visiting friends in Portland, Oregon. Benell was alone in the house. A servant comes in to clean up during the day. He's been eating his meals uptown."

"No dog?"

"No."

"Seems strange Benell would have opened his door at this hour of the night to people he didn't know," Brandon said.

"You forget that about the woman's voice," Ransome pointed out. "A woman could have made the stall that her car had broken down and she wanted to use the telephone."

"Uh-huh," the sheriff grunted skeptically.

Ransome pushed forward to open the door, then

stood back to let the sheriff and the district attorney enter first. They walked into a house furnished with excellent taste in modernistic fashion. The chairs were of chrome steel upholstered with blue leather. The lighting was all indirect. Wall vents showed that the house was air-conditioned. Through the French doors in the dining room could be seen the patio, which had been designed as a place for relaxation, with tiled porches, hammock-swings, chairs, well-kept plants, and a fountain which overflowed into a goldfish pond. The blue-colored indirect lights in the walls of the patio gave an effect of intensified moonlight.

"Quite a place," Brandon muttered.

Ransome led the way into a modernistic bedroom, a place of huge plate-glass windows, Venetian blinds, and streamlined furniture. There were twin beds, two closets, and a bath, two dressers and several chairs. The doors of both closets were open. One of them contained feminine garments. The other was well filled with expensively tailored men's suits.

One of the beds had been slept in. The covers had been turned back, and the sheet and pillows were rumpled. Over near the closet door, a suit of blue silk pajamas lay in a pile on the floor. Near by were bedroom slippers.

"Just as you found them?" Selby asked.

"Nothing's been touched," Ransome said.

Abruptly the telephone started ringing.

The men exchanged glances. Ransome said, "How about it, boys?"

Brandon shook his head. "There may be fingerprints on that telephone receiver."

Selby said, "We might pick the receiver by the upper end. That doesn't sound like an ordinary call to me, the way central keeps ringing."

"Tell you what," Ransome suggested. "We can go

across to the neighbors' house and get the call from there. You'll want to question the neighbors anyway."

"Good idea," Selby said. "Let's go."

They filed across to the adjoining house. An elderly couple, very evidently much perturbed, were getting an early breakfast. The aroma of coffee and frying bacon assailed Selby's nostrils, made him realize that he was hungry. Billy Ransome performed introductions. Brandon apologized for the disturbance, went to the telephone, and asked the operator about the call on Benell's line. She said, "I'll see. Hold the line, please." A moment later, the crisp voice of the long-distance operator said, "Tucson, Arizona, is trying to reach District Attorney Selby. The cashier at the bank said he'd be at Benell's. They say it's very important."

"Put the party on," Brandon said. "Selby is here."

Selby picked up the receiver in response to Brandon's nod, and a moment later, heard central say, "Go ahead," and Reilly's voice saying, "Gee, Selby, I guess I pulled a boner."

"What happened?" Selby asked.

"Well, I went out to Lacey's house—not right away after you'd left because I wanted to give him an opportunity to cool down. Well, I got out there, and there were no lights in the place. I pounded around on the doors for a while, and got no answer and concluded Lacey had decided to go to bed and let us go to the devil. I came back uptown, and kept thinking things over, and a half an hour ago got a brainstorm I shoulda had earlier. I remembered that Lacey had told me once about an aviator here named Paul Quinne. Said he was related to his divorced wife and asked me to give him a break on any county jobs that might come up. There hadn't been any county jobs, and I'd all but forgotten about him. But I went down to hunt up Quinne just to see if he knew anything.

Well, I found Quinne had pulled out of the airport about half or three-quarters of an hour after you'd left, and said he was going to fly to New Mexico and then on a cross-country tour. The interesting thing is he had some passengers—Jim Lacey, Mrs. Burke, and the baby."

Selby digested the information in silence. At length, he said, "Okay, Buck. Thanks for running it down."

"Thought I'd let you know," Reilly said, his voice anxious. "Guess I sorta let my sentiments get in the way of duty tonight."

"Forget it," Selby said. "You stood by me when Lacey's right hand got nervous. By the way, what relation was Quinne, do you know?"

"I checked on that," Reilly said. "He's Mrs. Burke's brother."

"Thanks," Selby said, and was about to hang up when the crisp voice of the long-distance operator said, "Mr. Selby, I know, of course, about what's happened, because of calls I've been putting in. I took it on myself to check the record of Benell's telephone to see if there were any long-distance calls you should know about. One of the operators on duty remembered that she'd put through a call to Benell from a pay station in Tucson, Arizona, tonight. Does that help any?"

Selby could feel his fingers involuntarily tighten on the receiver. "I'll say it helps," he said. "Who was calling?"

"It was a woman. She didn't give any name. The call was placed as a station-to-station call, and was paid for at that end."

"I don't suppose your operator listened in on any of the conversation?" Selby asked.

"No, except right at the tail end. She cut in to see if the line was clear and heard the woman say, 'shortly after midnight. Good-by.' "

Selby said, "Thanks a lot. We'll be down to check on that," dropped the receiver into place, and nodded significantly to Sheriff Brandon. "Looks as though we're getting some place, Rex," he said.

Chapter Ten

EIGHT O'CLOCK in the morning found Doug Selby seated across from Rex Brandon in a Las Alidas restaurant, with empty plates pushed to one side, and the two engaged in a low-voiced conference, running over the information they had uncovered.

Billy Ransome, who was very much married to a wiry little woman of five-feet-one who weighed a hundred and two pounds, but who never hesitated to announce that she "took no sass" from her husband even if he was the chief of police, had gone home to breakfast, almost tearfully pleading with them not to leave before he returned. Shrewd in the ways of small-town politics, he knew that it was excellent advertisement for him to be seen huddled in conference in a public restaurant with the sheriff and the district attorney, and only his wife's peremptory command over the telephone had dragged him away.

Selby crammed tobacco into his pipe, settled back in the somewhat uncomfortable bench seat, and contentedly puffed out blue wisps of smoke.

"Here's what we've got to go on," he said. "The Western Union office in Phoenix reports that the wire purported to have been signed by John Burke is a phoney. Someone telephoned it in, said they were calling from a certain telephone, and asked to have the wire sent and charged to that telephone. He gave the number and the Western Union operator asked him in whose name the phone was registered. The party gave the correct information. It's easy to do that. All one needs is a telephone book and a voice that radiates assurance. All right, that wire was a stall. All we know is that it was sent by a man, because the operator remembers it was a man's voice. Probably the same man who got the body cremated without identification.

"Mrs. Burke's telephone shows that she telephoned Lacey in Tucson twice, once Monday morning at eleven o'clock, and once Monday evening at seven-thirty. It also shows that she telephoned her brother, Paul Quinne, at the Tucson airport at eight-thirty Monday morning. At nine-fifty yesterday evening, some woman called Oliver Benell from the pay station in Tucson.

"Now this much is certain. Benell knew something about Burke. For some logical reason, he wanted the investigation on Burke's disappearance called off. In other words, he was connected with it in some way. *Perhaps* it was only because he wanted to grab that ten thousand dollars for the bank. It looked like it at the time. Subsequent events seem to indicate he may have had another reason. I'm inclined to think the crimes are all connected, and Benell was killed because of that information."

Brandon, rolling a cigarette, said, "Don't forget that something caused him to go to the bank somewhere around two or three o'clock in the morning. He didn't go to the bank in his own car. He went with someone. That someone made a good thing out of it. As nearly as the preliminary check-up shows, the bank is out almost fifty thousand dollars. That's a sizable haul."

Selby was about to say something when Bob Terry

came in, his face showing the strain of fatigue. He drew up a chair, ordered a waitress to bring him a pot of coffee, and then pulled a series of photographs from his pocket.

"Any luck?" Sheriff Brandon asked.

"Yes," Terry said, "but I don't know what it is yet. That thirty-eight caliber revolver had been wiped free of fingerprints. There wasn't a fingerprint anywhere on the outside of it. What's more, the numbers have been ground off so that we can't trace the gun sale. That makes it look very much like a professional job."

Selby said to Brandon, "Of course, Rex, it *could* have happened that Benell knew something about this other job, yet that his death had nothing to do with that."

"It commences to look that way," the sheriff admitted. "The numbers being filed off the gun and the fingerprints being wiped off are kinda significant."

Terry opened the bag which he was carrying at his side, pulled out the revolver, and said, triumphantly, "*But* I found something."

"What?" the sheriff asked.

"Sometime—there's no way of telling when, it may have been days, weeks, months, or perhaps years ago—someone was cleaning that gun. His fingers were moist, and one finger pressed against the inner surface of the hinged piece that throws the cylinder out. Look here."

He snapped the catch, jerked out the cylinder and showed a well-formed fingerprint outlined in dark, reddish etching.

"What's that?" Selby asked. "Bloodstains?"

"No, apparently it's just rust. Here's a photograph of the fingerprint."

He pulled out a photograph and spread it on the table. "I've been working in one of the local camera studios," he said, "and have my stuff pretty well developed. There were lots of prints out at Benell's house. Some of them were Benell's. Some of them weren't. Some of the more recent ones I found on the chrome-steel arms of a chair in the bedroom. I found some on the doorknob and one on the glass top of the dresser. That modernistic furniture is the cat's whiskers for fingerprints."

Terry produced a series of photographs from the bag and spread them out. "This is the haul," he said.

Selby and Brandon bent forward to examine the fingerprints.

"You've enlarged these?" Selby said.

"Yes, these are all enlargements."

"They all look the same to me," Selby said. "This one looks just exactly the same as the one I saw yesterday—the one that you brought into the office."

Terry interrupted with a smile. "They look the same to non-expert eyes, Mr. Selby, just as all makes of automobiles look alike to someone who doesn't know what to look for. But the trained eye looks at the slope of the radiator, the shape of the windshield, and the lines of the body, in classifying an automobile, just as the trained eye looks for points of distinction in a fingerprint. No two fingerprints are the same."

"I suppose so," Selby said, "but just the same I happened to notice those fingerprints of the dead man rather closely. Someone was pointing out to me the difference between a tented arch and a whorl and . . . Say, Bob, let's just check this with those fingerprints."

Terry hesitated for a moment as though disliking to interrupt the procedure with a useless gesture, and then said, "Very well, Mr. Selby," pulled several prints from his inside pocket, and finally selected a series of ten prints. "Incidentally," he said, "we've received a telegram from Washington. They don't have anything on this man. Whoever he was, he didn't have a criminal record."

"We've identified him," Selby said.

"Who was he?"

"John Burke who worked for the lumber company here."

Terry gave a low whistle. "Then he wasn't a hobo?"

"Not in the accepted sense of the word. He may have been starting out to be one," Selby said. "Here, Bob, show me where this fingerprint you've taken from the gun is different from the fingerprint of this middle finger on the right hand."

"Well, in the first place, Mr. Selby," Terry said, "we start making a pattern of the finger. We get what we call the 'core' and the 'delta' and measure the intervening ridges."

He put the two prints side by side, took a magnifying glass from his pocket, and a small finely divided scale.

"Now take this line on the core," he said, "and figure to the delta. Then we count the number of ridges which are cut by a straight line, and then we do the same on this other, and . . ."

He became abruptly silent.

"What's the matter, Bob?" Sheriff Brandon asked.

Terry faced them with startled eyes. "By gosh," he said. "They *are* the same."

Selby and Sheriff Brandon exchanged glances. Terry returned feverishly to a contemplation of the prints. After a minute or two he straightened and nodded to Selby. "A good hunch, Mr. Selby," he said. "They're the same."

"Then," Selby said slowly, "this gun with which the murder was committed was at one time in the possession of John Burke."

"That's right," Terry said.

"There's no opportunity for mistake?"

"Not the slightest chance of it," Terry said. "It's mathematical."

"What are those other prints?" Selby asked.

"Those are prints from various jobs," Terry replied, indicating the sheaf of photographs he had taken from his pocket. "Some of them are from the safe of the Las Alidas Lumber Company. Some of them are from a burglary job in a cigar store in Madison City, and one of them is a set of prints I got from the back of the mirror in that stolen car job. You remember I told you the steering wheel had been wiped off carefully; so had the door handles and the gearshift and the brake lever, but on the *rear* side of the rear-view mirror there were two dandy prints."

Selby said quietly, "Let's take a look at those prints and see if they match with any we have."

"Of course," Terry said, "I haven't tried to classify any of these yet. I've been too busy developing latents and getting impressions. And most of these prints came from things there in the house. That chrome steel made regular etchings of fingerprints. Let's see if any of these check . . . wait a minute, here's one that looks promising."

Brandon and Selby watched him in silence while he compared two prints, then straightened with a puzzled look, and said, "Look here, Sheriff. *These* two are the same. One of the prints on the back of that rear-view mirror on the automobile and one from the underside of the chair arm in that front room."

"Then the man who drove that car from Arizona was in Benell's house," Selby said.

"Well, you can't be certain it was the man who drove the car from Arizona. Those prints on the back of the rear-view mirror might have been there for some time. They may have been made by the owner of the car."

"Just check them with the prints of the dead man," Selby said. "I'm commencing to think this whole thing may fit into one pattern."

A few moments later Bob Terry said in an odd voice, "Gosh, Mr. Selby, I don't know what we're getting into, but you've called the turn. The prints on the back of that rear-view mirror were prints of the dead man we found yesterday morning in the wash, and this print which came from the underside of that chair arm is also from that dead man."

"Therefore we have his prints on the revolver with which the murder was committed, on the arm of a chair in Benell's house, and on the rear-view mirror of an automobile which was purportedly stolen from Tucson, Arizona," Selby said.

"That's right."

Selby and Brandon exchanged glances. "Look here," Selby said, "it's important to develop this thing all the way. Suppose we seal up that house tight as a drum, telephone Los Angeles, and get a couple of good fingerprint men to come up and help Terry out. Then let's go over every single article in that house and check every latent we can find."

"Terry's covered the ground pretty well already," Sheriff Brandon said. "I was figuring that if it was the work of a gang, they'd be pretty apt to have criminal records, and we might get enough fingerprint evidence to identify them."

"What would John Burke have been doing in Benell's house?" Terry asked. "He wasn't friendly with Benell, was he?"

"Not that anyone knows of," Brandon said.

"Well, he was there all right," Selby observed.

"Of course," Sheriff Brandon went on, thoughtfully, "he *could* have gone up there to ask for a loan—something he didn't dare to ask in the bank."

"You mean in case he'd been short in his accounts and wanted some credit to cover up?" Selby asked.

"Something like that," the sheriff said, "although I wouldn't put it exactly that way. It's reasonable to suppose Burke was hard pressed for cash. He probably had some property, something to show for his speculations. Naturally, he wasn't in a position to walk into the First National Bank during banking hours and ask for a loan on it, but he might have gone to Benell's house, made a clean breast of the whole situation, showed Benell where a little more money to carry him through would salvage enough to make good the shortage, and Bennell decided to finance him, and he and Burke drove up to the bank so Benell could get some money out of the vault. Then when Burke saw all that money in the vault, he lost his head and . . ."

Selby said with a grin, "That's darn sound reasoning, Rex, except that at that particular moment, Burke was dead and cremated."

Sheriff Brandon scratched the hair back of his ears. "That's so," he admitted. "Then those prints made by Burke couldn't have been made last night."

"No," Terry said positively.

"There's no chance of a mistake?" the sheriff asked.

"None whatever. Burke was in that house recently, probably some time after Sunday night, perhaps Monday night. He . . ."

"Well, now, wait a minute," Brandon said. "We may be getting somewhere after all. Suppose Burke *did* go to the house. Suppose Benell went to the bank and gave Burke ten thousand dollars. Burke was to rush it in to his broker in the morning. He took it down and left it in the lumber company's safe."

"Then dressed himself as a hobo, went out and got bumped by a train?" Terry asked.

Selby shook his head. "He wasn't hit by a train," he

said. "It wasn't an accidental death. It was cold-blooded murder, but there must have been a motive for that murder."

"Perhaps the person who killed him thought he had the ten thousand dollars on him, and didn't know he'd ditched it in the lumber company's safe," Brandon said.

Selby nodded. "Now, we're getting somewhere. But it still doesn't account for what happened to Benell last night."

"One at a time," the sheriff said.

"And don't overlook the fact that there are other fingerprints that were made after those of John Burke," Terry said.

"Let me take a look at them," Selby requested.

Terry shuffled out three or four photographs. "These," he said, "were found in the bedroom. I would say they were made last night."

Selby said, "They're entirely different from those others."

Terry said, "Yes, they're an entirely different pattern, and, of course, the measurements of the ridges are different."

"How much work did you do on Lacey's automobile?" Selby asked.

"I went over the steering wheel, gearshift, and brake handle. Then I took the rear-view mirror. Everything had been wiped clean except the rear-view mirror."

"Did you try any of the rear windows or handles on the rear doors?" Selby asked.

Terry shook his head.

"Try those," Selby said. "Let's not overlook a single bet. There's something mighty fishy here. . . . Say . . ."

"What?" Brandon asked.

Selby said, "It's just occurred to me that the only person who's identified this dead man as John Burke is his wife, and she admitted his appearance had been changed. Now suppose she *should* be mistaken."

"You got those photographs, Doug?" Brandon asked.

"Yes, I have a set in my brief case. Sylvia Martin got them for me."

"Well, let's go hunt up some of Burke's acquaintances," Brandon said.

Selby nodded.

Bob Terry, finishing the last of his coffee, said, doggedly, "I don't care whether he was John Burke or George Washington, but the man who was found dead there in the wash was in Benell's house, had the gun with which the murder was committed, and had very probably been the last one to drive that stolen Cadillac. You know, when a man gets into a strange car, one of the first things he does is to adjust the rear-view mirror —particularly if he's taller or shorter than the last driver."

"Yes," Selby said. "We can prove the same man was in all of those places, but before I can convict anyone of murdering John Burke, I've got to convince a jury that John Burke is dead. And in order to do that, I've got to show that the body is that of John Burke. Tell you what you do, Terry, go out to Burke's house and fingerprint everything you can find there. That should give us a lot of Burke's fingerprints. Then we could compare them with the prints of the dead man, and with Mrs. Burke's admission that it was her husband we'll have an airtight case."

"Let's try out those pictures on some of the people who knew him pretty well," the sheriff said.

The swinging door of the restaurant burst open as Billy Ransome came puffing importantly up to their table.

"Swell of you boys to wait," he said. "I didn't think I'd be so long."

"That's all right," Brandon said. "We were talking things over. Looks like we're making some progress. Listen, Billy, it looks as though John Burke was mixed up in this thing, and it looks as though a corpse we picked up day before yesterday that looked like a hobo who'd been hit by a train was really John Burke. Now we have photographs of that body. We want to identify those photographs if possible. Do you suppose there's any way . . ."

"Let *me* look at them," Ransome said. "I know Burke well."

Selby pulled out one of the eight-by-ten enlargements and Ransome gravely inspected it.

"Shucks, no," he said. "That isn't Burke. Burke had a little mustache and wore thick glasses and . . ."

"Wait a minute," Brandon warned. "Would it be Burke without his mustache and without his glasses?"

Ransome frowned, narrowed his eyes as he studied the photographs. "Funny thing," he said. "The man has thick glasses and a mustache, and somehow you always think of him that way. . . . Yes, by George, this *does* look like him. . . . Let's see that other photograph. . . . Yes, I guess it is. . . . Sure it is. That's Burke all right. He's changed a bit with that mustache off and without his glasses, but that'll be John Burke all right."

"That's fine," Brandon said. "Now we want to get a few more men to back up your opinion, men who have known Burke pretty well. Who could we get, Bill?"

"Well, let's see," the chief of police said thoughtfully, his manner reeking with the importance of the occasion. "There's Walter Breeden. He works in a cigar store. He should know."

"Did he know Burke intimately?"

"Yeah. They played a lot of chess together. Breeden was town champion until Burke showed up, and Burke could come in and trim him three games out of five. Breeden is a slow player. Burke's chain lightning."

"Anyone else?" Selby asked.

"Yes, there's Ella Dixon. She's the stenographer in the lumber company. She certainly should know. And then there's Arthur White, the next-door neighbor."

"Suppose we can round up some of these people?" Rex Brandon asked.

"Sure, I'll round 'em up," Ransome said. "You drive over to my office at the jail. I'll bring the witnesses in there. We'll get the photographs identified—but I don't think you need to bother. That's John Burke all right —what do you suppose he was doing with his mustache shaved? Trying a disguise?"

"Hardly," Selby said. "He must have been blind as a bat without his glasses."

"Yes, that's right, too."

"It looks," Selby went on, "as though he was murdered."

It was very evident that the announcement was not unwelcome to the big chief of police. "Well, well, well," he said. "Another murder, eh? Things certainly are looking up. They tell me that one of the Los Angeles papers is sending up a reporter and a staff photographer. Gosh, I've got to get shaved!"

Selby felt the stubble on his own chin and said, "Well, get these witnesses first, and then go ahead and get shaved."

Brandon winked at Selby as Ransome hesitated. "By the time the city newspapers get done with it," he said, "it'll be just a couple of sticks on an inside page."

"Don't kid yourself," Ransome retorted, "this is going to make the front page. Fifty thousand dollars gone slick as a whistle, and it looks as though they hadn't left a single clue. But we'll get 'em. I told the local correspondent that I . . . we was . . . were . . .

working on a hot lead and expected to have the whole gang under arrest within forty-eight hours. You know, that is, I didn't say that I was doing it. I told them the authorities—you know, I meant you boys, too."

"Yeah," Brandon said dryly, "we know. Well, we'll go on up to your office, and you can bring the witnesses in."

Up in the closed confines of the office at the jail with its battered furniture, barred windows, and the sickly sweet smell of jail disinfectant oozing out from the tank where curious prisoners forsook card games to peer at those who came and went, Doug Selby arranged the photographs and waited for Ransome to bring in the witnesses.

Walter Breeden was first, a man of around fifty-five with quizzical gray eyes held in a perpetual squint. He moved slowly and methodically.

"Take a look at these photographs," Selby said. "We want to identify the body. Mrs. Burke and Chief Ransome say it's John Burke. Of course, the mustache is shaved, and he isn't wearing glasses. What do *you* think?"

Walter Breeden looked at the photographs, fished a knife from his hip pocket, pulled out a plug of tobacco, slowly cut off one corner, placed it in his mouth, and mulled it around his teeth. He moved with slow, painstaking deliberation, and peered at each picture in turn, then went back for a second look. He pursed his lips as though holding back saliva, looked around for the cuspidor, found it, but waited until he had made another survey of the pictures before he turned, made a dead center shot on the cuspidor. Then he raised his eyes to Doug Selby, and said calmly, "Nope. That ain't him."

"It isn't?" Selby exclaimed.

"Nope," Breeden said. "That's not John Burke."

"Not with his mustache shaved and his glasses removed?"

"Nope."

"How do you know?" Brandon asked.

"Just from the appearance," Breeden said. "Just the way you'd know anything, just the way that I know you're Sheriff Brandon and know that this is District Attorney Selby. It ain't Burke."

"Why isn't it? Where are the features different?"

"I don't know, just a little something about the chin and the shape of the nose—and maybe the forehead."

"Of course," Selby said, "these are photographs and the man is dead. You have to take all that into consideration."

"Yeah, I know," Breeden said, "but it ain't Burke, not if you're asking my opinion."

"Well, we're asking your opinion," Selby said, "and it's very important that we don't make any mistake."

"Well, of course, it's hard to tell about a thing like that. As you've pointed out, the man's dead, and these are photographs, but I don't *think* it's Burke. I could tell if I could see the body."

"Unfortunately," Selby said, "that's . . ."

He broke off as Chief of Police Ransome waddled importantly into the office bearing in tow a very tall, thin girl with spectacles and large blue eyes.

"Ella Dixon," Chief Ransome announced. "Now, Ella, take a look at those photographs of John Burke. He's dead, and it may be something of a shock looking at those pictures that way, but . . ."

She paid no attention to him, but stepped quickly over to the table and looked down at the photographs.

She was somewhere in the late thirties. Her face showed the fatigue of years spent in office work. But there was a quiet competency about her. She was the sort who wouldn't lose her head in an emergency.

"Of course," Brandon explained, "these are photographs. The man's dead. His mustache has been shaved, and he's not wearing his glasses. Now . . ."

"I understand," she said quickly. "Let me study the photographs a moment, please."

She studied them for perhaps ten or fifteen seconds, and then nodded, and said, "Yes, that's Mr. Burke."

Walter Breeden said nothing. He pursed his lips and squirted tobacco juice into the cuspidor.

"Are you acquainted with Mr. Breeden?" Doug Selby asked.

She turned and nodded to Breeden. "I've seen him several times," she said. "I know who he is."

"Mr. Breeden knows Burke pretty well. He says it isn't Burke."

"I think it is," she said. "What makes you think it isn't, Mr. Breeden?"

Breeden mouthed the chew of tobacco for two or three seconds before he said; "I just don't think it is, that's all."

"I'm *certain* it is," she said. "I've seen him in the office day after day. Of course, I've always seen him with his glasses on and with a mustache, but I feel quite certain this is he."

"Looks like him—that is, it looks *something* like him," Breeden said. "Might be a brother or maybe someone with just the same sort of features. But it ain't Burke."

Chief Ransome said, "Sure, it's Burke, Breeden. What's the matter with you? Take another look at him. Why, his wife identifies him absolutely! And here's Ella Dixon that works in the same office with him, and *she* identifies him, and *I* know that it's Burke. Remember that a man looks different when he takes off his glasses and shaves his mustache. It might fool you, but it wouldn't fool me. Us officers are accustomed to dealing with people who wear disguises. We have to look at a man with a mustache and figure how he'd look without that mustache. We have to look at a man with glasses and figure how he'd look without glasses. Come over here and take another look at those photographs."

Breeden chewed once or twice tentatively at the tobacco, and said, "I don't need to take another look at the pictures. I looked at them. I ain't saying you're mistaken. I ain't saying you're off on the wrong track. You've got your opinion. I've got mine. That ain't John Burke—not if you ask me."

Ransome flushed. He started to say something else when an officer brought a nervous, slender man in the late thirties into the office. "Arthur White," he announced.

Arthur White came swiftly forward. "Good morning, gentlemen," he said.

Sheriff Brandon turned to him. "White," he said, "you work in the bank. You're a next-door neighbor of John Burke. You know him pretty well, don't you?"

"Well, I'm not exactly a close friend, but I . . ."

"I know, but you see him quite frequently."

"Yes."

"You see him in the bank?"

"Yes, I've seen him in the bank several times."

"And have taken a good look at him?"

"Yes, of course."

"He always wore a mustache and thick-lensed glasses?"

"Yes."

"Close your eyes and try to figure what he'd look like without his mustache and without his glasses."

White obediently closed his eyes, and, after a moment, said, "Yes, I think I know just what he'd look like."

"All right. Take a look at these photographs," Ransome interposed importantly, "and identify this body as that of John Burke, because there's no question that it *is* John Burke. His own wife has identified him. Ella Dixon says it's Burke, and *I* know it's Burke."

White stepped forward, started to nod his head, stopped, stared at the photograph, tilted his head first to one side, then to the other, then with his fingers covered up first the forehead of the face shown in one of the photographs, then the mouth. He moved his eyes from one photograph to the other, then straightened and said, "I don't care *who* says it's John Burke. These pictures are *not* those of John Burke. The man shown in these pictures isn't Burke."

In the silence that followed, Breeden's delivery of tobacco juice rattled against the sides of the cuspidor.

They were just leaving the jail when a car drove up, and George Lawler of the Las Alidas Lumber Company said, "I'd like to speak to you for a moment, Mr. Selby."

Selby excused himself and stepped over to the running board of the car.

"Lots of excitement in town," Lawler said.

Selby nodded, recognizing that the man was nervous and was trying to make some polite preliminary before plunging into a conversation about something which was preying on his mind.

Lawler went on excitedly, "A man by the name of Miltern is up here from Los Angeles, claiming that the ten thousand dollars that was in our safe is *his* money."

"What's the ground of his claim?" Selby asked.

"He says it was money Burke had to pay over to him, that it was all segregated in a parcel, and . . ."

"Where is he now?" Selby asked. "I want to talk with him."

"He's having a cup of coffee down at the Blue Whistle. Sam Roper's his lawyer."

Selby said, "Drive around to the Blue Whistle. I'll get the sheriff and join you there. I want to talk with Miltern."

Selby turned back to the compact little group which was standing in front of the jail and said to Rex Brandon, "Miltern, the stockbroker, is at the Blue Whistle. He has Sam Roper with him. They're trying to claim the ten thousand dollars that was in the lumber company's safe. I think it would be a good time to interview Miltern."

Sheriff Brandon's eyes narrowed. "If Sam Roper's his lawyer," he said, "it might be a lot better to talk with him when Roper wasn't there. Roper hates the ground you walk on, and it's a cinch he'll try to keep his client from giving any information which would be of any value."

"I know that," Selby said. "And I'm discounting it in advance. Miltern is a material witness, and I'd like to flash those photographs of the dead man on him, and get *his* reaction on the man's identity before word gets around there's a dispute about it."

"I get you," Brandon said. "Come on, get in the county car, and we'll go. How about Ransome? Want him along?"

"If he wants to come, yes."

Selby moved over to Ransome. "We want to interview another witness, Bill. Would you like to come along?"

The three officers climbed into the county car, and Sheriff Brandon drove to the Blue Whistle. Lawler, waiting just outside the door, pointed out Miltern sitting at a table with Roper.

Miltern was facing the door. He was around forty-three, a fat, sleek individual with wide-open, candid blue eyes, and a full-moon face. His eyes shifted to the quartet marching down the floor past the counter, and his lips moved as he made some quick comment to Sam Roper.

Roper, the former district attorney of Madison County who had been defeated by Doug Selby in a whirlwind campaign, was not one to forgive or forget. Tall, rawboned, his face was dominated by high cheekbones and a thin, wide mouth. Above those high cheekbones animated little black eyes glittered out suspiciously at the world. Roper was an opportunist, a man who had not scrupled to use his office for the purpose of feathering his nest. He had the inherent suspicion of other people which so frequently characterizes men who are conscious of some weakness in their own character, either of education, environment, or moral stamina.

Selby, taking the lead, said, "Good morning, Roper —Lawler tells me that you're making a claim on ten thousand dollars which was found in his safe."

Roper pressed his lips tightly together. "I am," he said, and then added, "on behalf of my client, Mr. Miltern."

He made no attempt to introduce his client, but Selby, overlooking the slight, extended his hand. "How are you, Mr. Miltern?" he said. "I'm Selby, district attorney of Madison County. This is Sheriff Rex Brandon and Chief of Police Ransome."

Miltern gravely shooks hands.

Roper, standing erect with his restless eyes in constant motion, saw the interest which was being created by the conversation, stepped around the side of his chair so that he would be nearer the center of the group.

"Might I ask," Selby inquired, "what are the grounds of your claim, Mr. Miltern?"

"Are you asking as Lawler's attorney?" Roper interrupted as Miltern apparently was on the point of answering the question.

"I'm asking as the district attorney of Madison County."

"What does that have to do with it?"

Sheriff Brandon started to make some retort, but Selby smiled, and said suavely, "Nothing, Roper. You asked me the capacity in which I was asking the question. I told you, that's all."

"I don't see how that has any bearing on the duties of the district attorney."

"That," Selby said, "isn't the first time we have had a difference of opinion as to the proper discharge of the duties of the office."

Back at the lunch counter somebody snickered, and Roper's black, hostile eyes flickered over in that direction.

"Any objection to telling us what your claim is?" Sheriff Brandon asked Miltern.

"I fail to see why there should be," Miltern said. "This man, John Burke, was known to us as Allison Brown. He was a customer who plunged rather heavily at times. We knew but little about him. A few days ago Mark Crandall, a man whom we had known for some time and who is one of our most valued clients, happened to be in the office when Allison Brown was there. I could see that he recognized Brown and could see also that he was uneasy. I decided to investigate, although I didn't tell Crandall I was going to do so.

"On the other hand, I didn't tell Crandall about our relations with Brown. We had given him a line of credit. After making some money, he had refused to take our advice and cash in at a profit. We had some difficulty getting in touch with him. After holding off as long as we dared, we closed out a part of his holdings. The situation was still far from satisfactory. He owed us ten thousand dollars in round figures, and I told him we were going to close out the balance of the account. He promised me faithfully that he would have ten thousand dollars in our hands the next morning. About eight o'clock Tuesday night he rang me up on long distance and told me that he had secured the ten thousand dollars, that he was putting it in a safe place for the night but would leave early in the morning so that he would have the money in my hands as soon as the office opened.

"On the strength of his assurance, we followed his instructions, and in following those instructions lost our collateral. In the meantime, we were looking him up. Shortly after noon yesterday we discovered that he was known here as John Burke and was employed by the Las Alidas Lumber Company."

"Suppose he was short in his accounts at the Las Alidas Lumber Company?" Selby asked.

Roper entered the conversation. "We don't give a hang about that," he said. "If the ten thousand dollars found in the lumber company's safe was the lumber company's money, that's one thing. If it was money that Burke owned personally and had put it in the safe just to keep it overnight, that's another. I don't care if the lumber company does figure Burke owed them around ten thousand dollars. Burke skipped out, owing my client around ten thousand dollars. If there's twenty thousand dollars in indebtedness and only ten thousand dollars with which to pay it, we'll each of us take fifty cents on the dollar."

"In other words," Selby said, "it depends entirely on the status of the money."

"That's right," Roper snapped, "and I'm not so certain but we can hold the whole ten thousand. Title had virtually been transferred in that telephone conversation, and when Brown put it in a safe place, he may have done so as the agent of my client. In any event, that was money Burke got to use as margin money. It wasn't money which belonged to the lumber company. The most *they* can claim is that they're a creditor of Burke. We've served a garnishment on the lumber company."

Selby, flashing a quick look at Rex Brandon, said, "Of course, that's presupposing John Burke and Allison Brown are one and the same."

"They are," Miltern said easily. "We've satisfied ourselves of that."

"Better take a look at these pictures of a dead body," Selby said, whipping the envelope of pictures from his brief case and handing them to the stockbroker.

Miltern looked at the photographs and frowned. "Is it," he asked cautiously, "your contention that Burke is dead and that he shaved his mustache before his death?"

"Yes," Selby said. "Also you'll notice that his glasses are missing."

Roper fidgeted uneasily. "Wait a minute, Miltern," he said. "I'm not certain I like this."

Miltern showed his opinion of Roper by brushing the comment to one side. He met Selby's gaze fairly and frankly. "That's the man we knew as Allison Brown," he said positively. "His appearance has been changed somewhat but I'd know him anywhere."

"Thank you," Selby said, slipping the pictures back in the envelope. "There's no question in your mind?"

"None whatever."

"Here, let me see those pictures," Roper said, suspiciously, stretching forth a gaunt hand. He took possession of the envelope and examined the pictures carefully. "I don't like the way they're asking those questions," he said to Miltern.

"Nonsense," Miltern said. "Our client, Allison Brown, was the same as John Burke. If Burke is dead, then our client is dead. These are the pictures of the man whom we know as John Burke alias Allison Brown."

"And you identify them?" Rex Brandon asked.

Before Roper could interpose any word of caution, Miltern said quickly, "I identify them—of course I identify them. My entire claim to that ten thousand dollars hinges on the fact that Allison Brown and John Burke were one and the same. If John Burke is dead, then Allison Brown is dead. I identify these as photographs of Allison Brown. I think, gentlemen, that covers my case. Brown and Burke are one and the same. Allison Brown owes us ten thousand dollars. He died with ten thousand dollars in his possession."

"In the safe of my lumber company," George Lawler protested.

"That makes no difference," Roper interposed coldly. "Burke certainly didn't *give* that money to you. As a matter of fact, he never intended that you should have it. He had access to your safe. He used it as a place to deposit his money, that's all. The title to the money remains vested in John Burke—unless the telephone conversation was sufficient to vest the title in my client. In any event, we're entitled to either half of it or all of it."

Lawler said to Selby, "How about that, Mr. Selby? Is that the law? Can he embezzle from us and then use that same money . . ."

"Not that *same* money," Roper interrupted. "This is money he'd obtained from some other source."

"What other source?" Selby asked.

"I'm not prepared to answer that question right now," Roper said.

Miltern said, "Well, I gathered he got that money from . . ."

"Shut up," Roper interrupted.

Miltern became silent.

"I think," Selby observed, "you were about to comment on a phase of the matter which I consider of the greatest importance. *Where* did you gather he'd obtained this money, Miltern?"

Miltern smiled. "I think from now on," he said, "you'd better ask questions of my attorney, Mr. Roper."

"Look here, Selby," Lawler said, thoroughly indignant, "they can't pull a stunt like this. Anyhow, that money was deposited in the bank and the bank paid off a note with it. Try and get around *that* one!"

"Where are those bills now?" Roper asked.

Lawler shrugged his shoulders. "I presume the bandits who looted the vault got them," he said. "It isn't *my* funeral. It's the bank's."

In the silence that followed, Selby and Brandon exchanged significant glances.

Chapter Eleven

BACK IN his office, before Selby had finished with the morning mail, his secretary announced Inez Stapleton. Selby pushed aside the mail and told Amorette to show her in.

Inez was crisply businesslike in a smart Oxford gray tailored suit. "Good morning, Mr. District Attorney," she said. "I understand you had rather a busy night."

"Got two or three hours' sleep," he admitted. "I'd probably be feeling better if I'd stuck it right through."

"They tell me murder cases are popping all over the county like fireworks."

He nodded, sensing that this was not merely a social call.

"I further understand that the grand jury is in session and is going to institute an inquiry into what happened."

This time he did not nod.

She raised her coolly competent eyes to his and said quietly, "Doug, I'm representing James Lacey and Mrs. John Burke."

Despite himself, his voice showed his surprise. "*You* are!" he exclaimed.

She nodded, and then, after a moment, asked, "Why not? I'm an attorney, you know."

"And did you know they're fugitives from justice?"

She shook her head. "They're here in Madison City."

"They'll appear before the grand jury?"

"If you subpoena them, yes. I want to have a subpoena served to make things regular. You can serve it on them at the Madison Hotel."

"And they'll testify?" Selby asked.

"I don't know."

Selby shifted his eyes from hers to drum thoughtfully on the edge of the desk for several seconds. Then he pulled out his pipe, filled it with tobacco and struck a match.

"Finished stalling for time?" she asked, as the first fragrant clouds of smoke came puffing from his lips to form a bluish-white haze about his face.

"No," he said shortly, "I haven't," and smoked for several more silent seconds before he said, "Look here, Inez, I probably shouldn't do this, but I'm going to tell you something."

"Don't tell me anything that you wouldn't want to disclose to an attorney who was representing Mrs. Burke and Lacey," she said.

He shook his head impatiently as though brushing her remark to one side. "Inez," he said, "I don't know what's back of this. I feel certain you don't. I have every reason to believe that James Lacey told a whole series of lies. He probably underestimates our ability to check up on his moves. I think he plans to go before the grand jury and try to cover up. I'm here to tell you he can't get away with it."

"Why not?" she asked.

"Because," he said impatiently, "I'm not going to let him. This is a murder case. I'm not going to let anyone play horse with me. If he's in love with his former wife and wants to protect her, he'd better co-operate with the law instead of getting at cross purposes with it. If he's a hot-headed customer who killed Burke because Burke was trying to kill his wife and then tried to cover up, he'd better put his cards on the table.

"I think it was a splendid thing for you to get admitted to the bar. I think the study of law is a fine thing for any woman who has a logical mind. But when it comes to the practice of law . . . well, Inez, I'm sorry to see you entering criminal law."

"What's criminal law?" she asked.

"Defending people accused of crime."

"When they're innocent?" she asked.

"Very few people accused of crime *are* innocent. The innocent ones are pretty well weeded out by the time the case gets to court."

"Thanks, Doug," she said breezily, "for the advice."

"What are you going to do?" he asked curiously.

"I'm going to represent Thelma Burke and James Lacey to the best of my ability. I'm going to leave no stone unturned to see that any charges you may prefer against either or both of them fall through. I'm going to take advantage of any technicality the law affords."

"Suppose they're guilty?" Selby asked.

She shrugged her shoulders, and said, "As I understand the law, they're innocent until you have proven them guilty beyond all reasonable doubt. And it's going to take the unanimous opinion of twelve jurors before either of them can be convicted."

She got to her feet. "I think that's all I have to tell you, Mr. District Attorney," she said.

She turned and started bravely for the door, then suddenly whirled to come back and face him across the desk. "Oh, Doug," she said, "I hate to do it, and yet I *have* to do it. It's inevitable. You and I had a wonderful friendship. It meant . . . it meant a lot to me. We used to laugh and run wild and do things on the spur of the moment. We had our little jokes, our little intimate understandings, and the world seemed just a big playground in which we were having fun.

"Then you became interested in politics and got elected to office. Since that time you've had your nose so close to the grindstone that you can't see anything except work. You've carried it to such an extreme that you've lost respect for me. . . . No, Doug, don't interrupt. I know what I'm saying, and I know you. You *did* lose respect for me, not perhaps as a woman, but as a friend. The world suddenly became a place for serious work, and your interest centered on the serious workers. I made up my mind the only way I'd ever be able to command your respect was to become a worker."

She hesitated for a moment, and her lips twitched as her mouth stretched into a peculiar, one-sided smile. "All right, Mr. District Attorney," she went on, *"you're going to notice me now.* You're going to notice me in a big way. Before you get through, you'll wish you could overlook me—and find you can't.

"Doug, I'd rather cut off my right hand than do anything to hurt you, but I'm an attorney and I'm representing my clients. I'm going to represent them to the best of my ability. I warn you to watch your step. This case is going to attract a lot of attention. Newspapers will be full of it. This is going to be just like one of our tennis matches, Doug. If I can beat you, I'm going to do it."

"Regardless of whether two criminals escape?" Selby asked quietly.

"Regardless of anything, Doug—and remember, you asked for it."

She turned back to the door and left the office without another word, leaving Selby seated at the desk staring with thought-slitted eyes at the door which was slowly closing behind her.

A few moments later Sheriff Brandon came in, and said, "Well, Doug, how you feeling?"

"A little groggy," Selby admitted with a grin. "What's new?"

"I've played the thing the way we planned it. I had two fingerprint men rushed up from Los Angeles. They went into Burke's house and went over everything, trying to get a complete set of Burke's fingerprints."

"What is the answer?"

Sheriff Brandon said, "Doug, I don't think that dead hobo was John Burke. I think the whole thing is a fake that was worked out to collect life insurance or, what's more to the point, a scheme that was worked by Burke himself to get out from under."

"What makes you think so, Rex?"

"The fingerprints prove it," Brandon said quietly. "We've gone through Burke's house from cellar to garret. We've taken fingerprints from mirrors, from door handles, windowpanes, liquor bottles—everything we could find to fingerprint. We've got a set of fingerprints we figure are those of Mrs. Burke and a set of fingerprints that *must* be those of John Burke."

"And Burke's fingerprints don't tally?"

"Not with the corpse, no."

"But his wife identified that photograph absolutely, Rex."

"Yes, so did a lot of other people. But Walter Breeden thinks it isn't Burke, and Arthur White thinks it isn't Burke. Now you know as well as I do that's going to lick us. We're in the position of having a bear by the tail. The grand jury will insist we do something. Right now we're behind the eight ball. If we arrest anyone for the murder of John Burke, we can't prove beyond a reasonable doubt the body was that of Burke. If we act on the assumption it *wasn't* Burke, we can't dig up any motive for the murder—not yet."

"But," Selby said, "we can identify that dead man sooner or later. He was friendly with Oliver Benell. He must have been in Benell's house. He must have driven Lacey's automobile."

The sheriff nodded glum acquiescence. "And that," he said, "doesn't help a bit. Oliver Benell was alive and well yesterday afternoon. That hobo, *whoever* he was, was dead as a doornail Wednesday morning. He'd been in Benell's house all right, but not late enough to do us any good."

Amorette Standish opened the door of the outer office to say, "Sheriff Brandon wanted on the telephone. It's long distance and important."

Brandon thanked her, picked up the telephone, said, "Hello," waited a moment, and then said, "Yes, hello, Ransome. . . . Oh, you have, eh? That's good. Let's have it. . . . Is that identification positive? . . . I see.

. . . That's good work, Ransome. It sure checks.
. . . Yeah, I'll see you get a break in the papers over
here. Why not drive over and bring him with you. . . .
That'll be fine. Okay. G'by."

Brandon pushed the telephone away, looked across
at Selby, and hesitated for a moment as though trying
to correlate the information he had received with the
facts as he knew them. Then he said, "A man by the
name of Light, who runs a taxicab over at Las Alidas,
got in touch with Ransome this morning and told him
he'd driven a man up to Santa Delbarra. His passenger
seemed nervous and under pretty much of a tension.
When he got to Santa Delbarra, he got off at the
Worthington Hotel, and paid Light off. But Light happened to notice he didn't go in the hotel, and has a
hunch he took another taxi some place."

"When was this?" Selby asked.

"Tuesday night."

"You said something about an identification?"

"Yeah. Lacey called on Ransome this morning to see
about his car. Light saw him talking with Ransome. He
says Lacey is the man."

Selby thought a minute, then said, "There are a
couple of charter planes at Santa Delbarra. Better get
the sheriff up there and see if he can find a charter
party that clicks."

"I will," the sheriff said. "Look here, Doug, suppose
we get enough to pin this on Lacey, and Mrs. Burke
wants to protect him. Can she change her identification of those photographs?"

"Why not?" Selby asked, wearily. "A smart lawyer
could fix that up easy. She'd say the light was poor or
she didn't have her reading glasses or it had a superficial resemblance to her husband or that she was hysterical and jumped at conclusions, that since she stud-

ied the photographs more carefully she's decided it isn't her husband."

"Think she'll have a smart lawyer?" Brandon asked.

"Yes," Selby said.

"Who?"

"Inez Stapleton."

Sheriff Brandon's eyebrows went up.

"Inez has been admitted to the bar," Selby went on. "She's out after my scalp for personal reasons. She won't stop at anything."

"You've talked with her?"

"Yes, she was in and warned me."

Brandon came around the desk and put his hand on the younger man's shoulder. "You're tired, Doug. Take it easy. Don't let Inez get you to pull any punches. She's green at the game. You can't afford to go easy on her."

"I know it," Selby said in a tired voice as Brandon moved over to the exit door. "See what you can find out from the airport."

When the sheriff had left, Selby put down his pipe, got up and walked restlessly around the office. For several minutes he stood at the window staring aimlessly, then put on his hat and started for the door. "For your private information," he told Amorette Standish, "I'm going to be at the barber shop. For the benefit of any taxpayers, constituents, and visiting pests, I'm out working on a murder case."

She grinned. "Pretty tough night?" she asked.

Selby nodded, pushed his hands down deep into his pockets, and walked down the long courthouse corridor. Halfway to the stairs he saw Sylvia Martin emerging from the county clerk's office. "Hi," she called, flashing him a bright smile and flinging up her arm in a salute.

Doug returned her salute, walked over to her, took

her arm, and said, "A new development of sorts coming up."

"How soon?" she asked.

"Probably within half or three quarters of an hour."

"Important?" she asked.

"I think it is. A taxi driver has identified Lacey as being a fare whom he drove to Santa Delbarra on the night of the murder."

"What did he want in Santa Delbarra?" she asked.

"An airplane, on a guess," Selby said. "We're checking on it."

"How about fingerprints, Doug?"

"From the fingerprints," he said, "the body *wasn't* that of John Burke—not unless someone has been clever enough to go all over Burke's house wiping off fingerprints and then putting on a new set for us to find."

"That could have been done, couldn't it, Doug?"

"Yes."

"You don't sound very chipper this morning."

"I'm not," he said. "I'm so low I don't have to open doors. I can walk right under the cracks—without taking my hat off."

"What's the matter, Doug?"

"I don't know. I have been going round and round on this thing, and it gets me. Every case I ever had before had something I could take as a tangible starting point. In this case I can't get a toe hold."

"I know, Doug," she said sympathetically. "You've got to buck up and stick out the old chin. You're in for a fight."

He said, "I can stand fighting all right. I only wish someone would start something."

"They're going to," she said.

"Tell me about it."

"Come on down here. . . . Come on in the supervisors' room. There's no one there this morning."

He followed her into the supervisors' room. She propped a hip on the rail which separated the supervisors' table from the spectators' benches, and said, "The grand jury's meeting, Doug."

She waited for him to make a comment. He, in turn, waited for her to go on.

"Jack Worthington is the foreman of the grand jury," she said. "He didn't take an active part in the campaign, but he was for Roper. He's still for him. I don't know just what Roper's angle is. Probably he's after that ten thousand dollars, but he's reached Worthington and Worthington's after your scalp."

"After *my* scalp?"

"Yes."

"Meaning what?"

"Roper's whispering it around that you've been lucky in that so far you've had a bunch of hand-picked cases. Naturally, he's jealous of your record. He'd like to see you come a cropper. He figures this is a good case for you to start."

"What does all this have to do with the grand jury?"

"Simply this," she said. "If the grand jury went off half-cocked and indicted Lacey, you'd have to prosecute him, wouldn't you?"

"I suppose so."

"Suppose they did it before you'd been able to work up a very good case?"

Selby said, "I could move for a dismissal if I thought the facts warranted."

"That would be playing right into their hands, Doug. They'd start whooping it up that you were yellow, that you didn't have the ability to go into court and convict a murderer unless it was a dead open-and-shut case."

130

"I'd have to take it," Selby said. "I wouldn't prose-cute anyone I thought was innocent."

She studied him with narrowed eyes. "You don't talk as though you were spoiling for a fight this morning."

"I'm not. I'm tired. I'm like the dog who's been chasing his tail around in a circle until he's tired out. Being aggressive is all right when you know that you're on the right track. The trouble with being a district attorney is that you don't want to prosecute an inno-cent person if you can help it, and above all, you don't want to convict one."

"Know who's going to represent Lacey, Doug?" she asked.

For a moment he had a tendency to avoid her eyes which he fought down, and met her solicitous stare. He nodded.

"Who?"

"Inez Stapleton."

Her eyes flashed. "So that explains . . . Doug Selby, if you let her . . . If you lay down on this because you don't want to get her where she'll be defeated—or dis-barred, I'll never speak to you again as long as I live. She's asking for it. You go fight her just as you would Sam Roper if *he* were the lawyer."

"I'll do my duty," he said.

"Duty nothing! If they indict Jim Lacey, you con-vict him! Inez Stapleton has no business mixing in this. She's desperate because you haven't been run-ning after her. . . . Hell hath no fury like a woman scorned, and she'd like nothing better than to pick you to pieces."

He shook his head. "She isn't like that, Sylvia."

"Why isn't she?"

"Because she isn't."

"You don't think she's going to fight you on this?"

"Yes," Selby said, "she is. She'll do anything she can to get her clients off. She warned me of that."

"Then why isn't she just like I said she was?"

"I can't explain it," he said.

Sylvia started to say something, then caught her breath. Her eyes flashed. After a moment she said, in a low, tense voice, "Doug Selby, you make me tired! If you think that woman . . . Oh, all right, I won't be catty. . . . But, Doug, *please* don't let her lead you around with a ring in your nose."

"I won't."

"Any comments about the grand jury meeting for publication?"

"When do they meet?"

"Two o'clock this afternoon, as I understand it. Worthington's position is there are some angles of this case that need independent investigation."

Selby nodded grimly. "He's probably right."

"But, Doug," she protested, "that's just a lot of political hooey. What they're after is to put you in a box. They figure this case is pretty well mixed up, and if they can push you into the middle of it where people can see you flounder around, it will be a cinch for the old ring to get back in the saddle next election."

Selby said slowly, "I have no objection to the grand jury interrogating the witnesses. As I see the situation at the present time, an indictment would be premature. I shall tell them that. I shall also tell them that if I see fit, I shall move for a dismissal."

"But, Doug, you *can't* do that, not with Inez Stapleton on the other side of the case. They'll yell frame-up and that you're lying down on the job because the woman . . . a woman . . . a friend . . ."

Selby took a deep breath, straightened his shoulders, and smiled. "I don't give a damn *what* they say. I'm going to run my office to the best of my ability. And, in the meantime, I'm going down to a barber shop and get a shave and plenty of hot towels."

Her apprehensive eyes were blinking rapidly as she watched him down the corridor.

Chapter Twelve

SELBY WAS still in the barber shop when Sheriff Brandon called him on the telephone. The barber peeled off the hot towels, and Selby, with the barber's covering sheet flapping around his knees, crossed over to the telephone, and said, "Hello, Rex."

Brandon said cautiously, "Doug, I think we're ready to go. There's some stuff I don't want to discuss over the telephone. How about meeting me at the Madison Hotel?"

"The hotel?" Doug asked in surprise.

"Yes, we'll be waiting in the lobby."

Selby said, "Okay, be right over," and started pulling the cloth from around his neck as he hung up the telephone. "Just give me a comb and brush," he said to the barber, "and I'll put the hair back in place. I'm on my way."

The barber, bursting with curiosity concerning the murders and anxious to get the latest news, hovered solicitously about as Selby ran a comb through his wavy hair, buttoned his collar, and knotted his tie into place.

"Must be pretty hard," he said, "to be up all night and get called out first thing in the morning."

Selby, holding his tie pin in his lips, muttered, "Mm-hmm."

"Some new developments?" the barber asked curiously.

"Just some witnesses," Selby mumbled.

The barber watched him take the scarf pin from his lips and insert it in his tie. "From all I can hear, guess that guy down in Tucson ain't sitting any too pretty."

Selby ignored the veiled inquiry and started for the door, the eyes of everyone in the barber shop upon him. The Madison Hotel was a block and a half down the street, and Selby, hurrying toward it, had to make excuses to half a dozen citizens en route, men who would be the first to criticize the district attorney for failing to solve a case, yet who wanted to take up his time in curbstone discussions for no other reason than to enable them to assume an oracular importance of first-hand information at other curbstone discussions.

Selby reached the Madison Hotel and encountered a little group in the lobby: Billy Ransome, the chief of police from Las Alidas, Rex Brandon, a man who was introduced as Sam Light and another whose name was Philip Crow.

Brandon's eye was ominously calm and steady. Ransome seemed excited. The other two were somewhat flustered at finding themselves catapulted into an official conference on a murder case.

"You knew the grand jury was meeting this afternoon, Doug?" the sheriff asked.

Selby nodded.

"Understand they're getting ready to make an independent investigation," Brandon said.

Again Selby nodded with the trace of a warning glance, cautioning the sheriff not to say too much in front of the witnesses.

"Well," Brandon said. "this is the man who took a

passenger from Las Alidas over to Santa Delbarra, and from Santa Delbara, Crow, the aviator here, was given a charter flying job to take him to Phoenix. Light has identified Lacey. Crow's description shows it's the same man. But when we came to make an identification . . ." The sheriff shrugged his shoulders, and his voice trailed off into significant silence.

"You mean he isn't here?" Selby asked.

"Gone," Brandon said. "They left a note for the manager of the hotel to be opened at five o'clock p.m. When I found out they weren't in and hadn't got back from breakfast, I got suspicious and told the manager to open the note. The note said they'd been called out on business and might not get back. If they didn't get back by five o'clock to pack their bags and store them. There was a twenty-dollar bill in the envelope."

Selby said, "Just a moment," and made a dive for the telephone booth. He called Information and said, "A Miss Inez Stapleton is opening a law office somewhere. Does she have a telephone yet?"

"Yes, Main 604."

"Let me have that number, will you, please, and rush it? It's important. This is Selby, the district attorney, speaking."

"Yes, sir," the operator said, and a moment later Selby heard the signal indicating Inez Stapleton's phone was ringing. He had hardly anticipated she would be in, and was conscious of a distinct feeling of relief when he heard her voice over the telephone, saying coolly and calmly, "Hello, this is Attorney Stapleton speaking."

"Doug Selby, Inez," he said.

"Oh, yes—hello, Doug."

"I understood your clients were going to be ready to testify before the grand jury."

There was a moment's silence, then she said calmly, "Did you subpoena them, Doug?"

"Not yet."

"I see," she said.

Doug felt himself flushing. "I'm down at the Madison Hotel now," he said. "They aren't here."

"No?"

"No."

There was a period of silence.

"Look here, Inez," Selby said savagely, "I understood those people were going to appear before the grand jury. Because you were the one who told me that, I didn't consider it necessary to break a leg slapping a subpoena on them."

"I told you to serve a subpoena if you wanted them, Doug."

"I went down to get shaved," he said.

"I see."

"You're not being very much help," Selby snapped.

"What did you want me to do, Doug?"

"I want to know whether they're going to be available for interrogation by the grand jury this afternoon at two o'clock."

"I'm sure I couldn't tell you."

"You mean you don't know?"

"I can't tell you, Doug."

Selby said, "I have some witnesses here. I want them to look at your clients to see whether they can be identified."

"Well, you can't do that very well if they aren't there, Doug."

Selby lost his temper. "Look here, Inez, you can stall around all you want to, but you're not playing a game now. This isn't tennis. This is murder. I grant that you've shown you're smart, but there's a lot about law you don't know. A young attorney never has the right perspective on ethics. Now if you've advised these people to get out, you're going to get into trouble. What's more, if your clients aren't there before the grand jury this afternoon, it's going to look like hell. You know what the grand jury will do. They'll indict them for murder. Flight is something that can be taken as an indication of guilt."

"But what are they fleeing from, Doug?" she asked calmly. "No one served a subpoena on them. You didn't tell them *when* the grand jury was going to meet. They appeared voluntarily in Madison City. If you wanted to question them, they were at the hotel until ten-thirty this morning waiting to be questioned. If you wanted to serve a subpoena on them, you could have done so. I told you where they were. Mr. Lacey is a man of large business interests. It's quite possible he's been called out on a matter of business . . ."

Selby said, "All right, Inez. You've stuck your chin out. Now don't yell if you get hurt."

He slammed the telephone receiver up savagely, strode out to the lobby. Brandon, taking one look at his flushed face, said to Ransome, "Nice work on your part, Ransome. I'm going to ask you two witnesses to be available when the grand jury meets this afternoon. We'll either have the people there for you to identify at that time, or we'll have some photographs you can identify. That'll be all now."

And with that as a dismissal, Brandon linked his arm through Selby's and led him back toward the telephone booth, leaving the chief of police of Las Alidas uncertain whether to feel rebuked at being excluded from their presence and herded with the witnesses, or flattered by the sheriff's compliment.

"Talk with Inez, Doug?" Brandon asked in a casual voice.

"Yes," Selby said. "And it looks as though she's

taken an unfair advantage. She told me her clients were here, ready to testify, and I could subpoena them. To tell you the truth, Rex, I feel as low as though I'd been run over by a steam roller. I went down to get shaved before getting the subpoenas ready. They skipped out."

Brandon said reassuringly, "They skipped out before you ever went down to get shaved, Doug. Inez is representing her clients. She can't turn them down and she can't back up. I think Lacey *was* planning to appear before the grand jury and testify. But when Light identified him and when we started checking the airports at Santa Delbarra, he knew the jig was up. Now here's some stuff I didn't want to spill in front of Ransome. Terry went over the rear of that Cadillac automobile the way you told him to. He found some fingerprints. He found some of those same fingerprints in Burke's residence and they tallied with some he'd got from the arm of a chair in Benell's bedroom. And the prints we got that we figure are Mrs. Burke's prints were also found in Benell's house. We found that Paul Quinne's plane was at the Las Alidas airport this morning. If he'd left Tucson around ten, he'd have got in there . . ."

Selby said savagely, "Go get Billy Ransome, Rex. Have him telephone over to Las Alidas and send an officer down to the airport. Grab Paul Quinne."

"Putting a charge against him, Doug?" Brandon asked anxiously.

"Anything that'll hold him," Selby said. "Assault and battery, mayhem, or first-degree murder—I don't care. He's their means of escape. If we can get him before they reach the plane . . ."

Brandon said, "I get you, Doug. I'll handle it." And Brandon's long legs carried him across the lobby to the door where he called down the street, "Oh, Ransome. . . . Hey, Billy. . . . Hey! Come back here."

Selby climbed the hill to the courthouse and entered his office. The despondency he had felt an hour earlier was giving way to cold rage. He paced the floor of his office, turning the facts of the case over in his mind. If he only knew who that dead man was. . . . How humiliating it would be to work up a perfect case of circumstantial evidence against Lacey, or Mrs. Burke, or both, have the motivation hinge on the identification of the victim as John Burke, and then have Inez Stapleton raise such a doubt as to the identity of the victim that the jury would reluctantly acquit . . . and *was* the victim John Burke, or was that a trap which the murderer had baited? Once Lacey had been tried and acquitted, he could never again be put in jeopardy for the same offense, no matter if Selby uncovered evidence proving to a mathematical certainty that he was guilty—and what a sweet spot *that* would put him in. . . . All right. If Inez wanted a fight, she could have it. If she . . .

The telephone rang.

Selby scooped up the receiver and heard Brandon say, "You had the right hunch, Doug, but we were ten minutes too late. Jim Lacey, Mrs. Burke, and the baby got in Quinne's plane and took off about ten minutes ago. Quinne told hangers-on at the field he was taking his sister on a tour of the country by air."

Selby said, "All right, Rex. Notify all landing fields. Get out a fugitive warrant. . . . No, wait a minute. We'll let the grand jury decide that."

Brandon said, "Remember, Doug, that ain't a friendly grand jury."

Selby said, "That's nothing. I'm not friendly myself," and hung up.

Chapter Thirteen

IT SEEMED that about half of the county had thronged around the courthouse, jamming the corridors, grouping in low-voiced clusters around the marble stairway. Sam Roper was very much in evidence, passing from group to group, shaking hands, "passing the time of day," and, wherever he could find the smoldering embers of incipient criticism, fanning them into a flame. By the time Selby left his office and had walked down the corridor to the grand jury room, he noticed several people who avoided his eyes as he walked toward them, only to whirl and stare at his back as he passed.

Jack Worthington, chairman of the grand jury, spoke to Selby with exaggerated courtesy. "How are you, Mr. Selby?" he said. "We feel that we owe you an apology for dragging you in here after you've had a sleepless night. But some of us feel that the present situation calls for prompt action. We don't want to work any hardship on you or Sheriff Brandon. None at all. If you'd prefer to stay in your office and let us call you when we need you, that'll be quite all right with us."

Selby said, "I'll stay right here."

He looked around at the assembled faces, saw many that were curious, some that were friendly, some that were hostile. He could read in their glances the effect of the whispering campaign which had been carried on up and down the street by Roper and his friends.

Worthington, a paunchy man with a flair for political oratory, ran a shoe store, and paid more attention to the intrigue of petty local politics than to his own business. He went on importantly, "The eyes of the entire country are upon us. The metropolitan papers are beginning to focus attention on this community. It's up to us to *do* something. We've had two murders; one of them, the murder of a man who may have been a hobo or who may have been a clerk. That's bad. But when the president of the First National Bank of Las Alidas is shot down in cold blood and a fortune is stolen, it's up to us to do something and do it fast. The bank examiners may even order the bank closed—unless you officials can recover the money."

Worthington looked around at the grand jurors. There were several nods.

"All right," Selby said, "go ahead and do something."

"We intend to," Worthington announced. "We want a report from you on what *you've* done."

Selby said, "I've been working with the sheriff in making an investigation."

"Will you please tell us exactly what you've discovered?"

Selby said, "I'll give you the high spots. On some things, I'm waiting for confirmation. On others, I'm waiting for developments."

Worthington said ominously, "We wouldn't want you to withhold *anything at all* from us, Mr. District Attorney. We feel that this body should have the facts."

Selby outlined what he had discovered and what he had done. When he had finished, Worthington started calling witnesses who had been subpoenaed. It was for the most part merely a repetition of the story Selby had told. Only the witnesses now, in place of relating the matter informally, were interrogated largely by question and answer. Selby, acting as examiner, put the witnesses on the stand one after another and let them tell their stories. But Worthington pressed them with additional questions when they had finished.

He particularly gloated in the conflict of testimony over the identification of the photograph of the dead man, and emphasized the flight of Lacey and Mrs. Burke.

Harry Perkins, the coroner, sensing the cold hostility of the inquisitorial body, lacked the nerve to stand on his own two feet, but hid behind Selby. He had, he said, gone to Selby for advice as to whether it "would be all right" to go ahead with the cremation. No—so far as he knew, Selby had made no attempt to have the body identified. He had taken fingerprints. . . . No, the county officers had taken no photographs. The Southern Pacific had done that.

Midway in the examination, Brandon sent in a note to Selby. Selby read it, crumpled the note, pushed it down in his side pocket, thought a minute, then turned to the grand jurors and said, "A report from Sheriff Brandon is to the effect that he's discovered an important item of evidence in the room of the hotel occupied by Mrs. Burke. Do you want to hear it?"

"We want to hear everything," Worthington said.

Selby nodded to the deputy at the door. "Ask Sheriff Brandon to step in," he said.

Once more Selby's hand sought the note and crumpled it. He didn't want the grand jurors to note the last sentence on it, to the effect that if Selby wished he could step out for a quick look at the evidence and then withhold it from the grand jury until after that body had recessed.

Brandon came in, flashed a quickly sympathetic look at Selby, held up his right hand, was sworn, took the witness chair, and in response to Selby's questioning reported that when it appeared James Lacey and Mrs. Burke had actually left the hotel leaving the baggage behind, he had gone to their rooms and instituted a complete search. His fingerprint expert had developed a set of latents which unquestionably were those of James Lacey. They did not coincide with the finger-prints which had been found on the rear-view mirror of Lacey's car but did with those which had been found in the house of the murdered banker and in the rear portion of the Cadillac. On searching Mrs. Burke's suitcase, Brandon had noticed a place where the cloth lining had evidently been cut and then sewed back into place. Cutting through that lining, he had found a piece of paper, a note with writing on it. The note was signed John Burke and was dated Tuesday last.

Brandon passed the note over, and Jack Worthington read it to the grand jurors:

My darling Thelma:
I cannot face it. I've decided to end it all. Before midnight I will have died by my own hand. I will try to make it look like an accident. This is the best way out for everyone. You can collect five thousand in insurance, and it'll be ten thousand if you can prove it was accidental death. My creditors can't touch that money. It belongs to you. It will be enough for you and the baby to get another start. I've known for a long time that your heart was with your first love. Go back to him. Don't be foolish and wait a year. Leave town so there won't be any gossip, and go to the man you love. Try and make little Airdre think her daddy wasn't all bad. Don't let her ever take the name of Lacey or think that Jim Lacey is her father. That's all I ask, but I mean it. I'm sorry, darling, but I'm making it up to you the best I can.

There was an interval of thoughtful silence following Worthington's reading of the note. Abruptly, the foreman of the grand jury said to Sheriff Brandon, "Why did she hide that note? Why didn't she give it to the authorities as soon as she found it?"

Brandon shrugged his shoulders. "I've found the note," he said. "I'm not a mind reader."

Worthington said, "That note's a forgery. They intended to make the death look like an accident. They planned to kill him and dress the body in the clothes of a hobo. Lacey came from Tucson wearing the hobo clothes which were to be put on John Burke. Then he flew back to Phoenix and went through the trickery which hoodwinked the officers of this county into disposing of the body so that an identification can never be made."

"You forget," Brandon said, heatedly, "that we took his fingerprints. *That's* the best way of identifying any person."

"But you haven't any fingerprints of John Burke."

"We've found some around the house that we think are John Burke's."

Worthington came out into the open. "Some that were planted," he sneered. "You men were hoodwinked on this thing. You acted like a bunch of amateurs. You walked right into the trap and cremated the only real evidence. You can't prove that man was Burke. You can't prove he *wasn't* Burke. The brightest legal mind in the county has advised me that you can't convict *anyone* of the murder of Burke until you can prove Burke is dead. You let yourselves get jockeyed into a position where you're stalemated before you start."

Sheriff Brandon said, "I think we're the judge of that, Worthington."

Worthington said truculently, "I think you forget, Mr. Sheriff, that you're addressing the foreman of the grand jury."

Sheriff Brandon's face darkened. "I'm addressing a two-by-four main street politician, a he-gossip, a guy who's 'half-smart,' a bird who's been teamed up with the opposition before our election and afterwards, a man who's been trying to hamstring this administration at every turn of the road, because he wants to get officers back into power who can be subject to crooked political influence."

Worthington jumped to his feet. "Sheriff," he shouted, "you don't know who you're talking to. You . . ."

Sheriff Brandon calmly pushed back the witness chair, strode across to stand towering over the pudgy, purple-faced foreman of the grand jury. "Don't tell me I don't know who I'm talking to," he said. "I'm talking to Sam Roper's stooge. I'm talking to the stool-pigeon of the crooked gambling interests who are trying to hamper a square administration by every means in their power. You called this meeting of the grand jury to put us on the spot. Sam Roper's jealous of Doug Selby's record of a hundred-per-cent conviction in murder cases. He's trying to get our scalps by having the grand jury dump something in our laps we can't handle. All right, go ahead and do whatever you damn please, but don't think *we* don't know who you are and *what* you're doing."

He turned and strode the length of the grand jury room to the door. At the door, he turned on his heel once more to glower at Worthington. "Don't tell me I don't know who I'm talking to," he said. "I know you like a book," and, jerking open the door, he banged it shut behind him.

Worthington swallowed twice, shook himself like a rooster who has been vanquished in battle and is trying to get his feathers back into alignment. He glanced about him at the faces of his fellow grand jurors, then glowered at Doug Selby. "We are trying to co-operate with the officers of this county," he said. "We are doing *our* duty. It looks as though you fellows haven't been big enough to handle a case that's bringing a lot of unfavorable publicity to this community. We're trying to help you where you've fallen down because of your inexperience. That's what *we're* here for."

Selby said nothing.

"Well," Worthington blustered, taking courage from Selby's silence, "go ahead and say something."

Selby said, "I am bearing in mind that I am not addressing an individual. As the district attorney of this county, I am talking to the foreman of the grand jury. I have, therefore, nothing personal to say. In case I had, I doubt if I could add anything to the comments of the sheriff. He seems to have covered the ground thoroughly."

Someone laughed. Worthington flushed, and said, "All right, I'm coming to you, Mr. District Attorney. You had the two most important witnesses and let them slip through your fingers, two people who could have been interrogated before this grand jury and given an opportunity to come clean. They'd either have got all tangled up in their stories and we'd have something to work on, or else they'd have kept silent on the ground that their testimony would have incriminated them. And that's all anyone would have needed to show their guilt. Just because your girl friend is attorney for this pair, and . . ."

Selby strode across to face him. "In your capacity as foreman of this grand jury," he said, "you're stepping outside of your official position. In your individual capacity, you're talking too damn loud and too damn much."

Worthington shriveled back into his chair under the cold glare of Selby's eyes. Where the sheriff had left him purple with impotent rage, Selby's controlled wrath, his cold scorn put Worthington in a position where he recognized the expedient of sheltering himself behind the cloak of his official position. "I think that's all we need from you, Mr. District Attorney," he said. "The grand jury is going to discuss this matter. Personally, I am in favor of indicting James Lacey and Thelma Burke for the murder of John Burke. I would then suggest that you get busy and *try* to investigate the death of Oliver Benell with more vigor and intelligence than you've yet shown."

Selby said, calmly, "If you're going to indict anyone for the murder of John Burke, you'd better find out, first, that Burke is dead, second, who killed him and, third, why. Those are questions which will have to be answered in front of a jury. If your purpose is to embarrass the sheriff and the district attorney of this county by a premature indictment, go to it."

"Good heavens!" Worthington said. "What do you want? You've got all the evidence in the world! Do you want an eyewitness who saw Burke slugged and dropped in that gully?"

Selby went on without raising his voice, "In order to convict anyone of murder we have to show motivation. We have to show premeditation. We have to show malice. It's up to us to prove our case beyond a reasonable doubt. We have to prove the corpus delicti before we can introduce any evidence tending to connect the defendant with the crime."

Worthington said, "We want this case solved. We want to help. We figure you need help. Now, men, here's my suggestion. I'm in favor of appointing Sam Roper as a special prosecutor to give Selby assistance. He's had a lot of experience in these cases. Selby hasn't. Roper's a professional where Selby's an amateur."

There were several nods around the table.

Selby said, "Now the cat's out of the bag. All right, get this: the district attorneyship is an elective office. As long as I'm district attorney, I'm going to discharge the duties of my office the way I see fit. I don't want any politically discredited former incumbent of the office sticking his nose into my business. You have certain powers, but only certain powers. If you want to indict anyone for murder, go ahead. When you do it, *you* take the responsibility."

Selby turned from Worthington to the members of the grand jury. "Men, we're working on these cases. There are a lot of things we haven't as yet been able to solve. I don't think *you* can solve them. It's a lot more dangerous to get off on the wrong foot than it is to wait. As district attorney of this county I deem it my duty to tell you that. I'm fully aware Worthington wouldn't adopt the position he has unless he'd already made an informal canvas of this body and learned its sentiments. I'm also aware that Roper has been doing a lot of talking. It's a lot easier to stand on the side lines and criticize than it is to get in and do something. Any time I'm unable to discharge the duties of this office, I'll resign. Any time I need help, I want someone who will give me *help*, rather than someone who will use the opportunity to stick a political knife in my back."

One or two of the members nodded. One of them said to Worthington, "You've got to admit that's right, Mr. Foreman. Roper's had a lot of experience, but if he got in there, he wouldn't be trying to help Selby."

Worthington sneered. "On the basis of Selby's promise to resign if he can't solve this case," he said, "we'll leave Roper out of it."

"That wasn't what he said," one of the members protested.

"It amounts to that," Worthington insisted.

"No, it ain't the same thing," the other said.

Selby strode toward the door. "Don't argue with him," he said. "He's so anxious to have Roper back in office he's falling all over himself to get me out. If you people want to help solve these murders, keep out of this and don't toss any more monkey wrenches into the machinery."

He jerked the door open and strode out.

Brandon was waiting for him in the corridor, still white-faced with rage. "Worthington's a dirty, two-faced double-crosser," he said. "He and Sam Roper have been doing a lot of whispering. They've got those jurors hypnotized. Some of those jurors are good men, but they figure they can help us by taking a hand. Word has been passed around that you're sweet on Inez Stapleton, that she's pulling the wool over your eyes and you're holding off on her clients just because they are her clients. . . . I had no business losing my temper, but I'm damn glad I told Jack Worthington just what kind of a snake in the grass he is."

Selby gripped the sheriff's shoulder. "It's okay, Rex," he said. "If we can dish it out, we should be able to take it."

Brandon shook his head. "I can't be that calm about it, Doug," he said. "I almost hit that little toad. I wanted to smash my fist right into his lying mouth."

"Forget him," Selby said. "We're working on bigger things. Anybody can fight when his blows are landing and the other guys aren't. The fighter who counts is the one who can stand up when every punch the other man makes is landing where it hurts, and still keep on fighting." He left Brandon, walked on down the corridor, past curious and unsympathetic eyes, to the sanctuary of his own office.

He heard nothing from Sylvia Martin.

Shortly before five o'clock *The Blade* hit the streets.

149

Amorette Standish brought him his copy without a word.

The Blade had utilized its opportunity and "gone to town." A headline spread across the front page read, "SELBY PROMISES TO RESIGN." Below it, in smaller letters, "IF HE FAILS TO SOLVE CRIMES."

Then followed a lurid account of the grand jury session. The fact was duly emphasized that on the night of Benell's murder the district attorney of the county was out of the state "looking for evidence," and, according to rumors, accompanied by a young woman. The friendship of the district attorney for Inez Stapleton was emphasized, also the fact that Inez Stapleton, an attorney, had completely hoodwinked the "young and inexperienced district attorney" by the clever expedient of voluntarily bringing her clients to Madison City and thereby lulling the officers into a false sense of security before the two accused persons resorted to flight.

The paper went on to state that "following the failure of the sheriff and district attorney to make any appreciable headway in the cases, the grand jury had gone into the matter, that it was understood the sheriff and district attorney had indignantly spurned any offers of help, apparently preferring to let the murderer or murderers escape rather than be deprived of any of the credit which might ensue should they stumble upon a solution of the cases—a situation which seems unlikely in view of the manner in which they have permitted themselves to be pushed behind the eight ball in the early stages of the investigation."

A separate headlined article gave an account of Sheriff Brandon's loss of temper, of his defiance of the authority of the grand jury; and an editorial comment was to the effect that while the people of the county were prone to be patient with these officials, recognizing that they lacked the years of experience of their predecessors, and that particularly Selby's youth made him somewhat vulnerable to the practices of shrewd and experienced criminal attorneys—or even to newly admitted fledglings of the bar—the people would not long put up with the high-handed arrogance of an inefficient officer who sought to mask his own inefficiency behind an assumption of dictatorial power, or with a bullying attempt to override the agencies of the people which had been duly created by the law those very officials were sworn to enforce.

At five-thirty the grand jury returned an indictment against James Lacey, charging him with the murder of John Burke, and reported that "in order not to hamper the investigations of the district attorney or prevent him from utilizing the evidence of Mrs. Burke, the grand jury had recessed, temporarily at least withholding an indictment against Mrs. Burke." Selby took the news without comment. A reporter for *The Blade*, trying to goad him into some statement which could be used as the basis for an editorial, succeeded only in eliciting the toneless comment, "Sheriff Brandon and I are continuing our investigations. I shall discharge the duties of this office to the best of my ability, and Sheriff Brandon will do the same. It is my sworn duty to prosecute the indictment returned by the grand jury. Aside from that, I have no comment."

Selby went out to dinner at six-thirty. Up to that time he had heard no word from Sylvia Martin.

Chapter Fourteen

SELBY, sitting in one of Madison City's cafés, toyed with the fried abalone, French-fried potatoes, and canned peas which comprised his meal. He was conscious of that mental and physical weariness which had been with him all day. There was a sense of disillusionment, a feeling of spiritual void as though the bottom had dropped out and left him suspended in air.

Abruptly he pushed away his half-empty plate. Was he, by any chance, trying to feel sorry for himself?

Inez Stapleton had turned against him. She hadn't done it surreptitiously. She'd given him fair warning. She was fighting to make him respect her, to make him notice her, and there was nothing half-hearted about Inez Stapleton in a fight. He remembered all too keenly the tricky cuts which she gave to tennis balls, the manner in which she would trick him out of position, only to slam the ball with sudden viciousness into the far corner of the court.

Sylvia Martin had not called, had not been near the office. She was, of course, disappointed. Many of his sympathizers were disappointed. He was cutting a sorry figure.

What of it?

Doug didn't finish his plate, didn't wait for dessert. He summoned the waitress, paid his check, went to the telephone and called the sheriff's office. Sheriff Brandon was home. Selby called the residence. "Hello, Rex," he said. "Hope you weren't taking an after-dinner nap and had to be dragged back to the world of murderers, grand juries, and newspapers."

"Not me," the sheriff said. "I won't be able to sleep for a week. I'd like to get the editor of *The Blade* in a dark corner and stuff that newspaper down his throat piece by piece, make him eat every damn word of it."

Selby didn't waste mental energy getting angry. "Any reports on Lacey and the Burke woman?" he asked.

"Not yet."

Selby said, "How about concentrating on New Mexico? That's the place Quinne mentioned when he took off at Tucson."

· Sheriff Brandon said, "Shucks, Doug. They're running away. The last place to look for them is where they said they'd be."

"That's just it," Selby said. "If they *were* there, they wouldn't be running away. A clever man might figure it that way."

"Not one chance in a million," Brandon said .

"Okay," Selby remarked. "It was an idea I had. It does sound a bit ridiculous when you put it in words."

There was a moment's silence, then Brandon said, "I get you, Doug. I'm a little bit worked up tonight, I guess. I'll see what I can do."

"Okay," Selby said. "Got any pictures of Jim Lacey?"

"Not yet. I wired for some, but they haven't shown up."

Selby said casually, "Well, don't let it worry you, Rex. I'm going to grab a little sleep. After all, we're in for it now. The indictment's been returned, and it's up to us to make out a case if we can."

"Or be laughed out of the county if we can't," Brandon growled.

"Better get some sleep, Rex. I'm going to," Selby said. "Good night."

"Good night, son," the sheriff answered, his voice suddenly softening with affection.

Selby strolled into the Madison City hotel, looked

up the condensed airline schedules east. A plane left Los Angeles at ten-thirty Pacific Time and arrived at Phoenix, Arizona, at one-fifty-five A.M. Mountain Time. He noticed that a plane left Tucson at ten-twelve P.M. and arrived at Phoenix at eleven-five P.M.

Selby went up to the office and put through a call to Buck Reilly at Tucson. When he had the under-sheriff on the line, he said, "What's new, Reilly?—Selby talking in Madison City."

"Not a thing, Mr. Selby," Reilly said somewhat rue-fully. "I'm afraid I talked you out of doing what you wanted to do last night, but . . . well, you know how it is."

"That's all right," Selby said easily. "How about Lacey? Have you any photographs?"

"Yes, I got a bunch of photographs, snapshots taken at picnics and out on the ranch, a portrait, a picture of Lacey standing by a bronco buster at one of the recent rodeos, and . . ."

"There's a plane leaving Tucson at ten-twelve P.M. It gets in Phoenix at eleven-five P.M. Put those pic-tures in an envelope, address them to Doug Selby at the airport at Phoenix. Have the pilot leave them at the desk for me to pick up. Explain to everyone along the line that it's important. Will you?"

"I'll do that little thing," Reilly promised. "Any luck at your end?"

"No," Selby said. "They walked out on us and van-ished into thin air."

Reilly made clucking noises of sympathy. "That," he announced, "is a tough break."

Selby asked, "You're keeping a watch on the house?"

"Yes."

"There's a chance they'll show up to pack some things," Selby said. "Keep your man parked out where he won't be seen. Keep his car out of sight, and . . ."

"I know," Reilly said. "We're doing everything, Mr. Selby. You can count on that. This is a bad break, and it kind of caught us off first base."

"All right," Selby told him. "Be sure and get those things on the night plane. Give them to the pilot to be left for me at the Phoenix airport."

"Check," Reilly said.

Selby called Harry Perkins, the coroner. Perkins was inclined to be apologetic. "Forget it, Harry," Selby said. "It was all my fault. It's something we do a dozen times a year. If we held every hobo's body in cold storage, we'd be criticized just as much. This just happened to be the wrong hobo. Get out that blanket roll. I want to look it over. I'll be right down."

He got out his car, drove to the coroner's office, looked over the bedding which had belonged to the dead man, a nondescript bunch of old blankets. One of them interested him. It was of a pure wool, long and narrow. A hole had been burnt in the center.

"Think I'll cut off a piece of this blanket," Selby said. "It's an odd shape."

"Uh-huh," Perkins said absently as Selby took out his pocketknife. When Selby had cut off a sample and put it in his brief case, Perkins suddenly thrust out his hand.

"Ordinarily," he said, "I try to straddle the fence. I've survived three changes of administration in this county. After this, count me in *your* corner. The way you've acted makes me feel like a heel."

Selby gripped the proffered hand.

"Thanks," he said, and went out, feeling that the heavy clouds of mental despondency which had gripped him were already breaking.

Driving into Los Angeles, Selby guided the car mechanically. His mind, completely absorbed in the case, snapped to conscious attention from time to time. At such times, he would try to remember whether he had passed through certain suburban towns, and would be unable to tell until he encountered some familiar landmark. Then, reassured as to his position, his thoughts would gradually drift back to the case, and he would once more guide the car without conscious volition, realizing fully what he was doing, but in the doing having no regard for time or distance.

He arrived at the Los Angeles airport with some fifteen minutes to spare. He purchased his ticket, went into the restaurant, had a cup of chocolate and some dry toast, boarded the plane, and remained awake only long enough to see it sweep down the cement runway, zoom up into the air, and circle over the lights of Glendale. Then the steady drone of the motors lulled his senses into dreamy restfulness. The stewardess wakened him, fastening his seat belt just before they came into Phoenix.

It was a cold, clear, star-studded night. Civilization and irrigation had pushed the desert far back from Phoenix, but at night, after people were asleep, the desert reclaimed its own. The calm silence, the dry cold which sucked warmth from the body along with humidity, the steady unblinking splendor of the stars were all of the heritage of the desert. The taxicab, driving through the dark streets, seemed utterly out of place.

"Where to?" the driver asked.

"Your best hotel," Selby said, settling back against the cushions, and remaining in a blissful state of mental relaxation, until the cab drew up in front of a large hotel built after the Indian type of architecture with terraces, ladders, and flat roofs. Selby entered the lobby where a crackling fire was burning in a big fireplace. A courteous clerk, behind a counter back of which were great Indian curios and fine Navajo rugs, took his signature and raised his eyebrows slightly. "No baggage?" he asked.

"No baggage," Selby said, and paid for his room in advance. He tipped the bellboy, closed the door, and took from his pocket the envelope which had been waiting for him at the airport. He hesitated for a moment whether to open it then or wait until morning, decided to wait until morning, tossed it in a bureau drawer, divested himself of clothes, which he threw carelessly over a chair, climbed into bed, and was almost instantly sunk in a deep peaceful sleep.

He wakened in the morning to find the room chill with desert dawn. He closed the window, turned on the steam heat, bathed, donned his clothes, and opened the envelope. The photographs were excellent likenesses.

There was enough of the lone wolf in Doug Selby so that his nerves gained the sustenance they needed from a sense of carrying on singlehanded warfare. How much of this was due to the fact that Sylvia had failed to be at his side in a moment of crisis, he didn't bother to analyze. Rex Brandon was a priceless friend and a valuable ally, but when it came to a showdown, Selby wanted to hunt alone. The solution of this case lay somewhere in Arizona, and Selby had decided to retire from circulation until he could solve the puzzle. He asked only to be left alone, to be free from interruption. He thought of calling on the local police for assistance, and then rejected the thought without knowing exactly why it was distasteful to him.

He had breakfast, purchased a safety razor, shaving cream, and brush, toothbrush, toothpaste, new underwear, socks, and tie. He threw his soiled garments away, and pushed the toilet accessories he had purchased into his brief case, together with the fragment of blanket.

When he walked out of the hotel room there was no necessity for him to return. He was traveling light and was ready to travel far and fast.

Selby went to a photographer's establishment, and showed him the portrait of Jim Lacey. "Can you take a picture of this portrait," he asked, "put on a sombrero and a leather vest, retouch a gray walrus mustache and then rephotograph it so it doesn't look like a fake?"

The photographer looked at him suspiciously for a moment, and then nodded. "Yes," he said, "I *could* do it."

"How soon?"

"You could have it by tomorrow."

"I want it in an hour," Selby said.

The man shook his head, but somehow the gesture lacked emphasis.

Selby took a twenty-dollar bill from his pocket, folded it around his fingers. "I'll be back in an hour," he said. "I'll pick up the photograph. Have it ready for me. At that time, I'll leave you the twenty dollars."

The photographer sighed, and reached for the photograph. "It's going to be a job," he said.

"I thought it would," Selby commented, and walked out.

For more than forty minutes he wasted time covering stores which could tell him nothing about the fragment of blanket, a blanket, which, from its shape, Selby concluded had been a saddle blanket. The manager of one of the harness and saddlery stores on which he called at the end of his forty minutes of fruitless search, said, "You might try the Hall & Carden Saddlery Company down on First. That looks a little like a job lot of hand-woven saddle blankets they had down in one of the Indian schools. I don't think the blankets turned out just the way they wanted, and they quit handling them. They furnished the yarn and tried to produce a porous, absorbent blanket."

"What was wrong with them?" Selby asked.

"Had to sell for too much money," the man told him. "People won't pay those prices these days."

Selby thanked him and walked down to a store marked "Hall & Carden's Harness and Saddlery." The window was decorated with sombreros, hand-tooled saddles, silver-inlaid spurs, chaps, gauntlets, leather coats, and vests made of cowhide. A clerk referred him to Mr. Hall, a thin, hawk-like individual who conveyed the suggestion of poised energy which is carried past middle age only by men who are thin and rangy.

Selby showed him the fragment of blanket.

"What about it?" Hall asked, studying Selby carefully.

Selby produced one of his official cards. "I'm district attorney of Madison County," he said. "I'm anxious to identify a body. I think identifying that saddle blanket will help me."

Hall shook his head. "I don't think it can be identified."

"Why not?"

"I couldn't tell you who had it."

"What do you mean?"

"There were a hundred of them," Hall said.

Selby's nerves tingled with excitement. "You mean that you sold this blanket?"

"Yes. We had a hundred made up, got the yarn for them, made according to our specifications, had an arrangement with one of the Indian schools to weave 'em."

"Were the blankets all alike? I notice there's a strand of colored . . ."

"Yes, they were all alike," Hall said. "We had the yarn made to our specifications. It was all the same."

"You sold all of those blankets?"

"No. I think we have some left in stock. They're rather expensive. They didn't move fast."

"How long ago was this?" Selby asked.

"More than a year ago," Hall said.

"How much more?"

"I could look it up for you, but roughly speaking you can figure it was a year ago."

Selby followed him to the back part of the store. Hall took down a blanket and held it out for Selby's inspection. "Nothing like it anywhere," he said. "You double it over, and it's light and porous. It lets the air through between the saddle and the horse. It absorbs perspiration from the horse—and it costs too damn much money. The difference between that and other blankets isn't worth the price."

Selby said, "I'll buy it. I want you to wrap it up and hold it in a safe place, put some identifying mark on the package so you can remember it."

He paid for the blanket, started to walk out, then turned, and said, "Do you by any chance have a branch store in Tucson?"

"Yes," Hall said.

Once more Selby tingled with excitement. "How many blankets went to Tucson?"

"I don't know, five or six," Hall said. "The Tucson branch manager didn't think as much of them as we did, and," he added after a moment, "he was right, and we were wrong."

Selby thanked him, and walked out. Five minutes later, the photographer handed him his original photograph together with a copy showing James Lacey with an iron-gray walrus mustache wearing a gray sombrero. Beyond a slight haziness, it was impossible to tell that there was anything unusual about the photograph.

Selby handed him the twenty dollars. The photographer sighed. "One of the hardest twenty bucks I ever made," he said. "I couldn't find anyone's photograph wearing a sombrero that I could swap faces with. I have to photograph the sombrero, paste the photograph on this guy's head, rephotograph it, dry the negative, retouch it, make an enlargement, do some art work, and then photograph the enlargement on cabinet size. Brother, I've been moving."

"So have I," Selby said absently, and then added, "Not that I'm ungrateful to you. Thanks a lot. I appreciate it."

He took his photograph to the Pioneer Rooms. All of the way, there was hammering at the back of his brain the knowledge that he should telephone Rex Brandon and let him know where he was, but Selby had a feeling that he was in a charmed circle. To talk about what he was doing would break the spell. He wanted to carry on—alone. Time enough to speak when he could ring Brandon, tell him that the mystery was solved, and the proof necessary to secure a conviction in his hand.

The manager of the Pioneer Rooms was a big-framed, hard-eyed, skeptical woman who regarded Selby without cordiality but with alert, intelligent eyes. Selby made known his identity and asked her about the man who had taken the room as Horatio Perne of the Inter-Mountain Brokerage Company.

She said wearily, "Lord, I'm tired of that man! The police have been asking questions and asking questions. For the life of me, I can't remember anything about him except that he was a man somewhere around fifty, or maybe not so old, with a cowhide vest, a Western hat, and one of those drooping gray mustaches. I think I noticed the mustache more than anything else."

"Wasn't there something about his eyes?" Selby asked.

"Yes," she said. "There *was* something funny about the eyes—the way they were held wide open. Those eyes reminded me of something, and I can't for the life of me recall what it is."

"You mean you've seen them before?"

"I don't think so, and yet I have the feeling that I have. There's something funny about them."

"You mean about the color?"

"No, about the shape, something about the slant of them."

"He had Oriental blood, perhaps?" Selby asked, groping blindly, a grow sense of disappointment gripping him.

"No. It wasn't that. I just don't know *what* it was."

"Can you tell how tall or how heavy?"

"No, I can't. And because I can't I guess he was medium size. Well, maybe a little taller than ordinary. You know how things are like that. We have forty rooms, and most of them are rented every night. People come and people go. I look them over just enough to see if they're apt to get drunk or noisy or do anything that will attract the police. I'm particularly careful about young women who travel in pairs. Aside from that I don't pay very much attention."

"Would you know this man if you saw him again?" Selby asked.

"Yes, I think I would."

"You can't tell me now what there was about his eyes that impressed you as being familiar?"

"No, I can't. It's something I've seen before somewhere—well, maybe, you know, I've seen the man's brother or sister, and . . . Now I wonder if it *was* that. . . . I'll tell you what I'll do, Mr. Selby. I'll think it over and see. There's a chance it was a family resemblance or maybe it just reminded me of someone I knew real well."

"Thanks," Selby said. "Now, how about his picture. Would you know his picture if you saw it?"

"I think I would."

Selby opened his brief case and took out the picture the photographer had given him. "Is that the man?" he asked.

She scrutinized it carefully. "No," she said, "that's not the man."

"Do you mean that you don't recognize him as the man who was here, or that positively and absolutely that isn't the man?"

She said slowly, "I won't say positively and absolutely that it isn't the man. It looks something like him, and then again it doesn't look something like him. It . . . oh, wait a minute . . ." She lowered the picture, blinked her eyes rapidly, and said, "I know now what those eyes look like."

"What?" Selby asked.

"I knew a woman one time who had some work done on her face. They didn't want her to use her facial muscles because it would stretch the skin. So they put some strips of adhesive tape that ran from her eyes back up to her forehead—you know, not from the eyes themselves, but from the temples. It pulled the skin back tight, and her eyes had a tight, staring look. That's what this man reminded me of."

Selby grew excited. "Then you'd say that his forehead had been taped so as to change the expression of his eyes and the look of his face?"

"Well, I wouldn't go so far as to say that, but his eyes reminded me of that woman. I *knew* there was something about them. I just couldn't place it."

Selby said, "Look at that photograph again. Now, suppose the eyes had been pulled up by strips of adhesive tape, stretching back from the ears up to the top of the head. Would that make it look like the same man?"

"Yes," she said slowly, "I think it would, but that's just a think. That isn't a positive statement. The sombrero, the vest and the mustache make the face look somehow familiar—if the eyes were different."

"I understand," Selby said. "Now I want you to quit thinking about this entirely. I think the man who was here was disguised. I think the mustache was false. I think he'd changed the shape of his face by strips of adhesive tape concealed under the hat. I'm going to try to show you a picture of the man I think was here, with his face made up just the way it was when he was here, and until then, I want you to dismiss it from your mind. Don't try to figure what the man in this picture would look like if his eyes were different. Do you understand?"

"Yes," she said. "I'll do that, Mr. Selby, and I'll be right here whenever you want me."

Selby left her and went to the telephone office where he put through a call to Rex Brandon.

Brandon's voice showed surprise. "You're over in Phoenix, Doug?"

"Yes," Selby said. "I'm trying to run down this Arizona angle of the case."

"The officers there have gone over everything," Brandon said. "The testimony of the landlady who owns the Pioneer Rooms ain't worth much. The Phoenix police did the best they could with her—and got nowhere much."

"Anything new at your end?" Selby asked.

"We've got Lacey," the sheriff said. "That was a swell hunch you had, Doug. I telephoned the authorities in New Mexico before I went to sleep. The authorities there covered the landing fields. They nabbed

Lacey, Mrs. Burke and the pilot in an Albuquerque hotel."

"Where are they now?" Selby asked.

"Right down here in jail," Brandon said. "They tried to pretend they were intending to come back when you needed 'em, and weren't running away and all that hooey, so the New Mexico authorities got 'em to waive extradition and flew 'em back— They were registered under assumed names at the Albuquerque hotel."

"What's Inez Stapleton doing?" Selby asked.

"She's tearing the roof off of things," Brandon said. "Claims that it's an outrage to have a young innocent child polluted by having the mother held and is probably going to try for a writ of habeas corpus. I wish you were here, Doug," he added after a moment. "There's going to be some legal fireworks, and it won't look good to have you outside the county."

"I'm not outside the county," Selby said promptly. "I'm sick. I've got a bad cold. The doctor has advised me to seek complete seclusion for at least twenty-four hours. There's nothing Inez Stapleton can do which will come to a head before Monday. Simpy sit tight and let her get her writs or anything else she pleases. I'll be back sometime tonight, perhaps this afternoon. Today is Saturday, a legal half holiday. I'm entitled to a week end—when I'm sick."

"Take care of yourself, son," Brandon said solicitously. "How are you feeling?"

"Swell," Selby said. "I'll be seeing you, Rex," and hung up. He hired a car to drive him to Tucson. The local manager of the Hall & Carden store was a saddle-bronzed, bowlegged, quiet individual who wasted few words. He looked at the sample of blanket Selby handed him, looked at Selby's card, and said, "Yes, that came from one of our blankets."

"How many of them did you have?"

"Four."

Selby met his eyes. "To whom did you sell them?"

"I don't know that I can recall offhand."

Something in the steadfast hostility of the man's gaze gave Selby his cue. "Did you," he asked, "sell one to James Lacey?"

The man's eyes grew colder. "Lacey," he said, "is a customer of ours. If you want to know anything, ask him."

Selby walked over to the telephone, called the sheriff's office, got Reilly on the phone, and said, "I'm in town, Reilly, having a little trouble with the local manager of Hall & Carden's store. I wonder if you'd mind coming down."

"I'll be there in five minutes," Reilly promised.

During the five-minute interval, the manager seemed to be thinking things over. He grew more and more uneasy. Once or twice he made as though to talk to Selby but Selby held himself aloof. The door opened, Reilly came in, shook hands with Selby, then went over and shook hands with the manager. "What's the matter, Tom?" he asked.

"I don't want to give out information about a customer of the store—Jim Lacey."

"Phooey," Reilly observed. "You don't want to be put in the position of not helping the law, do you, Tom?"

"No, I guess I don't."

"I didn't think you did," Reilly said. "As far as Lacey is concerned, he's a friend of mine. He's important politically. I'm not going to make an enemy out of him. I'm in office to do my duty. I'm going to do it. This man's asking you a question. My office is co-operating with him. That means *I'm* asking you the question. Are you going to answer it?"

"Yes," the man said.

"What's the question?" Reilly asked Selby.

Selby indicated the piece of blanket. "I want to know if James Lacey bought one of those blankets through this store," he said.

The manager nodded.

"When?" Selby asked.

"Around a year ago, right after they came in. I knew the blanket was too expensive to sell to our regular trade, and dudes don't ordinarily buy their own saddle outfits. The dude ranches furnish them. Lacey was different. Nothing's too good for a horse that Jim Lacey owns. I told him about the blankets. He bought two of them."

"Two of them!" Selby exclaimed.

"That's right."

"Can you tell me exactly when that was?"

"Not exactly . . . Yes, I can, too, if I look it up. But it was last year, and my books have gone on to the Phoenix office."

"He'll look it up and let me know, and I'll get in touch with you," Reilly said to Selby. "You've been a pretty busy individual, I see, Selby."

Selby nodded.

Reilly's glance was significant. "If you're all finished here," he said, "come on up to the office. I want to talk with you."

Selby walked out to Reilly's car, but Reilly didn't drive to the office. He drove about a block, then parked the car, and said, "How important is it to identify that blanket?"

"Damned important," Selby said. "I want to tie it up directly with Lacey. The way things stand now, I can't do it. I've got circumstantial evidence, and that's all. There were a hundred of those blankets. Lacey got two of them."

Reilly said, "I have a hunch I could help you out on that."

"How do you mean?" Selby asked.

"Ride horses any?" Reilly asked.

"No, not much."

"Thought so," Reilly said abruptly. "Think you're overlooking the best bit of evidence you've got."

"What's that?" Selby asked.

"I noticed a couple of horsehairs embedded in that blanket. I presume that piece was cut from a blanket you're holding as evidence. That right?"

"Yes," Selby said.

"Want to take a ride?" Reilly asked.

"Where to?"

"Out to Lacey's place. Think we might find something."

"Let's go," Selby said.

Reilly drove out at high speed. The place was locked with no one in sight. "We had a man out here until early this morning," Reilly explained. "Then your sheriff telephoned he'd taken Lacey into custody. . . . Understand your grand jury indicted him for first-degree murder."

Selby nodded.

"There must have been more evidence against him than I thought," Reilly said. "He's hot-headed enough to shoot if he's crowded. You saw that. Sorry I talked you into going easy with him. Well, let's do a little exploring."

He went around to the stable where a Mexican was cleaning out some stalls. Reilly spoke to him in Spanish. After several moments the Mexican reluctantly led the way to a room which opened on the back of the stable and which was locked with a padlock. The Mexican took a key from his pocket, fitted it to the padlock, and opened the door, disclosing a series of saddletrees containing some fifteen saddles. Again there was more conversation between the Mexican and the under-sheriff. The stablehand indicated a saddle of hand-tooled leather, mounted with silver. A blanket was flung across the top of this saddle.

Reilly went over and took the blanket down. "Okay, buddy," he said to Selby. "Perhaps I can make up for throwing you off the track the first time you were out here. The boy tells me this here is Lacey's favorite saddle and this is his saddle blanket. It's the mate of the one you were talking about, ain't it?"

Selby studied the blanket and nodded. "Can you find out what happened to the other one?" he asked.

Reilly launched into voluble Spanish, indicating the saddle blanket, then indicating the piece in Selby's hands. The Mexican answered, for the most part in surly monosyllables. Finally he offered information in a brief sentence which called for a torrent of speech from Reilly. Again the Mexican talked, gradually becoming more loquacious. At the end of five minutes, he was waving his hands, gesticulating, and talking.

Reilly turned to Selby. "This blanket that you're trying to identify," he said. "Did it have a hole burnt in it?"

He read the answer in Selby's face.

"Well," Reilly said. "Looks like you've got all you need, buddy. This boy has been with Lacey for two years. He remembers when he got the saddle blankets. He says there were two just alike. The other one got a hole burnt in it when Lacey took it on a pack trip back into the high mountains after deer. One of the men was using it for a blanket and slept too near the fire. A spark popped out and burnt a hole in it."

"And what happened to it after that?" Selby asked.

Once more Reilly talked with the man in Spanish,

then said to Selby, "It was around here for a while, but he hasn't seen it lately."

"What does he mean by lately?" Selby asked.

"I asked him that, and he said, 'Oh, perhaps a week.' You know how these people are in regard to time. It doesn't mean very much to them."

Selby said, "Look here, Reilly, this is going to be important as the devil. I don't want anything to happen to this man. I don't want him to skip out, and I don't want his testimony changed."

"Okay. We'll take care of that," Reilly said. "I had another idea, too, Selby, that might help."

"What?" Selby asked.

"Horsehairs," Reilly said. "Now hairs of different horses are all different. How about taking this other saddle blanket back and checking it and the one you have. I think you'll find a good man with a microscope could find hairs from the same horses in 'em."

Selby gripped his arm with sudden enthusiasm. "Reilly," he said, "I owe you a drink."

Reilly grinned. "We get it at Tucson," he said. "Come on."

Chapter Fifteen

SELBY caught an afternoon plane to Los Angeles. With the difference between Mountain and Pacific Time in his favor, he was able to get back to Madison City before dark.

It was Saturday afternoon, a legal half holiday, but the merchants' busiest time. People from the outlying ranches were pouring into the city. There were no parking places available anywhere on Main Street. Crowds thronged the sidewalks. Traffic congested the streets. Selby had to drive slowly because of the traffic. He parked his car at the courthouse, ran up the steps to the sheriff's office, and was relieved to find Sheriff Brandon tilted back in his official swivel chair, his booted feet on the desk, a corncob pipe clamped between his lips.

"Hi, son," Brandon said.

Selby grinned. "You look happy."

"I am."

"What happened?"

"We took Lacey's fingerprints. They match with the ones we thought were his. Now then, we can prove he was in Burke's house and was in Benell's house. We can show the time they took off from Tucson. They landed at Las Alidas—and they took chances doing it. That's not much of a field for a night landing."

"It was moonlight," Selby pointed out.

"I know," Brandon said. "Anyway, they landed. They must have gone to Benell's house."

"What are they saying?" Selby asked.

"Nothing."

"Nothing at all?"

"Absolutely nothing," the sheriff said. "We don't care. We'll put this fingerprint evidence in front of a jury and then they'll *have* to talk."

"How about the aviator?" Selby asked. "Is he Mrs. Burke's brother?"

"Yep."

"What does he say?"

"Nothing."

"Why did they go to New Mexico?" Selby said.

"Just the way you doped it out, son," the sheriff said, proudly. "They figured it was the last place anyone would look for them because there's where Quinne said he was going when he left Tucson. They registered in a hotel under assumed names."

"But what does Quinne say?" Selby asked. "What does he say about that telephone call from Mrs. Burke?"

"He says nothing," the sheriff said. "They all say nothing. Inez Stapleton says she'll do the talking for the three of them. And all the talking *she* does you can put in your eye."

Selby frowned. "Only Lacey is accused of crime. We can bring the other two before the grand jury and . . ."

"Nope," Sheriff Brandon said. "We'll bring them to trial. That fingerprint evidence is going to lick 'em."

Selby said, thoughtfully, "I wish we could absolutely prove that body was Burke. . . . I ran on to some swell evidence down there in Arizona, Rex. If we can prove the body was that of Burke, then there'll be nothing to it. We can forge a chain of circumstantial evidence which Lacey can never break."

Brandon puffed contentedly away at his corncob pipe.

Selby started to pace the floor. "Hang it," he said. "I don't like it. I don't want to send a man to his death on circumstantial evidence. Do you know, Rex, I have a feeling that if Lacey killed him, he did it in self-defense or in trying to protect Mrs. Burke. And if he did, it's high time for him to say so. If he waits much longer, people will never believe him."

"Well, he's got Inez Stapleton to thank for that," Brandon said. "We've done our duty. Tell me about what you found in Arizona, Doug."

Selby produced the blanket, told him about what he had discovered.

Brandon's chuckle was as ominously dry as corn

husks rustling in the wind. "Let Attorney Stapleton figure *that* one out," he said. "It's her move now."

There was a knock at the door. Brandon frowned and said, "Sounds like Sylvia." He took the pipe from his mouth and called, "Come in."

Sylvia pushed open the door, saw Doug, and said, "Oh," quickly, as one makes an involuntary exclamation. Then, without taking her eyes from Selby, she said, "Hello, Sheriff," and walked across the room to put her hand on Doug's arm.

"Where were you last night, Doug?" she asked. "I rang your phone and rang it and rang it."

Selby heaved a deep breath, which seemed to lift a heavy load from his mind, "*You* did?"

"Yes, where were you?"

"Chasing around Arizona," Rex Brandon said, "getting evidence that's going to hang a first-degree murder charge right slap bang around Jim Lacey's neck."

"Oh, *were* you, Doug?"

"I dug up some things that Lacey will have quite a time explaining," he said.

"Oh, Doug, why *didn't* you let me know?"

Selby grinned somewhat sheepishly. "I thought you might be off me, Sylvia, thinking that I left Inez Stapleton pull the wool over my eyes."

"Oh, Doug, that was what I was afraid you'd think. I was out trying to get a line on where Lacey and Mrs. Burke were. I thought I was on a red-hot lead, and then it turned out it was a false alarm. I called you just as soon as I got back, and I couldn't get an answer."

"Sorry, Sylvia," Selby said. "I guess I was feeling just a little sorry for myself or something and wanted to strike back. I couldn't figure any way of doing it except going out and digging up evidence."

"I'll say he dug it up," Sheriff Brandon said. "You

can talk about the identification all you want to, Doug. As far as I'm concerned, it's a dead open-and-shut case. And you mark my words, a jury hereabouts is going to feel exactly the same way about it. Figure it out for yourself, Doug. If Jim Lacey takes the stand, you're going to be able to rip him to pieces with cross-examination. If he doesn't take the stand, you know what a jury is going to figure *that* means."

"Under the law, jurors can't take that into consideration," Selby said. "A man has the right to remain mute and force the prosecution to prove . . ."

"Bunk," Brandon interrupted. "They may pretend to themselves they're not taking it into consideration, but they sure do—in this country anyway."

"Would it be too much to ask you to tell me the evidence you have?" Sylvia asked.

Selby showed her the blankets, explained the manner in which they had been acquired. Sylvia Martin's eyes danced. "Oh, Doug," she said, "I knew you'd do it! That's wonderful! That gives me an opportunity to smash *The Blade* right between the eyes. Have you seen their paper tonight?"

Selby shook his head.

"Well, promise me one thing," Sylvia said.

"What?" Selby asked.

"That you won't read it until after you've had dinner."

"I promise," Selby said.

Brandon said, "The Missus said to bring him over to my place for dinner. Then he's going home and get a good night's sleep."

"You'll be over at Sheriff Brandon's?" she asked.

Selby nodded enthusiastically. "Dinner at Brandon's" he said, "is a feast for the body and a rest for the soul."

"If I hear anything, I'll let you know there," she

174

said. "Oh, Doug, just wait until you read the way I'm going to lambast that *Blad* story tomorrow."

Her heels click . . . click . . . click . . . clacked on the marble floor of the corridor as she hurried out. Sheriff Brandon grinned across at Selby, and said, "Friends like that are worth having, Doug. Let's eat."

Selby nodded. In his car, he followed the sheriff's machine to Brandon's house where Mrs. Brandon received Selby with the pride of one welcoming a favorite son.

Selby always enjoyed his dinners at Brandon's. There was a homey atmosphere about the place, a simple, rustic sincerity that made no attempt at masquerading under false colors. Mrs. Brandon occasionally did some political entertaining, but she absolutely refused to "put on airs" as she termed it. When she had a meal, her food was plain, wholesome, and ample. She placed steaming dishes on the table, slipped off her apron, sat down, and as she expressed it, "ate hearty."

As Doug rested his tired nerves in the atmosphere of friendliness which permeated the place, he thought back with a smile of how he had felt the night before —alone, crowded into a corner, almost against the ropes, physically and mentally wearied, spiritually numbed. He had asked, and asked in vain, for an opportunity to fight back at the adversaries who were so intangible that he couldn't touch them—Sam Roper, whose activities had been so smugly surreptitious that it was impossible to pin anything on him; Jack Worthington, the fat hypocrite, who had greased the skids under Selby; *The Blade* with its warped, unfair presentation of the case, its subtle manner of clothing Sam Roper with the dignity of experienced wisdom and putting Brandon and Selby in the light of inexperienced amateurs floundering around hopelessly out of their depths; and, last of all, the murderer who had conceived and carried out his crime with such diabolical cleverness that there seemed to be no tangible starting point for a solution.

Selby sighed with contentment after the meal, and lit his pipe. "How about *The Blade*, Rex?" he asked.

Brandon shook his head. The smile faded from his eyes. "Not until you've finished your pipe, Doug," he said. "That's part of a man's dinner."

Selby stretched out his feet, crossed his ankles, and puffed contentedly at his pipe. It seemed impossible that any disturbing event could pierce the atmosphere of calm tranquillity which bathed him in its warm glow.

Mrs. Brandon busied herself with the dishes. Sheriff Brandon spilled golden flakes of tobacco into a brown paper, rolled the cigarette with one hand, snapped a match into flame, and joined Selby in puffing out clouds of tobacco smoke.

The telephone rang.

Selby heard a cessation in the clatter of dishes in the kitchen, then Mrs. Brandon's voice answering the telephone, heard her say, "Yes, he's here, but he can't be disturbed. He's going over some important . . . Oh, yes, I'll tell him, Miss Martin."

She opened the swinging door from the vestibule. "Sylvia Martin on the phone for you, Doug," she said.

Selby thanked her, walked to the telephone, and heard Sylvia's excited voice. "Doug, how tired are you?"

"Not very," he said. "Why?"

"I want to see you. I want to talk something over with you."

"When?"

"Right away, just as soon as you can get here. Oh, Doug, it's *frightfully* important."

Selby said with a grin, "I haven't read *The Blade* yet."

"To thunder with *The Blade*," she told him. "That's history. Read the *news* in Sunday morning's *Clarion*. It may interest you. . . . Oh, Doug, please come. I think I'm on the trail of something."

"Fifteen minutes?" he asked.

"Could you possibly make it in ten?" she countered.

"We'll compromise on seven," Selby said. "I'll be over at your place."

"I'll be waiting at the curb, Doug. You have your car?"

"Yes."

"That's fine," she said. "I'll be all ready to jump in as you drive by."

Selby went out in the kitchen and thanked Mrs. Brandon for the dinner. To the sheriff he said, "Sylvia's on the trail of something new."

"Hate to have you go out again, Doug," Rex Brandon said, looking at him with shrewdly speculative eyes. "You've had quite a siege of it."

Selby laughed. "I could never go to sleep feeling there was anything left undone," he said.

"Don't let that case worry you, son. It doesn't worry me. You've got a conviction, hands down."

"Well," Selby said, "we'll see what we can find out. I'll keep you posted, Rex."

"Think I should go along?" Brandon asked.

Selby shook his head. "Sylvia and I work well together," he said. "You'd better hold yourself available in case anything turns up here. I'm supposed to try cases, not investigate them, so I can be out of reach without attracting so much adverse comment."

Brandon walked to the door with Selby, put his hand on the younger man's shoulder, said, "Good luck,

Doug. If Sylvia thinks she's got something, it's pretty apt to *be* something. You can trust that girl."

Selby nodded, dashed down the stairs, across the strip of lawn to where his car was parked, and roared it into motion. Three minutes later he was braking it to a stop at the curb where Sylvia was waiting.

She jumped in beside him with a quick, lithe motion, a swirl of skirts, and a flash of legs. "Let's go, Doug," she said breathlessly.

"Where?" he asked.

"Los Angeles."

"What's the idea?"

"I want to talk with a girl."

"What about?" Selby asked.

"About . . . about . . . about why she lost her job."

"Want to tell me about it now?" Selby asked.

She placed her hand briefly over his where it rested on the steering wheel. "No, Doug, if it doesn't pan out, it's going to be too much of a disappointment. If it does, it may mean something."

"Okay," Selby said with a smile. "We devote our attention to driving the car. What's the name of the young woman we're going to see?"

"Carmen Ayers," she said. "I have her address. And please don't ask anything more about her until we get there."

"Think she'll be in?"

"Yes, I feel certain she will. I've fixed that up. Let's not talk about it, Doug."

He grinned, and said, "Okay."

Sylvia surveyed his profile with tender eyes. "That," she announced, "doesn't mean that the conversation is necessarily confined to silence."

Chapter Sixteen

CARMEN AYERS lived in an apartment house that presented an ornate entrance of stucco and grille work. Once inside the reception hallway, however, the architecture faded into drab corridors, a small, rattling automatic elevator, and the close smell which comes from poorly ventilated passageways that get no sunlight.

Selby, accustomed to living in a rural, sun-saturated community where fresh air and sunlight were as much a part of life as breath itself, frowned at the close, stale mustiness of the corridor.

Carmen Ayers lived on the third floor. Sylvia led the way to the door of the apartment, knocked gently. Almost immediately the door was opened by a girl whose slender yet shapely limbs and figure gave her the appearance of being slightly above average height, although when Sylvia stood beside her, the girls were of the same height, hardly higher than Selby's shoulder. "I'm Sylvia Martin, Miss Ayers. May we come in?"

The girl nodded, calmly stood to one side, and held the door open. She had the appearance of perfect poise. She was blonde, with finely chiseled features, steady blue eyes in which there seemed to lurk a smile, and a shapely mouth with rather full lips. Her voice was well modulated, the evenly spaced words being pronounced slowly, almost with a drawl, as she said, "Good evening, Miss Martin, do come in. Won't you please be seated?"

When they were seated, Carmen Ayers glanced across at Sylvia. There had been no introduction of Doug Selby, and the young women did not seem to expect any. She was, Selby concluded, a woman who had been educated in the school of live and let live.

If Sylvia wished to introduce her male companion, well and good. If she didn't, Carmen Ayers would not indicate by either word or gesture there had been an oversight.

Sylvia seemed somewhat embarrassed as she said, "I am going to be most horribly impertinent."

"Yes?" Miss Ayers asked in a calm voice.

"I believe you worked for the brokerage firm of Miltern & Miltern at one time?"

Carmen Ayers hesitated for a long moment before she said shortly, "Yes, I did."

"You left their employ about a month ago?"

"You seem to have been taking quite an interest in my affairs," Carmen Ayers said, and just a slight accent upon the possessive pronoun carried a note of rebuke.

Sylvia rushed on, "While you were there, you knew an Allison Brown. I believe you saw him in the office and . . . outside, did you not?"

Carmen Ayers looked steadily at Sylvia, picked up a carved wooden box containing cigarettes and offered one first to Sylvia then to Selby. She took one herself. Selby held a match. "Three on one match?" he asked.

"Certainly," Carmen Ayers said, "so far as I'm concerned. I have no time for superstitions."

Selby lit his cigarette. The blond young woman who seemed so much at ease blew out a cloud of smoke and raised a coral-tinted nail to pick a grain of tobacco from her lower lip.

"I think," she said to Sylvia Martin, "you've pried quite enough into my private affairs, Miss Martin. Of course, if there's any good reason . . ." She let her voice trail off into silence and gave a slight, almost imperceptible shrug of the shoulders.

Sylvia looked at Selby, then took a deep breath, and inched forward to the edge of her chair. "Look here,

Miss Ayers," she said, "I'm going to be frank with you. This is Douglas Selby, the district attorney of Madison County. I'm with one of the newspapers there."

For a moment there was a quick flicker of expression in the eyes of Carmen Ayers. Then her face became as a mask. She had perfect control over her speaking voice, and there was no faintest trace of surprise in it as she said, "Well?"

"I wonder if you've read in the papers about a John Burke being found dead—murdered."

"I don't think so," Carmen Ayers said.

"We have reason to believe," Sylvia said, "that the person we knew as John Burke and the person you knew as Allison Brown are one and the same."

"Murdered, did you say?" Carmen Ayers asked.

Sylvia nodded.

"And you're with a newspaper?"

"Yes."

Carmen Ayers shifted her eyes to Doug Selby. "Is this visit official?" she asked.

"I am calling on you for the purpose of getting information which I think may help us solve a crime," Selby said.

"I'm sorry, Mr. Selby," she observed in a tone of courteous finality, without showing the slightest sign of emotion. "I have no information which would be of the slightest assistance to you."

Sylvia said, "Oh, but you have, Miss Ayers! The identification of the body of the murdered man has become exceedingly important. During his lifetime, John Burke wore a small mustache and thick-lensed spectacles. When his body was found, there was no mustache and he was wearing no spectacles. Under the circumstances . . . well, people differ on the question of identification."

"Can't you put the spectacles back on," she asked, "and put on a false mustache . . ."

"Unfortunately," Selby said, "the body has been cremated. It was cremated before we had any intimation there might have been foul play. However, I have some photographs, and . . ."

"No, no, Doug," Sylvia interrupted. "Not that."

She turned to Carmen Ayers. "I'm going to talk frankly to you, Miss Ayers," she said. "I'm going to tell you how I happened to know about you and why I came here. Mr. Selby is my friend, my very close friend. A great deal depends upon his identifying that body. It may mean that his career is at stake. There's a situation which I can't explain. I mention it to show you how important it is.

"The sheriff and the district attorney were trying to identify the body as that of Burke by working on Burke's friends and acquaintances. I happened to know that Burke had gone under the name of Allison Brown down here and had been a customer of Miltern & Miltern. I started in trying to find out all I could about him at this end. One of the girls told me that there was an ironclad office rule against any of the girls going out with any of the men customers of the firm, that you had violated that rule by going out with Allison Brown, and Alfred Miltern had discovered it and discharged you."

"Yes?" Carmen Ayers asked, raising her eyebrows.

Selby started to say something, but Sylvia motioned him to silence. "My information," she went on, "was that you went with him quite a bit. I . . . I know you were swimming at Ensenada and . . ."

Carmen Ayers said, "I think you've said all you need to say, Miss Martin—probably too much. I have nothing to offer. I am sorry that you considered it necessary to fan a lot of gossip into flame by talking with girls who were at one time my office associates."

"Oh, *please* understand," Sylvia pleaded. "It's *so* important. It means so much. This body can't be identified. Some people say the photographs are those of Burke, and some say they aren't Burke. The district attorney has a job on his hands trying to prove a murder. He has to prove the identity of the body. He has to prove his case beyond all reasonable doubt. All the defense has to do is to raise a doubt. Doug Selby could put on a hundred witnesses who would testify that the body was that of Burke, and if the defense put on one reliable eyewitness who could testify it wasn't, the jury could either believe that one witness or else figure there was reasonable doubt and . . ."

"Why spill your troubles in *my* lap?" Carmen Ayers asked with a sudden flare of anger.

"Because," Sylvia Martin said, "you were on the beach at Ensenada swimming with him when—when Alfred Miltern happened to see you."

Carmen Ayers said bitterly, "And Alfred Miltern never even bothered to give me a chance to explain. He tried to pretend he didn't see me. The next day I was called on the carpet and given the sack. Don't think that Alfred Miltern himself had the nerve to do it. He had Mrs. Wait, who was in charge of office personnel, call me in and hand me a check for two weeks' salary in lieu of notice, then whisk me out of the office as though I had leprosy. Her face looked as though she'd been sucking on a very sour lemon."

"But look," Sylvia Martin pleaded, "I want you to understand what I'm after. The murderer who killed John Burke tricked the authorities into disposing of the body before it had been identified. It's something that was easy to do because the death seemed accidental and the man seemed to have been properly identified by a relative. It looked like a case of a hobo being hit by a fast train while he was walking along the trestle. Naturally, they didn't make a very close examination, but there was *one* thing the coroner happened to notice. The body had a little black mole in the shape of a pear on the back just below the left shoulder blade. Now we thought . . . that is . . . oh, *can't* you understand how much it means to us?"

"I see," Carmen Ayers said. "I walk on the witness stand, raise my right hand and say that I knew John Burke; that he had a pear-shaped mole on his back just below the left shoulder blade. The attorney for the defense comes up and sneers at me in front of the jury and asks me whether I knew the gentleman in question was married, how many times I went out with him, where I went with him, whether it's my practice to go out with married men—and smears me all over with a crimson brush. No, thank you. I've had enough of Allison Brown. I was on the up-and-up with him and thought he was with me. Try and make a jury believe *that*. Try and make Alfred Miltern believe that."

Sylvia's voice showed disappointment. "Oh, I'm so sorry," she said. "I thought . . . I hoped . . . Look here, Miss Ayers, that mole is the only means of identification we have."

Carmen Ayers regarded her quizzically over the tip of her half-consumed cigarette. "I see," she said. "So you hoped I'd prove a perfectly scarlet woman whose reputation could be kicked around the courtroom like a football. Is that it?"

Sylvia said, "I hoped you'd be interested enough to tell us the truth. We can prove John Burke and Allison Brown were one and the same person. . . . After all, this is murder. A man is arrested for that murder. If he's guilty, you don't want him to go free. We hoped you could at least—at least tell the truth."

Carmen Ayers flicked ash from the end of her cigarette. "Well," she said, "I'm sorry that my natural reluctance to be stripped of the last shred of my reputation stands in the way of Mr. Selby's career, but apparently it does. Allison Brown is a closed chapter in my life. I'm going with a young man now who is a square-shooter. I don't think he'd care to read the story of Allison Brown's courtship in the daily press. Too bad you had to take a long drive down here. I won't detain you any longer."

She ground out the tip of her cigarette, got to her feet and moved toward the door.

Sylvia, blinking back her tears, started for the hallway. Selby crossed to Carmen Ayers and held out his hand. "I'm sorry we bothered you," he said. "Naturally, I'm sorry you can't help us, but I see how it is. I see your point. I, for one, certainly don't want to drag you through a mess of publicity. Good night."

She took his hand, looked into his eyes, hesitated, glanced toward the door, and said, "Wait a minute. Let's come back and have a drink. I want to think a bit."

There was swift hope in Sylvia's eyes as she turned away from the door. Carmen Ayers said, "Sit down. Make yourselves comfortable. I've got some Scotch out in the kitchenette. It's good Scotch, but it's just Scotch. There's no charged water with it. You can have it with ice and water, or you can have it straight. Don't all speak at once."

"About half and half," Sylvia said, "if you don't mind."

"Straight," Selby observed with a grin. "Make it just about cover the bottom of the glass."

She whirled from the door of the kitchenette to stare at him. There was a trace of scorn in her eyes. "Too pure to be corrupted, Mr. Selby?" she asked.

Selby met her eyes. "Too cagey," he said, "to be placed in a position where my political opponents can check up on what happened here and describe it in the rival newspaper as a drinking orgy."

Her eyes softened into a smile. "Thanks for the tip," she said. "I guess I could use a little more prudence in *my* life. I suppose you'd really prefer it if we dealt you out."

"I would," Selby admitted with evident relief.

"All right, Miss Martin and I will do the drinking for the crowd. I'll do a little thinking while I'm mixing up the drinks."

A few moments later, she came back with two glasses, handed one to Sylvia, looked across at Selby, and said, "All right, you win."

Sylvia heaved a tremulous sigh of relief.

"Exactly what," asked Selby, "do I win?"

"You win all the way along the line," she said. "I knew Allison Brown quite well. He had a pear-shaped black mole on his back just below the left shoulder blade."

Selby could hardly conceal his excitement. "You're certain?" he asked. "You'd . . ."

"Of course, I'm certain."

Selby opened his brief case. "This isn't going to be easy, Miss Ayers," he said. "You'll have to remember that I'm showing you the picture of a dead man and . . ."

"Go ahead," she invited. "I've seen dead men."

"And I have every reason to believe that it's a photograph of your friend," he said.

"Pass it over," she invited calmly.

Selby handed her the three photographs. She looked them over carefully, one at a time, then nodded coolly and said, "That's Allison. The mustache has been shaved, and, of course, you have to make some allowances for changes in the angle of the jaw due to death. But that's Allison Brown."

"You're certain?" Selby asked.

"Quite certain, and if that man had a pear-shaped black mole below the left shoulder blade, I'm *absolutely* certain."

Selby couldn't keep the excitement from his voice. "This," he said, "is going to change the entire case, Miss Ayers. It . . . it means a lot to me."

"It means a lot to me, too," she said.

Selby put the photographs back in his brief case, stood looking down at her, and then said, slowly and thoughtfully, "By George, it does."

"Thank you," she said.

Selby frowned at the carpet for several seconds in silent concentration. "Look here," he said, "I'm going to try to leave you out of this. I think I can do it."

"Thanks again."

Selby said, "His widow is being held as a material witness. She had a child by him. She certainly knows about that pear-shaped mole. Of course, I could have put her on the stand and asked her the question direct; but if she'd denied that he had any such mole, I'd have been in an awful fix. I couldn't have impeached her because she was my own witness. That is, not very well and without laying myself wide open to a lot of legal mud-slinging. And I wouldn't have had anyone who could impeach her testimony. Now, if I can use you, I can tell her frankly that I have a witness I'm holding in abeyance and that if she lies on that essential point, she'll find herself indicted for perjury. I think it will be sufficient to identify the body."

"Then I won't have to go on the stand?"

"Not in that event," Selby said.

She turned to Sylvia. "But you're representing a newspaper, Miss Martin?"

"A newspaper, not a scandal sheet. I can't begin to tell you how much you've done for us—particularly for Mr. Selby. You can bank on me. I'll not even breathe a word of it unless you're called as a witness, and you can gamble that if Doug Selby tells you he won't call you unless he has to, he'll move heaven and earth to keep from putting you on the stand."

Carmen Ayers stared contemplatively at the glass which she held in her hand for a second or two, and then said slowly, "I fell pretty hard for Allison Brown. Naturally, I had no intimation that he was John Burke, and didn't know he was married. There was an office rule that we could never go out with a male customer. Allison Brown caught me one Saturday noon when I was feeling pretty low. I don't know whether it was deliberate or whether he just happened to eat in the same restaurant that I did that Saturday. I suppose he'd followed me in there. Anyway, we became acquainted. He was witty and entertaining, and said he had a Saturday afternoon to kill and suggested we drive down to the beach. It was a beastly hot day. East wind blowing in from the desert. My apartment would have been like a bake oven. I had no place to go and nothing to do. I'd always resented that office rule. I felt that I gave the firm value received in my work. I saw no reason why they should feel they had a right to control my private life.

"Anyway, we went. I don't remember whether it was then or later on that I noticed his car was registered in the name of John Burke at Las Alidas. I remember asking him about it. He said Burke was his brother-in-law, but asked me not to say anything about it at the office. Naturally, I didn't.

"Allison was a fast worker—that is, I mean he rushed things quite a bit. The first thing I knew I was going out with him quite frequently, shows, dinners, and dancing. He seemed on the up and up, and finally told me that he'd been married; that his wife had an interlocutory decree of divorce which would be final in about three months; that he wanted to marry me as soon as the final decree was granted. I didn't say yes right away because I wasn't certain that I cared for him quite that much. I told him I'd think it over. Apparently he had enough money to support me. He told me that we'd go to Europe on a honeymoon and that he'd go into business when we returned. He said his divorce had broken him all up and that he'd given up his business and was simply playing around with a few investments; that he thought he'd never have faith in women again but that I'd changed all that. . . . Oh, why is it that a woman who tries to be square and on the up-and-up meets men like that, while some gold digger who has her eye only on alimony never seems to have any trouble meeting and marrying a square-shooter?"

"Did you ever ask him about his business, his investments, or his connections?" Selby asked.

"No," she said, "that is, I asked a few questions when I first knew him. He told me that some day he'd tell me the whole story, but that it was too sore a subject to be opened up right then. He said his brother-in-law, John Burke, was a swell egg; that he was in Mexico somewhere and had left his car."

"Did you gather John Burke was his sister's husband or his wife's brother?" Selby asked.

"His wife's brother. He said John Burke was swell and knew what a rotten disposition his sister had; that the whole family sympathized with him in the divorce."

"When did the affair break up?" Sylvia Martin asked.

"When I got fired," Carmen Ayers said bitterly.

"Alfred Miltern caught us at Ensenada. I was bounced the next day. That was the last time I ever saw Allison Brown. I realized then that all he wanted with me was to get tips on what was going on at the office, and just as a diversion—and then one of those things happened that make you believe in Santa Claus. I met a fine young man, a man who hasn't any money to speak of, but he has a job, he has ambition, and he has character. I . . . he hasn't asked me yet, but I think he's going to. And there won't be any honeymoons to Europe. I'll have to keep on working—that's why he hasn't come right out and asked me to marry him. He's dropped one or two hints. He doesn't want his wife to work . . . but it isn't what you want in this world, it's what you get. He's been hoping he'd get a raise and—well, the raise just hasn't materialized. I think he's going to have a frank talk with me pretty soon. He's frightfully proud. Well, when he talks with me he'll find out that I'm perfectly willing to keep on working; that it's the only sensible thing to do."

"You didn't have any difficulty getting another job?" Sylvia Martin asked.

"Within three days," Carmen Ayers smiled. "I long ago made up my mind that if I was going to work for my living I'd be competent. There are lots of girls who are about fifty per cent efficient, and most of them are out of work. I've never been out of work over a month in my life, unless I wanted to be. . . . Now then, you see my position. I have a mother who's sick. I'm supporting her. She lives up north. She reads the papers, devours them, in fact. I have this boy friend who's proud and sensitive. You put me on the witness stand in Madison City and that trip to Ensenada and the engagement and all of that is going to sound like the devil. The reporters will brand me as 'the week-end woman,' or 'the bathing-suit girl,' and photographers will be chasing me with cameras, begging me to pose and show a little leg. . . . Well, you know how it is."

Selby got to his feet. "Miss Ayers," he said, "you're a square-shooter and a straight-shooter. I'll be just as square and just as straight with you. I'm going to do everything in my power to keep your name out of this case, and I think I can."

She wrapped firm, capable fingers around his hand. "Thanks," she said. "You register."

Sylvia said, "Miss Ayers, I can't begin to tell you how grand I think you are, and you can count on Douglas Selby."

"I know that already," she said, and, as she let them out into the hallway, added, "All you need to do is telephone me when you want me. Don't do it unless you have to; but if you telephone me I'll be there."

Out in the corridor when the door had closed, Sylvia said to Doug Selby, "Isn't she grand, Doug. . . . I find myself getting jealous. She fell for you. I'd never have got to first base by myself."

Selby said, "I think she knows I'm going to give her a square deal."

"How are you going to do it, Doug?" Sylvia asked.

Selby's lips tightened. "I'm going to Inez Stapleton."

Chapter Seventeen

IT WASN'T until Monday afternoon after the arraignment that Doug Selby had his opportunity to talk with Inez Stapleton. He found her in her office. "Hello,

Doug," she said, her eyes flashing into quick animation. "Did you come in to look me over?"

He nodded. "Always pay my respects to the new lawyers," he said with a smile.

She showed him her offices; the law library with its array of digests and legal encyclopedias, the volumes of reports, annotated codes, and volumes of recent citations of earlier decisions.

"Fine to have plenty of money," Selby said with a grin. "I remember my office when *I* opened up. I had the California codes, a book on forms, and a typewriter, none of them new."

She laughed nervously. "In some ways, it *does* seem like taking an unfair advantage of my position, Doug. But you see, you've had so much more experience that I have to even things up in some way. Come on in and sit down, Doug."

He sat down, facing her across the handsome mahogany desk with its hand-tooled leather blotting pad, its bronze book ends.

"Present from Dad," she said, noticing his eyes.

"Certainly is class," Selby agreed easily. "I see you pleaded Lacey not guilty."

"What did you expect me to do? Plead him guilty?" she asked, raising her eyebrows.

"I didn't know," Selby said.

She composed herself with an effort. Some of the animation faded from her eyes. "We're going to talk business?" she asked.

"Yes," Selby said.

She looked out of the window for several seconds, then said after a moment, "I should have known this was a business call. Go ahead, Doug."

Selby said, "I don't know just why you took up law. I thought at the time it was because you wanted something to do. I'm not certain now but what you wanted to kill time, and didn't know what else to do."

"Can't you please leave me out of it?" she asked.

Selby said, "No, Inez, I can't. I think you're looking at it as a game. You've mentioned once or twice that this was going to be like our old tennis matches. It isn't. We aren't playing with a ball. We're playing with justice. We're playing with human lives."

"All right," she flared. "I'm playing the game according to the rules. I don't care *what* we're playing with. All I want is that you play according to the rules, and may the best man win."

"Exactly what I'm trying to get at," Selby said patiently. "It isn't the best man who wins. It's the cause of justice, of truth."

"Bosh!" she stormed. "Do you believe that the law is perfect? At times, don't you think the law is just as rotten with politics, with personalities, with trickery, with . . ."

"I'm talking," he said, "about abstract legal principles."

"Then I'm afraid you'll have to put me down as a realist."

"Very well, I'll put you down as a realist," Selby told her. "Now then, I came here to give you fair warning. You're going to play according to rules."

"What do you mean by that, Doug?"

"Simply this. If you cut corners so far as ethics are concerned, you're going to be sorry—mighty sorry. If your clients think *they* can cut corners, they have another guess coming. You think it's going to be smart to stand up in court and outwit me. That's all very well. But when and if you do, you aren't outwitting me, you're outwitting justice. I don't propose to have you do it. You think that you can mix this case all up by casting doubt on the identity of the dead man. I want you to know that I can now prove absolutely and beyond a doubt that the dead man was John Burke. Please bear this in mind. Mrs. Burke has already stated that the body was that of her husband. We have another means of identification. One of my first witnesses is going to be Mrs. Burke. I'm going to ask her if that was the body of her husband. If she says it was not, I'm going to ask her detailed questions. If she tells the truth, she will be forced to admit that it was her husband's body. If she lies, it'll be perjury."

Inez said gravely, "Thanks for the warning, Doug."

"Are you," Selby asked, "going to stipulate that the body was that of John Burke?"

"No. . . . And, Doug, *please* don't go to trial. If you do . . ."

"Are you going to let Mrs. Burke deny that it was John Burke's body?" he interrupted.

"I'm not going to have her state or deny anything. She is being held as a material witness. You probably have the right to do that. It seems unjust to me. You go ahead and call Mrs. Burke if you want to, but . . . but, Doug, if you do, I warn you . . . No, Doug, I've said enough. You and I understand each other. We're adversaries."

Selby picked up his hat. "I understand why you want an immediate trial," he said. "After a man has once been acquitted, he can't be tried again for the same offense no matter what additional evidence is uncovered. You think we haven't got enough on Lacey to convict him, that the grand jury returned a premature indictment. You think you can get him acquitted and after that, when I discover additional evidence, you can laugh at me."

Inez ignored his statement. She said, "If you want to release Mrs. Burke and her daughter, we'll agree to a reasonable continuance, otherwise we're going to insist upon an immediate trial." Selby started for the door. "Go ahead and insist," he said, "but remember, I've warned you."

"And remember *I've* warned *you,* and ... Doug ... "

"Yes?" he asked.

She was blinking her eyes rapidly. "Why not come in and see *me* sometime, Doug—just to see me, not to give me warnings or make threats?"

His eyes failed to soften. "I will," he said, "after this case is over," and stepped out into the corridor, letting the door close behind him.

Two days before the trial, *The Blade* announced that it had retained the services of Sam Roper to act as commentator on the murder trial. The paper called to the attention of its readers that when it said *the* murder trial, it meant, of course, the trial of People versus James Lacey. There was no other murder trial in the offing, nor was there likely to be any. The murderers of Oliver Benell had quite apparently proven themselves too smart for a sheriff who, no matter how good a horseman or ranch manager he might be, was possessed of limited experience when it came to dealing with professional criminals of the type that had pulled off the robbery of the First National Bank and killed its president.

And so events swept rapidly onward to culminate in the day when Doug Selby walked into court, and sat separated from Inez Stapleton by only a few feet and heard her answer, "Ready for the defendant," in response to his statement that the people were ready in the case wherein the People of the State of California were plaintiff and James Lacey was defendant.

Getting the jury was almost a matter of routine. Inez Stapleton's attitude was calm, aloof, and impersonal. She asked but few questions. At first she had evidently been somewhat embarrassed, but as her stage-fright had worn off, her voice came in low, well-modulated tones which, without seeming loud, were audible in the far corners of the courtroom. It became apparent almost from the outset that she had a natural speaking voice and courtroom manner.

Selby adopted the position of being a just but resolute prosecutor, asking only for the law to take its course. The prospective jurors tried hard to qualify themselves. The result was that a jury was selected by noon, and the court recessed until two o'clock.

Selby had lunch with Sylvia Martin.

"Watch her, Doug," Sylvia warned. "I don't know much about law, but I know something about women. She's loaded with something—some form of legal dynamite."

"She can't be," Selby said confidently. "I'm sure of my ground. While I haven't an absolutely mathematical case, I have a case which will go to the jury. The decision rests in the hands of the jury itself."

"No, no, Doug," she said, leaning across the luncheon table. "You have to win. You simply have to. You can't afford to have that jury bring in a verdict of acquittal."

Selby's lips tightened. "You forget, Sylvia," he said, "that this isn't a battle between Inez and me. This is the trial of a murder case. The grand jury have indicted this man. I'm not certain that I would have proceeded against him at that stage of the game. However, it's up to me to prosecute. I'll prosecute to the best of my ability. If the jury figures the evidence proves him guilty beyond all reasonable doubt, I want the jury to convict him. If the jury figures that the evidence does not warrant a conviction, I want them to turn him loose."

Sylvia Martin didn't argue with him, but her silence was eloquent of contradiction.

Promptly at two o'clock Selby made his opening statement to the jury, and called Harry Perkins as his first witness.

In a courtroom which was tense with interest, Perkins gave his testimony, the finding of the body, the identification by the supposed brother in Phoenix, the telephone conversation, the arrival of the money, the inquest and the cremation. He testified further that Southern Pacific investigators had appeared and photographed the body. Selby introduced photographs to be marked for identification. Inez said she had no cross-examination.

One of the Southern Pacific investigators testified to the receipt of a report that a man had been struck by a Southern Pacific train. Following routine, he had arrived on the scene and investigated. As a part of his investigation, he had taken photographs of the body. He examined the photographs which had been identified by the coroner, and pronounced them to be prints of his negatives. Selby had them introduced as exhibits of the people.

Once more there was no cross-examination.

Selby called Sheriff Brandon and showed that fingerprints of the dead man had been taken, and introduced those fingerprints in evidence.

This caused a sharp hissing of whispered conjecture about the courtroom, whispering which was promptly silenced by the bailiff's gavel.

Then Selby announced dramatically, "I call as my next witness, Mrs. John Burke."

She came forward proudly and defiantly. When she put out her hand to be sworn, the court attendant shifted uneasily under her smoldering eyes. He even forgot to ask her to remove her red gloves.

"Mrs. Burke," Selby said, "I am calling you as a witness on behalf of the prosecution. I understand fully where your sympathies lie. However, at present you are not charged with any crime. You are held as a material witness. I am going to ask you questions, and I warn you that I shall expect truthful answers. I am going to show you the photographs of the body which have previously been introduced in evidence and ask you if those photographs show the body of your husband, and if you did not so identify those photographs when you first saw them at the residence of James Lacey in Tucson."

Inez was on her feet. "Just a moment, Your Honor," she said. "I object to this witness giving any testimony whatever in this case."

The judge raised his eyebrows. "On what ground?" he inquired.

"On the ground that under section 1322 of our penal code neither husband nor wife is a competent witness for or against the other in a criminal action or proceeding to which one or both are parties, except with the consent of both."

"But surely," the judge said, "you don't contend that Mrs. Burke is the wife of Mr. Lacey, the defendant in this action? While there has been no evidence directly on that point, I assume that there is evidence which can and will be introduced showing that she was duly married to John Burke. That, I believe, is a part of the People's case, is it not, Mr. Selby?"

Selby nodded.

Inez said calmly, "I think Your Honor fails to understand my point. This witness was at one time married to the defendant. A divorce was granted. The fact is, however, that while a divorce was granted, there had been no service on the defendant, James Lacey. Subsequently, at the instance of the plaintiff herself and upon due proof that there had been no service of process, the divorce action was set aside. That was done the day the defendant was arrested in Albuquerque. Therefore, this witness is the wife of the defendant, James Lacey, and as such wife she is incompetent to testify for or against the defendant in this case without the defendant's consent."

Selby was on his feet, struggling to keep his composure, conscious of the eyes of the spectators and of the restless motion of bodies behind him in the packed courtroom. "Your Honor," he said, "this comes as a distinct surprise. Counsel has not seen fit to communicate this to me, nor has the witness. May I ask, inasmuch as the objection is made by counsel for the defendant, that she proceed to substantiate the point?"

And Selby sat down with a frantic glance at the clock, hoping that he could stall matters along until the five o'clock adjournment.

Inez was prepared. Calmly competent, she introduced certified copies of records, duly attested. The judge received them in evidence, studied them in frowning concentration, and passed them to Selby without comment. When Selby had read them, the judge said, "Apparently this proof is conclusive. In the absence of some counter showing on the part of the prosecution, the court will be forced to rule that inasmuch as this witness is the wife of the defendant, she is incompetent to testify in this case except with the consent of the defendant, and, as I understand, that consent has not been forthcoming."

"No, Your Honor," Inez Stapleton said, "it has not. It is the desire of the defendant in this action to keep the woman he loves free of the notoriety incident to her appearance in such a case."

Selby was on his feet. "Your Honor," he shouted, "I object. Counsel can confine herself to the statement that permission has not been granted. This is no time to seek to influence the jury by any statements as to the purported motives of the defendant. If the motives of the defendant are going to be considered, we are prepared to show that, far from desiring to keep the woman he loves from being dragged into this case, he is trying to hide behind her skirts. It is an attempt on his part to . . ."

The judge interrupted Selby. "That will do, Mr. District Attorney," he said. "The court is inclined to agree with you that the motives of the defendant are not to be taken into consideration by the jury. The jury, therefore, will disregard any statement made by counsel for the defense as to motives of the defendant and disregard any statement of the district attorney as to *his* interpretation of the defendant's motives. You will leave the witness stand, Mrs. Burke . . . er, Mrs. Lacey, and you, Mr. District Attorney, will call your next witness."

Selby, sparring for time, called two of the Las Alidas witnesses who identified the photographs of the dead body, stating it was that of John Burke. These witnesses, as was to have been expected, sensing that a battle was in the offing on the question of identity, were somewhat vague and less positive in their statements made under oath than they had been in their statements made to Selby. And under Inez Stapleton's adroit cross-examination they admitted that it was merely their opinion, and finally, that it was their "best guess."

Selby realized then that there was no course open save that he should call Carmen Ayers. To do that it was necessary that he first lay a proper foundation showing that the Allison Brown who had traded with Miltern & Miltern was one and the same person as John Burke.

Reluctantly he embarked on that means of identification by calling Mark Crandall to the stand.

Crandall came forward and was sworn. He testified that he had know John Burke in his lifetime, that he had last seen John Burke in Los Angeles in the brokers' office of Miltern & Miltern, that at that time he was advised the man's name was Allison Brown. There was no chance he had been mistaken in his identification. He had known Burke for many years, and he had recognized both Burke and his voice. He took the pictures which Selby showed him and unhesitatingly identified them as photographs of the body of John Burke.

His calmly capable, quiet air carried conviction with the spectators. Selby could sense that men everywhere were accepting Crandall's words at face value, and wished he had been shrewd enough to put Crandall on the stand first, so that Crandall's positive identification would have stiffened the morale of the other witnesses.

And Inez also realized that this man's positive identification was having weight with the jury. Calmly she started making notes, preparing for a vigorous cross-examination.

Things were going so smoothly that Selby was surprised to hear the even voice of the judge saying, "It appears to be time for the evening adjournment. The court is going to place the jurors in the custody of the sheriff inasmuch as this is a murder case and in the opinion of the court the interests of justice will be served by holding the jurors together." Whereupon the court swore the deputy sheriff, admonished the jurors, and adjourned court until ten o'clock the next morning.

Selby left the courtroom to confer behind closed doors with Sheriff Brandon. "I could kick myself all over the block," he announced, "for not having checked back on that divorce action. I found out that the divorce had been filed and granted and paid no attention to what had been happening afterward.

That's why they went to Albuquerque. The divorce had been granted there, and Inez Stapleton planned that move right from the first. I felt like a schoolboy standing up there with my whole case tumbling down about my ears."

Sheriff Brandon said, "Stay with it, son. You're doing fine. . . . But, gosh, did you ever see anything like the way Inez takes hold? You'd think she was a veteran courtroom lawyer."

Selby nodded. He crammed tobacco into his brier pipe and started pacing the floor. There was a knock at the door. Brandon opened it.

Sylvia, accompanied by a man in overalls, leather jacket and grease-stained slouch hat, stood in the doorway. Her eyes were wide with excitement. "Sheriff," she said, "this is Brantley Doane. He knows something about this case. I want him to tell you in his own words."

The man extended a diffident hand, which remained limp under the clasp of the Sheriff's hard, brown fingers.

"And Douglas Selby, our district attorney," Sylvia Martin said.

Doane inclined his head awkwardly, made no effort to shake hands.

"Sit down," Sylvia Martin said, kicking the door shut. "Now, Mr. Doane, I want you to tell your story to the sheriff and the district attorney."

Doane avoided their eyes, sat down in a straight-back chair, inarticulate and ill at ease.

"Go ahead," Sylvia urged.

"I don't know nothing," Doane said.

Sylvia glanced meaningly at Doug Selby. "He does too, Doug. He's a gypsy truck driver. He actually saw the murder committed."

"No, I didn't," Doane interposed, quickly on the defensive.

Sylvia went on rapidly, "He told something of his story to a waitress in a roadside café that's patronized by truck drivers. I've been quite friendly with her and she told me about it. He won't talk with me. I had a lot of trouble getting him to come here."

Doane raised his eyes to encounter the steady inquiry in the sheriff's eyes, then hastily averted his gaze.

Selby dragged his chair over closer to Doane. "Have a cigarette, Doane," he said, handing him a package of cigarettes.

Doane started to reach for a cigarette, then said, "It's the last one you got."

"It's all right," Selby said. "Go on and take it. I only smoke them during recesses when I'm in court. I use a pipe when I have the time to enjoy my tobacco."

Doane took the last remaining cigarette, crumpled the package, and dropped it in the wastebasket. Selby struck a match and lit the cigarette. "Gypsy truck driving must be pretty much of a job," he said sympathetically.

"I'll say it is," Doane agreed.

"You're out on the road quite a bit of the time, aren't you?"

Doane took a deep drag at the cigarette and raised his eyes. "I'll say I am. The regular truck drivers have it bad enough, but at least they get their sleep. Us fellas who are bucking the big companies have to take things as they come. The only way to make a living is to keep pushing the miles under the old crate. It's just plain hell."

"Get through this country frequently?" Selby asked.

"Yeah. I've been hauling oranges back and forth from Imperial Valley."

"Make the trips mostly at night?"

"Uh-huh. You gotta load during the daytime, then you take your bill of lading and hit the highway in to Los Angeles, unload, get a receipt, drive back all night, and pick up another load the next morning."

"On the night of the murder," Selby went on, "you were headed back toward the Imperial Valley?"

"Naw. I was running in to Los Angeles with a load."

"Pretty cold ride, wasn't it?"

"I'll say it was. I was so damn sleepy I couldn't keep my eyes open."

"What do you do," Selby asked, "pull off to the side of the road and go to sleep?"

"Sometimes. Sometimes I pick up a hitch-hiker and find out if they know how to drive. If they do, I let 'em take the wheel long enough to find out if they're good drivers. If they are, I doze off to sleep. . . . Now, listen, I know I ain't supposed to do that. A man driving truck is supposed to have a special license. . . . But you can't blame a guy for cutting corners when he has a living to make."

Selby's nod was sympathetic. After a moment, he said, "So you picked up this hitch-hiker?"

"No, I didn't," Doane said.

"Why not?" Selby asked.

"I didn't get the chance."

"Tell me about it."

"Well," Doane said, "I don't want you boys to hold this against me. There ain't nothing I could say which would help—not much anyway. But I don't want to put my neck in a noose."

"Go ahead," Selby told him. "You're among friends."

Doane became more expansive. "Well, it was this way. I hadn't had much sleep to speak of for forty-eight hours. I had this load to get in to Los Angeles, and then I wanted to get back for another load. It was colder than the milltails of hell. I don't know just what time it was. I guess I was kinda groggy. I'd stop and get black coffee, then drive on for a ways, then stop for more coffee. Well, a car went whizzing by me—I didn't think nothin' of that, but the car pulled up a couple of hundred yards ahead of me and stopped. A hobo got out of the car—leastwise he had a roll of blankets—and stood there talking with the man that was driving the car. As I passed the two guys shook hands. This hobo looked to be sort of dependable, and I slowed down, thinking he'd flag me, but he didn't. So I went on. A minute or two later, the car started up. Us truck drivers have side mirrors to show the road behind, and I saw the lights switch back into the center of the road, and then the car passed me going some place in a hurry. I took a look to see if the hobo was in the car with the driver, but he wasn't, just one man at the wheel.

"Well, I figured the hobo had got a ride part way but the bird in the car had dumped him off, so I stopped my truck a couple of hundred yards on and waited for the hobo to come along. And then I saw this car ahead of me slam on the brakes and swing into a turn. And here it came, headed back, going like the devil. I seen it had an Arizona license, and was a big Cadillac. Well, the car passed me going fast back toward Las Alidas. Then, all of a sudden, it swerved off to one side and slammed on the brakes, and I heard something bang just after the lights all went out. I kept waiting and says to myself, 'I wonder if that guy hit that hobo, or whether he's picking him up again'—and I guess I dropped off for a minute, I don't know, but it seems like I did because all of a sudden I saw the lights on this car come on again and heard it drive away. Well, there was a wide place in the road and I turned around. I knew I had to have someone to spell me for a mile of two anyway. So I went back and I couldn't find hide nor hair of this hobo. I was good and mad then, and cussed myself for turning around. So I turned around all over again and started back toward Los Angeles. But I couldn't see no hobo. About ten miles farther on I picked up a hitch-hiker and he spelled me for a ways and I went on in."

"This hobo had vanished?" Selby asked.

"Yeah. But what made it look funny was the fact that I seen the marks of this guy's tires where he'd slammed on the brakes when I was coming back the second time. I stopped the car and seen a spot on the pavement that looked like blood, but the funny thing is that that spot was before the guy had put on his brakes instead of afterwards. . . . Well, I guess I should have reported it, but you know how it is. A man reports those things and the police tell him he has to testify at an inquest and make him be there at a certain time without no regard for his business and he loses maybe a couple of loads and doesn't get a dime out of it. I figured after all the guy with the car would report it—probably had loaded him in and taken him to a hospital. So today when I was coming through I stopped off at my favorite restaurant and asked the waitress had there been a hobo killed on the road that night, and how did it happen. She told me there wasn't any road accident, but a hobo had been hit by a railroad train. Well, I never thought, and I said, 'The hell he was hit by a railroad train. Some guy ran over him, accidental, and planted the body on the railroad track so it would look like a train had done it.'

"I didn't say no more about it, and she didn't. I got in my truck and started for Los Angeles, and then the next thing I knew, just as I was getting into the city, this girl came along in a car. She asked me questions, took me in to dump the load, and then made me ride back here with her—I ain't wanting to mess into things, and if I'm gonna lose time from my work, somebody's got to pay me."

Selby strove to keep excitement from his voice. "That's right," he said. "I'm going to have to subpoena you as a witness, but I'll see that you get paid for your time."

"When do I have to be a witness?" the man asked.

"Tomorrow morning at ten o'clock," Selby said. "I'll have to serve a subpoena on you to make it regular so you can get your money."

"And you ain't going to bear down on me about letting someone drive my truck that ain't regularly licensed?"

Selby said, "That's out of my department. I'm not even going to ask you about it. After all, this man didn't drive your car, and I'll just ask you about what you saw, and that's all you need to say."

"Well, thanks a lot," Doane said.

Brandon pulled a blank subpoena from a desk drawer and started scribbling. "Had any sleep lately?" Selby asked.

"Oh, some. I never get enough," Doane complained.

"What's the license number of your truck?" the sheriff asked.

"I have it here," Sylvia said, passing across a slip of paper.

Selby took five dollars from his pocket. "All right, Doane. You go down to the Madison City Rooming House, get yourself a room, and go to sleep. Don't talk with anyone. Don't tell what you've seen or that you're to be a witness. Just go to sleep."

"And I'll get paid for the trip I miss?" Doane asked.

"Yes," Selby said. "We'll fix that up all right."

Doane's face showed relief.

Sheriff Brandon handed him the subpoena. "Now,

listen," he said, "you're regularly subpoenaed in this case. You have got to be there. If you are, things will be all right. But if you ain't there, it's going to make lots of trouble. You understand that?"

"Sure," the man said. "I know the law all right. I've got to be there. That's all there is to it."

Selby said, "You didn't get the license number of that automobile?"

"Naw. I wished I had afterwards, but you know how those things are. I just noticed it was an Arizona license plate. I told that from the color. You know how it is when you're on the road. You get to know all the different licenses and you sort of recognize 'em unconsciously."

"And it was a Cadillac?"

"Yeah. It was a big Cadillac. I know that. Some sort of a dark color. A Cad sedan. . . . Well, I'll be there tomorrow morning at ten o'clock all right—and you won't make no trouble about my license?"

Selby shook his head, escorted Doane to the door. "And remember not to talk," he cautioned.

"I've talked too damned much already," Doane mumbled, shuffling out into the corridor.

Selby kicked the door shut, came back and hugged Sylvia, triumphantly patted her on the back. "Sylvia," he said, "we're going to have to put you on the payroll."

"Best little deputy I ever had," Brandon observed, his voice choking with emotion. He fished out a cigarette paper and spilled tobacco into it with a hand that shook.

Sylvia said, "Oh, Doug, I hope it works. It will, won't it?"

"I'll say it will," Brandon exclaimed triumphantly. "It gives us everything we want. You can see what happened. Lacey knew that Burke was short in his accounts. He arranged with Mrs. Burke to cover the shortage, but he didn't let Burke know he was doing it. Burke was going to skip out. Lacey brought up this hobo outfit for Burke to use as a disguise. He was going to drive Burke out of town a few miles and drop him on the road. He did it. The two men shook hands and then Lacey went on ahead to find a place to turn the car around. Maybe he didn't intend to kill Burke right at the time, but when he came back, he saw a chance to get Burke out of the picture and make it look as though the hobo had been run over by a railroad train. . . . Probably he intended to do it all along. He switched off the lights, crashed into Burke, loaded him into the automobile, and beat it. He took everything out of Burke's pockets, planted this indentification card, and dumped the body."

Selby stood with his arm around Sylvia Martin's waist, staring thoughtfully at the carpet. "Hang it, Rex," he said, "I wish you hadn't reconstructed the crime just that way."

"Why, son?"

"It doesn't sound like Lacey," Selby said thoughtfully. "Lacey's hot-tempered, impulsive, and would probably shoot a man who crossed him, but I can't figure him as planning a deliberate crime like this in quite this way."

Sylvia swung free of his circling arm to face him with blazing eyes. "Doug Selby, you make me tired. How do *you* know what Jim Lacey would have done? Everything he's done so far shows a clever schemer, a subtle, selfish man."

Brandon said, "Snap out of it, Doug. You can't tell what a man would do for love. Lacey was still crazy about Mrs. Burke. He wouldn't have had much chance with her as long as John Burke was alive, and he knew it. But he figured he could fix things so it would look as though Burke got hit by a railroad train right after he started walking the ties, or maybe jumped in front of the train to commit suicide. .. . . Shucks, Doug, that's what Burke's note showed he intended to do."

"That's right, Rex. Mrs. Burke didn't release that note because it showed Burke was an embezzler and she didn't want the child to have the stigma of a father who was an embezzler," Sylvia said.

"I suppose so," Selby said thoughtfully. "One thing's certain; a jury will believe that story. The only reason it seems dubious to me is that it doesn't square with the impression I formed of Lacey's character when I was talking with him."

"Doug Selby," Sylvia Martin said, "you're going into that courtroom tomorrow and get a first-degree-murder conviction. Don't you . . . don't you let . . . Inez Stapleton . . ."

Indignant tears filled her eyes. A catch in her throat shut off her voice.

Selby stood, hands pushed deep into his pockets, staring moodily down into the sheriff's wastebasket. "Yes," he said, thoughtfully, "I suppose you're right— you have to be right."

"Oh, Doug," Sylvia pleaded, "can't you understand that you're a prosecutor? You can't be so chicken-hearted. You've simply got to get a conviction. Jim Lacey is so guilty that . . ." She broke off as a knock sounded on the door. Brandon said, "Take it easy now, son." And then, reassuringly to Sylvia, "It's all right, Sylvia. Doug just wants to be sure, that's all."

"Sure!" she blazed. "My heavens, what more does he want?"

Brandon crossed over and opened the door. Mark Crandall stood on the threshold.

"Why, hello, Mark," Brandon said. "Come on in. Anything we can do for you?"

Selby smiled as he shook hands with Crandall, and said, "I presume Crandall wants to tell us that he has a business appointment for eleven o'clock tomorrow morning and we'll have to agree that he can be excused as soon as he gives his testimony."

Crandall smiled somewhat sheepishly and said, "Well, not exactly, Selby. I've stumbled on to something I think you two should know about." He glanced apprehensively at Sylvia Martin, took a package of cigarettes from his pocket, selected one, and tossed the package over to the sheriff. "That one of yours is about done, Sheriff," he said "Try one of mine."

"No, thanks," Brandon grinned. "I prefer to roll my own—don't want to get accustomed to these tailor-made cigarettes—not on my salary. What's on your mind, Mark? . . . Sylvia Martin's all right. She's one of the family. You can say anything you want to in front of her."

"What was it you stumbled on to, Crandall?" Selby asked, cramming tobacco into his pipe.

"It's the defense Inez Stapleton is going to make in case she can't get the judge to instruct the jury to acquit when your evidence is all in."

"Go ahead," Brandon said. "Let's hear it."

Crandall hesitated. "I got it in strictest confidence. I shouldn't tell you, and yet . . ."

"Never mind that," Brandon interrupted. "They've taken every advantage of us. If you know anything about this case, it's your duty to tell us."

"Well," Crandall said, "the story, as I get it, goes like this. John Burke was short somewhere around ten thousand dollars at the lumber company. He didn't know the exact amount. He told his wife about it and said he was going to skip out. She swore that he was going to do nothing of the sort. She said she could get him ten thousand dollars in cash, if she had to, in order to protect the baby's good name, but that she'd never live with him after that. When Burke was out, she telephoned Lacey at Tucson and explained the circumstances to him. She said she was through with Burke, that she only wanted the shortage covered because she didn't want her child to be taunted about having a father who was in state's prison.

"Ten grand was nothing at all to Lacey. He told her he'd get the money and be right up. She told him he'd better take a roll of blankets and park the car a ways down the street and come to the door as a hobo. Then, if her husband was home, Lacey could pretend he was a hobo, asking for something to eat, and slip Mrs. Burke the money when she handed him a plate of food.

"In the meantime, Burke tried to do some more plunging and lost. He left a note to his wife telling her that he was going to end it all, that he'd been unworthy of her, and a lot of that stuff. Mrs. Burke found the note when she came home, but she didn't say anything about it because she figured he didn't have the nerve to kill himself, but was going to duck out for a while until the thing blew over. Lacey came up as a hobo. Burke had gone, leaving the suicide note behind. Mrs. Burke thought he wouldn't be back. So Lacey went into a bedroom and shed his hobo clothes. He had a business suit under the rags. Then they went to call on Benell. Lacey had a letter to Benell from his banker. They swore him to secrecy. They didn't go to Lawler because they were afraid Lawler might try to profit by claiming the shortage was larger than it was.

"Mrs. Burke had Burke's keys and knew the combination of the safe. They went to the lumber company and put the money in the safe. Lacey had left his hobo clothes in the house and also the roll of blankets. Burke unexpectedly came back for something, shortly after they'd left. He figured the hobo outfit would be a good disguise for his getaway. He shaved his mustache, put on the clothes, picked up the roll of blankets and started out. When Lacey and Mrs. Burke got back to the house and found the outfit gone, they realized, of course, what had happened.

"Burke had left this suicide note, probably as a bluff, but since it was a confession of embezzlement, they decided to suppress it for the child's sake. In the meantime, Lacey was to go back to Tucson, and Mrs. Burke was to stick around, blaming her husband's disappearance on a nervous breakdown. Someone stole Lacey's car while they were gone. Lacey had to get a plane to take him back. Then Mrs. Burke read about the dead hobo and figured Burke actually *had* committed suicide. In a panic, she rushed to Lacey. Before they could plan anything, you came along. After you left, they flew up to see Benell. He advised them to consult Inez Stapleton. . . . That's the story the way they told it to Miss Stapleton—the way they'll tell it to the jury."

Brandon said, "Let them tell it. It's a story that won't hold water. We've got Jim Lacey dead to rights."

Crandall's face showed relief. "I'm glad to hear it," he said. "You folks have been mighty nice to me, and there's quite a lot of talk going around the county. Well, if Inez Stapleton gets her man turned loose, it'll be an awfully bad thing for you boys."

Selby, puffing his pipe, stared moodily at Crandall. "Could you tell us how you happened to learn about this Crandall?"

Crandall seemed uneasy. "No," he said, "I can't. Mrs. Lacey talked to a close friend, and the close friend passed the information on to someone who gave it to me in confidence. . . . How was my testimony, Selby? Did it suit you?"

"You made a swell witness," Selby said. "I wish now I had put you on the stand earlier."

"Well," Crandall promised, "they aren't going to shake me any in cross-examination." He got to his feet, glanced apprehensively at Sylvia. "You boys will protect me in this?" he asked. "See that it never gets out that I tipped you off?"

"Don't worry, Mr. Crandall," Sylvia assured him. "I'm here, not as a reporter, but as a friend."

"Well, I'll be getting on," Crandall said. "I don't feel so happy about being a talebearer, but you fellows started in on this case trying to help me, so I sort of figured it was up to me to do my share. That story sounded pretty plausible to me and had me worried. I wanted you to know about it, Selby. Forewarned is forearmed, you know, and you'll pardon me for my attitude in regard to you, Miss Martin. You know there aren't many newspaper reporters you can trust with a confidence. Well, so long, boys."

When he had gone, Sylvia said bitterly, "I'll bet Inez Stapleton made that story up out of whole cloth."

Selby said thoughtfully, "It's a dangerous story so far as a jury is concerned. It accounts for everything."

"It may account for everything," Brandon said, "but this truck driver is going to drop a monkey wrench in their legal machinery. Gosh, Doug, I'm so excited over this. I can hardly wait to have you walk into court tomorrow and slap Inez Stapleton between the eyes with that truck driver's testimony."

Selby said, "Rex, let's look at this thing from a detached viewpoint, without passion, without prejudice, but as reasonable men.

"When you come right down to it, we haven't any testimony directly connecting Lacey with the murder. Lacey drove his car at Las Alidas. He claims it was stolen. There's some chance it was. The murder, in all probability, was committed by a man driving a Cadillac car with an Arizona license. We can't prove, except by implication, that it was the same car. We can't prove, except by implication, that Lacey was driving it."

"But you can prove it by implication," Sylvia Martin said.

"Yes," Selby admitted, "we can."

"And what will a jury do with that proof?" Brandon asked.

Selby said, "They'll convict Lacey of first-degree murder. If Lacey hadn't lied to us, if he hadn't tried to disguise Mrs. Burke as a servant, if he'd told his story freely and frankly right at the start, the grand jury would probably never have indicted, and a trial jury would never have convicted him.

"As it is, I have it in my power to send that man to the gas chamber. I'll have to use Carmen Ayers as a witness to do it. Inez Stapleton will fight that identification. When she loses out on that, she'll fall back on this story."

"I thought Mrs. Lacey couldn't be a witness," Sylvia Martin said.

"She can with her husband's permission. So far, that permission hasn't been granted. Once we prove a prima-facie case, he'll change his mind."

"And *that* won't help him any with the jury," Brandon pointed out.

"That's just the thing I'm trying to emphasize," Selby said. "The responsibility rests with me. Lacey should have told his story when he first had the opportunity."

"He thought he could beat the rap," the sheriff said.

"Yes," Selby admitted, "but on the other hand, he *might* have been trying to protect Mrs. Burke's little girl."

Sylvia glanced anxiously across at the sheriff, and said, half jokingly, "What'll we do with him, Rex?"

"Darned if I know," the sheriff said, apprehensively, trying to match the banter in her voice. "Guess I'll have to take him over my knee and spank him."

"He'll feel better after a night's sleep. Won't you, Doug?" Sylvia said, turning to Selby.

Selby didn't answer her. After a moment, he said musingly, "I wish I could reconcile what I've seen of Lacey's character with the evidence in this case. I . . ."

Bob Terry opened the door, saw Brandon was in conference, said, "Excuse me," and started to close the door. Selby called to him, "Come in here, Terry. I want to ask you something."

Terry came in and closed the door. Selby said, "I'm still concerned about those fingerprints. It certainly seems reasonable to suppose that the body was that of John Burke, but if that's the case, why don't the fingerprints check?"

Brandon said, "Leave the fingerprints out of it, Doug. Good heavens, son, don't try the case for the defense. Lacey has his own lawyer."

"Why do you suppose he went to Inez Stapleton?" Sylvia asked.

"Through Benell," Selby said. "Lacey was consulting with Benell. Benell figured Inez could get my ear. He didn't realize that she was laying for me with a club."

"Well, Doug, you take that club right out of her hand," Brandon advised, "and beat her into submission with it. Son, you've got to do it. Your whole political future is at stake."

Selby crossed to the wastebasket, knocked the ashes out of his pipe, stooped and picked up the empty cigarette package which Doane had crumpled and dropped in the wastebasket. He took it over to the table where the package of cigarettes Crandall had tossed to Sheriff Brandon lay near the sheriff's elbow. Sylvia watched him nervously. Sheriff Brandon was frankly worried. Bob Terry, puzzled, stood near the door, glancing from one to the other.

"See Crandall and I smoke the same cigarettes," Selby said. Suddenly he straightened and said, "Look here, folks. I'm not satisfied with this proof. I think we worked up the case against Jim Lacey just as well as it can ever be worked up. Lacey's story would have held water if he'd told it at the right time and to the right people. Now it won't. He'll be convicted of first-degree murder, but when you analyze things, it'll be because of the manner in which the jury will be prejudiced against him, because of the way he's acted and the lies he's told, and not because of any inherent strength in our own case.

"I don't like that.

"When a district attorney sends a man to his death, it should be because the evidence points to one thing and one thing alone. Our case simply doesn't jell. Now when that happens, it's because there's something wrong with the very fundamentals. When a case almost holds water, but there are one or two leaks you can't plug up no matter what happens, it means that it's time to re-examine the fundamentals."

Selby ignored the disapproving silence of those about him and stood staring thoughtfully down at the table. Suddenly he whirled, his eyes glittering.

"Look here," he said. "Let's look this thing squarely in the face. A body is found. Someone makes a cunning and determined effort to keep us from identifying that body. Under ordinary circumstances, the body would have been cremated and there would have been no clue remaining as to its identity, but because we take fingerprints as a matter of routine and because the Southern Pacific sent investigators to take photographs, there was something remaining. What would the murderer naturally do when he found that out? There's only one answer. Now then, we come to a peculiar set of circumstances. The fingerprints don't tally with the identity. . . . I know, Rex, you've got lots of theories about it, but the fact remains that if that body *had* been that of John Burke and we had taken John Burke's fingerprints, they would have tallied with *some* fingerprints found in Burke's house.

"They don't.

"Why?

"We became so anxious to speed things up in order to get evidence against the persons we thought were guilty, that we failed to give proper consideration to that one salient fact.

"I can convict Jim Lacey of murder on the evidence that we have, not because that evidence is strong, but because the jury will be prejudiced against him and stampeded into placing too much importance on the evidence of this truck driver. . . . Rex, I'm sorry, but I'm not going to send Lacey to his death on the strength of that evidence. . . . I'm going to ask for time to develop the case further. If Inez won't consent to a continuance, then it's her funeral."

"Doug!" Sylvia exclaimed reproachfully.

Brandon's silence was eloquent of disapproval.

"There's one other solution which has just occurred to me," Selby said. "It's so startling that I can't think it's true, but yet . . ." Abruptly Selby took his knife from his pocket, bent over the table, his back concealing what he was doing.

Behind his back, Brandon frowned, started to say, "Doug . . ."

He stopped as his eyes caught Sylvia's determined shake of the head.

Abruptly Selby handed a sheet of cellophane to Bob Terry. "Bob," he said, "dust that cellophane with powder, develop the latent fingerprints, and let me know if they're fingerprints that figure in this case."

Holding the sheet of cellophane by the corner, Terry wordlessly left the office.

Brandon said, "Doug, my boy, you can't do it. It would be political suicide."

Selby said, "I don't care what it is, Rex. I can't ask for a death penalty against a man who *may* be innocent."

"But he isn't, Doug. He . . ."

Sylvia interrupted tearfully, "Don't, Sheriff. Nothing you can say will have any effect. Nothing I can say will have any effect. This is something Doug has to fight out with his own conscience. I respect him for it, and . . . and I *hate* him for it."

Selby stared at her moodily, then refilled his pipe.

His friends watched him solicitously during moments of silence. Seated on the table which served as Sheriff Brandon's desk, Doug scowled into the blue wisps of tobacco smoke which emanated at regular intervals from his lips.

Twice Brandon made as though to speak. Each time he thought better of it. Sylvia Martin kept her eyes on Selby. There was pleading in those eyes, but she was as silent as though she had lost her voice.

Suddenly the door from the outer office burst open. Bob Terry, so excited he could hardly speak, said, "They're there."

"What's there?" Brandon asked.

"The fingerprints of the dead man," Terry said.

Selby came to his feet.

Brandon said excitedly, "You mean that the truck driver left fingerprints on Selby's cigarettes, that . . . that they're the prints of John Burke . . . that a man who's dead . . . Doug, what the devil are you getting at?"

Selby heaved a sigh, a sigh of relief from strain. He removed his pipe and said, "All right, folks, come on and get in the car. We're going places and doing things. I'll explain as we go."

Chapter Eighteen

THE COUNTY car rocketed its way through the streets of Madison City, Bob Terry at the wheel, Sheriff Brandon beside him screaming the siren into noise as the car dashed across intersections, pedestrians, frozen in their tracks, staring open-mouthed at the apparition of the county officers roaring past. In the back seat, Sylvia's hand slid across to Doug. "Forgive me, Doug," she said softly.

"For what?" he asked.

"For doubting you."

"I haven't explained yet," he told her.

"You don't need to," she said.

"Straight to Las Alidas?" Sheriff Brandon asked.

"Straight ahead along the main highway," Selby said grimly.

"Doug, what are you after?"

"Got your gun?" Selby asked.

"Yes."

"Be ready to use it if you have to," Selby said. "I'll explain later."

The car flashed across the last street intersection, hit the main highway, and the speed mounted. Selby leaned slightly forward in the seat, watched the cars they overtook. It was dusk, and the motorists were just commencing to turn on headlights. Sylvia asked no questions, kept her hand snuggled into Selby's. Bob Terry gave his attention to driving the car. Brandon, in between moments of pressing the button which sent the siren screaming into action, said, "Any time you're ready to explain, son, I'm ready to listen."

In between blasts of the siren, Selby said, "It's mathematical, Rex. . . . Benell's murder is connected with the murder of John Burke. . . . We haven't accomplished a single thing toward the solution of Benell's murder. . . . That should have shown us we were on the wrong track. . . . It was the theory that Benell must have been taken to the bank forcefully. . . . There's no evidence to that effect. . . . There was one man and probably only one man who could have got him to go to the bank at that hour in the morning. . . . And, unless I'm mistaken, he's in that car ahead. Slow down, Bob, and pull alongside. Rex, I don't know what's going to happen. Get your gun ready. Sylvia, get back of me."

Sylvia's laugh was nervous. "Get back of you nothing, you big egg," she said. "I'm a reporter. Move over so I can see."

"All right, Bob," Selby said calmly, "now."

The tires screamed on the road as the speeding car slowed to pull abreast of the automobile on the right. That automobile, traveling slowly, came to a stop. Mark Crandall's expression showed puzzled bewilderment as Selby opened the door and jumped to the pavement, a step in advance of Rex Brandon.

"What's the idea?" Crandall asked. "Something happen?"

Selby said, "Nothing in particular, Crandall. I just wanted to ask you if you'd have any objection to giving us your fingerprints."

Crandall blinked his eyes. "*My* fingerprints!" he said.

"Yes."

Crandall said, "Good Lord, what do you want my fingerprints for? Are you folks crazy?"

Bob Terry, who had slid from behind the steering wheel, came walking around past the headlights of the county car.

Selby said evenly, "Yes, Crandall, your fingerprints. We want to see if they're the fingerprints of the dead man who was found by the railroad track."

Crandall said, "My God, Selby, have you gone crazy?"

"I don't think so," Selby said.

Crandall fumbled with the ignition switch. "Well, I think you have. Do you want my fingerprints here on the county road or do you want me to drive over to . . ." Suddenly he straightened. The muzzle of a revolver slid over the side of the door. It barked once. The county car lurched up into the air, then settled as the front tire exploded. Crandall's gears clashed into noise. His car shot ahead, hind wheels spinning under the impetus of the power he was pouring into them.

Selby yelled, "Get down, Sylvia. He's going to shoot," and started running in a fruitless effort to catch Crandall's car. Sheriff Brandon's bronzed hand streaked into a motion as swift as that of a striking snake. His big range gun, jerked from its shoulder holster, nestled into the competent fingers. He shot without raising the gun to the level of his eyes, without seeming to take aim. With the roar of the second shot, Crandall's speeding car swerved drunkenly. The hind tire collapsed. The rim pounded on the cement pavement. Crandall, still pouring power into the throttle, strove to control the car.

Brandon shot again.

The car slued sideways, skidded for a moment, swung up on two wheels, hung precariously balanced, and then inclined over. A big truck, coming toward them, set its brakes—too late. The toppling car crashed into the side of the truck. The impetus of that sideswipe sent the hurtling sedan into the ditch. The shrill noise of tearing metal, rising above the sound of the impact, was followed by the tinkling sound of breaking glass falling to the pavement. The truck driver stared in open-mouthed consternation at the four figures who came racing down the highway. He slid from behind his wheel, clambered down, and said to Sheriff Brandon, "What the devil . . . Look out with that gun, man!"

Brandon paid no attention to him, dashed over to where the sedan lay, a crumpled pile of twisted wreckage. One of the front wheels, bent out of alignment, continued to turn slowly.

In the wreckage could be seen a huddled, inert figure.

Sheriff Brandon took charge. Red flares from the county car warned passing motorists who formed in a curious ring of gawking spectators. The sheriff commandeered reluctant help, lifted, dragged the inert figure of Mark Crandall from the wrecked sedan.

The red spotlight of a speeding ambulance showed in the distance. The wail of its siren grew to a scream.

"Rush this man to the hospital," Sheriff Brandon said. "We'll follow you in."

He commandeered one of the cars which was headed toward Madison City. The excited driver tried to keep up with the speeding ambulance and failed.

Selby, with the calm certainty of conviction, outlined his case as the car speeded toward Madison City.

"The dead man was John Burke," he said. "The dead man's fingerprints weren't those of John Burke. Fingerprints don't lie. But we were so firmly convinced we were on the right track that we closed our eyes to the evidence of those fingerprints.

"Think back on what happened. We took the finger-prints of the dead man. Bob Terry was up at San Quentin delivering a prisoner. We waited for his return. Someone else *must* have substituted fingerprints. Who *would* have done it—the murderer, of course. Who *could* have done it—only Mark Crandall.

"You remember, Rex, when you came into my office to talk with me about Crandall. You told me you'd showed Crandall all through your office, that you'd showed him the fingerprint equipment. The prints of the dead man were undoubtedly lying on Terry's desk marked 'Fingerprints of dead man found near Southern Pacific trestle.' "

"They were," Brandon admitted.

"Put yourself in Crandall's position, Rex. He'd gone to elaborate precautions to commit a murder, feeling that he could only get away with it by disguising the identity of the corpse. He'd laid careful plans to make sure the body was cremated before anyone knew who it was. Then he comes to your office and finds that we have fingerprints of the corpse. There was only one thing for him to do. Get rid of the fingerprints. If they'd disappeared, we would have known that they'd been stolen. You then would have checked up on every-one who had had an opportunity to have taken those fingerprints. Crandall couldn't simply destroy the fin-gerprints. The only thing he could do was to sub-stitute others, and the only way he could do that was the way he adopted. While you were in my office, he grabbed another sheet of paper, inked his own finger-tips and left those prints instead of the ones taken from the corpse. It was a simple matter to write on a sheet of paper, 'Prints taken from Corpse found near Southern Pacific Trestle,' and we never thought of checking the handwriting to find if it was made by the coroner."

"But why," Sylvia asked, "would he want to get rid of the fingerprints?"

"That," Selby said, "goes back to the motivation of the whole murder. It must be because John Burke had a criminal record. Crandall knew that when those fingerprints were sent to Washington, we'd get a file by return mail. The name probably wouldn't mean anything to us, but there'd be a photograph of John Burke attached to that file. Can't you see what that means? Burke never did work for him ten years ago. Burke was a crook, and he had some hold on Crandall. He used that hold to make Crandall get him a job, but he didn't stop there. He blackmailed Crandall until he bled him white. Then, when he had all of Crandall's money, and that still wasn't enough to finance his speculations, he started embezzling from the lumber company. He ran his string out. Then he confessed to his wife. She telephoned Lacey. Lacey was willing to make the shortage good, but naturally wasn't going to do it until Burke had left. Otherwise Burke would simply have embezzled that ten thousand.

"Burke cleaned the safe of every cent of cash, not even overlooking the stamp drawer, and left—Mrs. Burke thought for good. Lacey was to make good the embezzlement. Mrs. Burke had him come to the house disguised as a hobo in case her husband should happen to be home when he arrived. Under the guise of asking her for something to eat, he could have handed her the money. When he arrived, she thought Burke was gone. She embraced him and told him they hadn't a minute to lose in getting the money to the lumber company's safe. People were getting suspicious of Burke. At any moment they might start an audit.

"Lacey jumped out of his hobo outfit. He must have

had a business suit on underneath or else wrapped in the roll of blankets. He and Mrs. Burke dashed up to the lumber company. She had learned the combination of the safe from her husband. Burke came back while they were gone. He was going to make a getaway. He saw the hobo outfit and appropriated it. He knew then that Lacey was calling on his wife, but didn't, of course, suspect he'd brought the money to cover his shortage. He evidently knew more about Lacey than they thought. His wife had taken their car, so he appropriated Lacey's. He had no trouble recognizing it from the Arizona license. Before he left, he hunted up Crandall to make one last touch, and probably to threaten Crandall with exposure unless Crandall forwarded him more money to some address they had agreed on. Crandall was to drive him out of town. He did so, using Lacey's car. We know what happened after that. Crandall simply returned the car to the place where Burke told him he'd found it, but in the meantime Lacey had been looking for his car, found it gone, and assumed someone must have stolen it. He reported it stolen as soon as he returned to Tucson. Naturally, he had no idea it would be found in Las Alidas, but did assume that it had been taken to some distant point."

"And how about Benell?" Brandon asked.

"Don't you see? Burke's embezzlement would start an investigation. It would probably show his record, show that Crandall's recommendation was false and lead inevitably to an investigation of Crandall's own record, which wasn't openly criminal, because his fingerprints, weren't on file, but was sufficient to have ruined him in Las Alidas. And to make matters worse, Lacey appealed through his banking connections to Benell and told Benell the whole story. Crandall had to act fast. He probably didn't intend to kill Benell, but he asked Benell to meet him at the bank on a matter of the greatest importance, probably intending to find out how much Benell knew. Remember, Crandall was a director in the bank. It's quite possible he asked Benell to open the vault so he could identify the numbers on those thousand-dollar bills or substitute them in some way so that the bank wouldn't lose possession of them.

"But when Benell opened the vault, Crandall had temptation confronting him, and Benell probably let the cat out of the bag by asking embarrassing questions predicated on information he'd received from Lacey and Mrs. Burke. Remember, Benell had tried to get me to drop the investigation, probably at Mrs. Burke's request. In any event, Crandall suddenly realized he had only to make Benell's death look like the work of robbers to walk away with a cool fifty thousand. He needed that fifty thousand. He needed Benell out of the way."

The speeding car dashed into the city limits of Madison City. "Go to the hospital," Sheriff Brandon said. "Straight down this street for four blocks, then turn to the right."

The relieved motorist slid the car to a stop in front of the hospital. Selby, Sylvia Martin, Brandon, and Bob Terry debouched to run up the steps. The ambulance driver was waiting for them. "He's conscious," he said, "but he's going fast, and he knows it. He says he'll talk—if you get there in time."

It was midnight when Selby parked his car and let himself into his little apartment.

The nervous stimulus which had upheld him while he was working on the case, while they were taking Crandall's dying confession, had vanished. He found himself suddenly weary, so tired that it was a physical effort to climb the flight of stairs which led to his room.

He stood at the window for a moment, looking down the hill to survey the sleeping city.

Out on Main Street the glow of neon signs marked the location of the through highway, showed all-night cafés and hotels which catered to the through night traffic on the main artery of travel. Close by, the fronds of stately palm trees were turned to greenish gold by the glinting moonlight. The residence section was dark. People were sleeping in the security of a rural community—sleeping peacefully, secure in their slumber because there was law and order. And Selby thrilled with the realization that he was a part of that vast, far-flung machine which safeguards liberties, protects property, and checks violence. He . . .

His thoughts were interrupted by the ringing of the telephone. He turned from the window. His eyes, adjusted to the brightness of the moonlight, required a groping moment of readjustment before he could find his way to the telephone, pick up the receiver, and say, "Hello."

It was Inez Stapleton's voice that answered.

"Doug," she said, chokingly, "I'm so glad that I caught you. I've been ringing at ten-minute intervals. . . . You . . . Doug . . . You've beaten me at my own game."

"It isn't a game, Inez," he said. "It's law, and justice. Can't you understand that it *isn't* just a game?"

There was something savage in her voice. "Doug," she said, "I could have beaten you in that case, and I'd have done it. I . . . I had a perfect defense, and now you've robbed me of my triumph, by . . . by outflanking me."

There were tears in her voice now as she said, chokingly, "Doug, I'm going to make you respect me because . . . because I l-l-love you. You're going to r-r-r-respect me. You can't ignore me. I'm here to s-s-stay."

And suddenly the line went dead as she hung up her telephone.

Selby stood for a moment, looking at the dead instrument. Then he quietly replaced the receiver, and returned to the window to stare out over the sleeping city, to look up at the lopsided moon, at the brighter stars which gazed steadily down in the unwinking splendor of a universe rolling majestically on its course through eternity in response to the unchanging majesty of divine law, a law which functioned smoothly and impersonally.

Down there in the lighted district, he knew that Sylvia Martin was pounding away at her typewriter, writing an account which would make political history in Madison City.

And the warmth of her kiss still tingled on his lips.